D0880140

SLUMPED

A Novel By

Jason Brent

Good2go Publishing

Slumped

GOOD2GO PUBLISHING
7311 W. Glass Lane
Laveen, AZ 85339
Copyright © 2013 by Silk White
www.good2gopublishing.com
twitter @good2gobooks
G2G@good2gopublishing.com
Facebook.com/good2gopublishing
ThirdLane Marketing: Brian James
Brian@good2gopublishing.com
Cover design: Davida Baldwin
Typesetter: Harriet Wilson
ISBN: 9780989185967
Printed in the United States of America
10 9 6 7 6 5 4 3 2 1

In the Beginning

*H*ow did I get to this point in my life...I asked myself looking down at my feet...one last lick...that's all it was supposed to be...in and out and get as far away from Sacramento as I could...Now I'm going to have to bury this nigga along with my past....I don't need anyone or anything linking me to this shit... Slump thought looking at his boy Tee. *Old friends become new enemies.*

Slump had been laying shit down for as far back as anybody getting money could remember. If you were a hustler, you had better have both eyes on the boogieman. That's what the streets had named Slump. He had this way of stepping out of nowhere almost magically. The grimiest of the grimiest. A predator to only predators. Growing up the black sheep of a big family, all he wanted to do was get away. Start over fresh somewhere where no one knew him. Somewhere the Boogieman didn't exist.

The Day It All Began

Prologue

"**J**aylon! JAYLON MUTHAFUCKIN DREW! I know you hear me calling yo' nappy headed ass, boy. If you don't get yo' black ass in this room."

"I'm coming, ma. Damn!"

"What you doing in that room anyway?"

"You always up in my shit. You don't never go through Shawanna or Lee's room. You always up in mine." Jaylon said while walking in his room...and as soon as he did, he knew it was over. On his bed laid his bag of toys...two twin rugger P89D's with thirty round clips, a box of bullets, a ski mask, a pair of leather murder one's, and a little less than a pound of Blu Dragon, some of the best weed to hit the streets of Sactown in the Catpiss and Grapes.

"Boy you still live in my house and I will go in any room up in this bitch whenever I feel like it. Now, where this shit come from and why is it in my house?"

"Damn, you ask too many questions."

"What you say, boy?"

Slumped

"Nothing!" Jaylon said putting everything back in the bag, all except for one of his twins, which he tucked into his waistline. He went to his closet and pulled out his black Rockman hoodie and a Jordan box off the top shelf.

After putting his hoodie on, he opened the Jordan box, which held $16,000. Counting out $5,000, he gave it to his mom and started to walk out the door of his room.

"Where you going?" Momma K asked.

"I don't know, but when I get there, I will let you know. Until then, I'll be around. But if you ever need me, Lee will know how to find me." Jaylon said as he walked down the hallway.

"Big Bro, where you going?" His younger brother Lee asked, peeking his head out of his room.

"It's time, bro. I got to get what I got coming and get the fuck away from this place."

"Boy, quit talking crazy and come back here!" Momma K yelled. She had been hearing things about her oldest son since he got out of CYA, California Youth Authority a year ago. But the eyes don't lie and those big brown eyes she had loved so much when he was younger had turned dead cold.

Almost as if he could hear what she was thinking, he looked at her and said, "Don't believe everything you hear about me, Momma," as he walked out the door.

However, before he could all the way out of the yard, his little brother ran out of the house, stood in front of him, and said, "Slump or be slumped."

Chapter 1

"**S**o you sure with this shit lil' nigga? Because if not, get yo young ass out the car right now." Tee said to Slump.

"I'm gon' keep it real Tee. I don't think you really know me because if you did, you would never have said that shit. So to answer that question, all I gotta say is drive cuz I can show you better than I can tell you." Slump said cocking his twins remembering the last thing his little brother Lee said to him before he left…*slump or be slumped.*

"Yeah. Alright." Tee said. "Show me lil' nigga," he said before pulling close to the corner.

""That's the nigga spot right there."

"Remember in and out."

"How we gon' get in. The nigga Munch got all them bars and shit all over the place?" Slump said looking at the house.

"I got it all under control. Now watch. Hello? You ready? Alright." Tee then walked to the house. "Open says me." He said and the door to Munch's dope spot opened up. Out of nowhere came one of Munch's workers, a little skinny kid named Black who had been trying to prove his worth to T for a long time.

"Look Tee, it's another nigga in the back room counting up Munch's money. He got a thang and I don't think Fat Mack is scared to use it." Black said using his hand to act like a gun. Then he looked over at Slump. *Oh shit, this nigga looks psycho. Tee better watch his back. Shit, I better watch mine. Slump don't play.* Black thought giving Slump another once over. "Um Tee, I did my part. I'm out. Holla at me later." Black said trying not to look at Slump again.

"Alright get up outta here." Tee said as Black walked away. Then T turned to Slump. "I think he scared of you."

"Why you say that man?"Slump asked confused.

"As soon as he realized who you were, all the fake gangsta left his young ass." Tee said laughing.

"Well you know what they say. All the kids are scared of the Boogeyman." Slump said getting out of the car.

"Where you headed?" Tee asked.

"Give me a few minutes. I'll be right back." Slump said walking into the house.

That's one cold-hearted young nigga. He can't be no more than 5'9" and a buck sixty-five soaking wet, but you would think he was a giant with the reputation he got. T thought as he waited for his next come up.

Chapter 2

"**B**lack! Black! Is that you?"Fat Mack called out. *This young ain't good for nothing but rolling and smoking weed.*

"Naw, it's the Boogieman!" Slump said, pointing his twin P89's.

Fat Mack looked at Slump and said, "I stopped looking under my bed and in my closet a long time ago." Looking at Slump, Fat Mack thought, *Ain't no way I'm gonna let some rookie rob me. I'm Fat Mack.* "So what you gon' do boy?"

"The money and the work for yo' life." He could see all the bricks of cash and the drugs sitting in front of Fat Mack.

"Oh yeah, well you bet…" was all Fat Mack got out before he was pinned to the chair by the hail of black talon hollow tip slugs coming from the twins.

Yeah I woulda killed you anyway. Slump thought. He got all the money, which looked to be about $150,000 and ten bricks of raw cocaine. He put everything in a duffle bag that was next to the table and left like nothing ever happened.

When he made it back to the truck, he said, "That was too easy," and lit a blunt of Blue Dragon. He then inhaled deeply. Just when he felt the burn in his lungs, in exhaled the smoke, looked over at Tee, and said, "I love you like a brother. Been knowing you since before I can remember. But the next time you question my gangsta, we gon' see if you are as hard as you say you are. Now let's go get to the spot, count this doe, and see what the rest of the day looks like. I might even hit 3 Kings and have a few drinks tonight.

Slumped

"Nigga, you ain't even 21 yet, talking about the club." T said.

"I know, but I know the nigga working the door so I'm good.

***

After counting the money up at Tee's baby momma house, they came away with sixty stacks each.

"Damn Slump. That nigga Munch was getting bread on that block. Sixty stacks each and five birds. I didn't think it was going to be like that. What you going to do with your half?" Tee asked.

"I don't know. Probably take momma some of it so she don't have to be hurting for no doe. Take my bro and little sis to get a few fits for school. But other than that, I don't know. I still got that Blue Dragon left from the last lick and a little over ten stacks." Slump said. "I need to get me a spot since I left momma's, which I know I should have. But I'm a grown ass man and I can't be having Mom's all up in my shit every time I turn around. And on top of that, all them old gossiping ass bitches she play Bingo with always telling her shit they done heard about me and she always on my back. I don't need that shit man. You feel me?"

"Yeah." Tee said. "But all she wants is to see you doing the right things. And you know young Lee look up to you."

"I know. That's why I got to get away before he turn out like me. He already think he the next Billy the Kid. I caught that lil' nigga trying to roll a joint the other day."

"Stop playing." Tee said.

"Real shit. So I rolled up a fat blunt and made the lil' nigga smoke it. But the crazy thing is that I don't think it was his first time smoking. The way he hit that motherfucker fucked me up. So I took it and he looked like he wanted to see me about something. He only 14."

"Look who his big brother is," said Tee.

Slumped

"Yeah but I don't want him out here living like me. My time on this earth ain't gon' be that long if I keep doing what I'm doing." Slump said looking Tee in his eyes.

"I feel ya my nigga. I feel you. So what we gon' do?" Tee asked.

"Take what we want and don't give nothing back. We about to hit shit harder than that earthquake that broke the Bay bridge back in the 80s and then I'm getting the fuck outta here and starting over where don't nobody know me and ain't never heard of the Boogieman.

Chapter 3

"Oh shit. What's up young Jaylon." Sam said and Slump walked up to the door of 3 Kings.

"Not shit. Trying to get up in there and have me a few drinks."

"Well you know I ain't supposed no one under 21 up in here, but since it's you, I will. But you gotta do something for me."

"What's that?" Slump asked pulling a knot of one hundred dollar bills out his pocket.

"I don't want your money, my nigga, but I can't let you up in here with yo' heat.

"How you know I'm heated." Slump said putting his money back in his pocket.

"Come on, Slump. When do you ever be without?"

"Alright, you got me. Hey Tee, let me see your keys so I can tuck my heat. I'll meet you at the bar."

"Alright." Tee said handing the keys to him.

"I'ma go get us a table VIP. Fuck the bar. We gon' bring the bar to us.

"Alright." Slump said. After tucking his twins, he went and found Tee at a black table in the VIP lounge with three bitches, a bottle of XO Remy and another bottle of Grey Goose at the table. As Slump sat at the table, he noticed Nicky on the dance floor doing her thang with a few of her girls. Noticing the gazed look that came in his eyes, Tee followed to see what he was looking at.

"Aw shit nigga. When is you gon' talk to her. You never say shit but every time we see her, you stuck on stupid."

Slumped

"I'm gonna talk to her one of these days, but I got to be ready. And I'm not ready yet."

"Nigga you got a pocket full of money. You can do whatever you want to but you ain't ready. I don't that." Tee said. Slump looked at Tee, opened his bottle, and took a long drink.

"That's a woman Tee. She got all her own shit. Don't need a nigga for nothing. I gotta be on my grown man when I get at her. Because once I get her, I ain't never letting her go."

"Damn, she must be special." One of the bitches said. And I was trying to take you home tonight." She said.

"Oh yeah. So what's your name, Miss Lady?"

"Lexas." She said sliding over towards Slump. Lexas was 5'6", 140 pounds of all ass and titties. She was light skinned, long hair, and eyes as green as jade. She looked good but Slump could tell she was nothing but a sack chaser.

"So you wanna take me home, huh?" Just then, Nelly's *Tip Drill* was coming from the speakers.

"Oh that's my song." Lexas said." C'mon Slump. Dance with me. She was basically fucking him on the dance floor. *Slump thought, I hope her pussy is as good as she looks.* As the song ended and they walked back to their table, Nicky and her girls CC and Torey walked up.

"Jaylon, can I talk to you for a minute?" Nicki said.

"Yeah, go on to the table. Lexas, I'll be there in a few minutes."

"Alright." She said looking Nicki. up and down.

"Don't take too long baby."

"What's up." His heart beating so hard he thought he could hear it.

"Every time I see you somewhere ,why you always looking at me but you never speak." She asked.

"I just be admiring beauty from a distance that's all." Slump said. "Besides, what's a nigga like me going to say to a woman like you. I'm not your type."

Slumped

"How do you know what my type is. You never even speak to me. I'll tell you what, I'm going to give you my number. Call me and let me be the judge of you being my type or not. But don't take forever calling." She said locking her number in a cell phone. "But don't take forever to call me he said locking her number his cell phone I'm not going to take up too much of your time since you got her over there waiting on you."

You can have all the time you want. Slump thought. "Alright. I'm gonna all you."

"Bye Jaylon." She said as her and her girls walked off. Lexas was talking big shit when he got back t o the table. All Slump said to her was, "Don't play yourself." He wasn't even thinking about her anymore. Compared to Nicki, she wasn't shit. All he could think about was her 5'8" frame. Nicki a caramel complexion. Her hair was so silky and hung down to the center of her back. Her body was out of this world. Everything about it was perfect. Her ass made Kim Kardashian's look normal. Her DD's had no sag at all to them. And her dark brown eyes were mesmerizing. He was definitely going to call. Hearing Tee's laught brought him back out of his daydream.

"What's so funny nigga?" Slump asked.

"You sitting there like you in love. And Lexas all mad like she yo' bitch or something."

Slump looked over to Lexas, "Yo, you mad at me , ma? Don't be like that." Slump said when she didn't respond. "Let me make it up to you."

"And how you gonna do that?" Lexas asked with a little bit of attitude.

"I think I can figure out a few ways." Slump said with a seductive look in his eyes. They stayed at 3 Kings until about 3a.m. before leaving and going to the Holiday Inn and getting two suites that connected.. Tee in one room with the other two girls that were with Lexas, Porsha and Jazzmine, while Slump and Lexas were next door getting it on.

"So what's up with you and that stuck up ass bitch anyway." Lexas asked.

"First ain't no reason for you to be up in here being all disrespectful and shit. And second it ain't none of yo' business. It ain't like there is some kind of love connection going on between us anyway. You got what you wanted and to be honest, the more you speak about her the uglier you become to me. I planned on chilling with you and maybe taking you some place but I changed my mind. Matter of fact, you keep this room. I'm done in here."

"Leave then nigga!" Lexas screamed. "I don't fuck with little boys anyway you bitch ass nigga." Before she had time to think of anything else to say or build up a scream, Slump had his hands around her throat.

"Listen because I'm only going to say this once. The next time you ever think about disrespecting me, you better think about everything you love because on that day, your love will be no more." Slump said, letting her neck go. "Now pick yourself up and go next door before I lose my cool and do something I regret. And by the way, the pussy was trash. Just for the record." Slump said with a smile on his face that didn't quite reach his eyes.

Once Lexas went next door with Tee and her two friends, he pulled out his cell phone and before he knew what he was doing, he heard a sleepy Nicki say, "Hello."

"Look I don't know what I'm doing right now, but I just need somebody to talk to."

"Jaylon? Is that you?"

"Yeah." Slump said.

"Boy do you know what time it is?"

Looking at his phone, he said, "5a.m. Damn, you right. I didn't even realize what time it was. My bad. Go ahead and go back to sleep. I didn't mean to bother you."

"No. Wait a minute." Nicki said. "I'm up now and didn't you say you needed to talk to somebody?"

Slumped

"Naw. It was nothing like that. I was just up in this room and for some reason, I just started thinking about my life and what it's been missing."

"Where are you?" Nicki asked.

"Why?"

"Because I asked. Why nigga?"

"Well I'm at the Holiday Inn."

"Who are you there with?"

"Nobody."

"Why you ain't with that big booty girl I saw you with at the club?"

"I was, but not anymore. She had no respect for herself or others for that matter. But what's up with all the questions. I called you to talk."

"She didn't seem like your type. She was too ghetto." Nicki said without answering his question.

"You think you know my type, huh."

"Yeah."

"So tell me what it is."

"Me!" Nicki said without thinking.

"Nah, Nicki. You too good for me. I'm not who you think I am."

"And who do you think I think you are, Jaylon."

"I got issues."

"Don't we all?"

"Besides, I'm not looking for someone to save me. I'm looking for someone to get to know and maybe spend some time with. So you want to get to know me Nicki?" Just then, the door adjoining was being banged on.

"What's that?" Nicki asked.

"Let me call you back."

"Jaylon, are you sure you're alright?"

"I'm good. Let me call you back." Before she could say anything else, he hung up the phone. Walking to the door, he unlocked it, and Tee came in.

"What's good, hood? Tee said.

Slumped

"Not shit. About to tuck a towel under the door and burn one."

"So what happened with you and ol' girl? She all shook up and shit."

"Nothing. She just need to watch how she talk. She's hella disrespectful. Punk ass bitch called me a little boy. And on top of that, a bitch ass nigga. Now you know me, Tee, and if them other two bitches wouldn't been around, I would have made that bitch pay with her life for those three little words."

"Yeah, I know. Sticks and stones may break my bones but your words will make me kill you." Tee said. "So what we gonna do?"

"Give them hoes cab money and get up out of here. Don't your baby momma still manage them apartments. What are they called?"

"Water crest." Tee answered. "Yeah she do. Why?"

"I need to get me a spot. You think she can hook it up?

"For you, you know she will. "

"Alright, well, now all we gotta do is shake them chicken heads."

"Don't trip. I got it. Now let me hit that blunt.

Chapter 4

After being up all day doing them, before Tee and Slump knew it, they were both passed out and probably would have slept forever if it weren't for Tee's phone ringing and the cleaning lady banging on the door to let them know it was check out time.

"Damn nigga. Last thing I remember is asking to hit the blunt." Tee said. "And ain't that some shit!" he said, looking in the other room. "These hoes is still here."

"Fuck them bitches. Let's get our shit and leave they asses."

"You is a cold nigga Slump. I'm glad I'm on your side." Tee said grabbing his shirt and putting on his shoes, looking at the naked Porsha and Jazzmine laid out on the bed. *Them two hoes sure knew how to fuck. I hate to fuck off another nigh with them,* Tee thought after leaving a hundred dollar bill for them to catch a cab.

Walking through the parking lot to Tee's truck, Slump's phone rang. "Now who the fuck could this be?" Slump said answering it.

"Hello?"

"Jaylon?"

"Yeah, who else is it going to be answering my phone? Who is this?"

"So you don't know my voice?" Nicki said. "And you can't call me back either, huh. It's not cool to start off lying."

"Oh shit. My bad beautiful. I fell asleep. So what's up with you this morning?"

"Nothing. Getting ready for work and thought I would call and make sure you were alright since you weren't going to call me back."

"So now you checking me. I hope you know what you getting yourself into Nicky. I told you I'm not like the rest of these cats."

"C'mon Jaylon. You don't have to play the tough guy with me. I see through all that bullshit."

"Oh yeah. Well what's on your agenda after work?"

"Nothing, why?"

"Can I take you out?"

"And where we gonna go?"

"It don't matter to me. Anywhere you want."

"Anywhere?"

"Anywhere!"

"Alright. I'm going to call you when I get off work. I get off around 7:30 so don't just be talking."

"Call me and find out."

"I will."

"I'll be waiting."

"Alright, talk to you later."

"Who was that?" Tee asked.

"Nicky." Slump said.

"Hold on, wait a minute. Did I miss something? When did you start talking to her?"

"I called her last night...well this morning after I choked that disrespectful ass bitch Lexas out and we talked for a minute before you came banging on the door like the cops or something."

"Well, it's about time. Shit!" Tee said.

"Before I do anything, I need to go holla at ya BM. I can't be out here going from telly to telly." Slump stated.

"I got you baby boy!" Tee said. "Matter of fact, let's do that now, then hit one of these tow yards because I'm not gonna be your motherfucking taxi."

Slumped

"Yeah, I was thinking the same thing. We got a nice chunk of change and some work so once I get my shit together as far as a spot and some wheels; I'm back at it like a crack addict my nigga." Slump said.

Chapter 5

After talking to Tee's baby momma, Vicki in Water Crest apartments and getting a spot hooked up to move in, Slump and Tee hit a few of the local tow yards. But being Slump, he couldn't see himself riding around in something that someone else had so after a while, they said fuck it and hit a car lot. After an hour and a half of talking to the dealer and $6,300, Slump pulled off the lot in a black on black Audi A8, which he leased for a year. He figured by this time next year, he'd be ready to upgrade to bigger and better.

"So now that you got a new apartment and car, what you got planned?" Tee asked.

"Well, my spot needs a woman's touch so I figure I'll let Nicky handle that. But right now, I'm gonna go get my momma and then take that lil' sis and bro to get some gear. After that, I'm gonna try to find a place to push this work."

"So why don't you call Stone out there in Texas and see what it's looking like in Crockett."

"Remember last time we were out there, it was on fire. Plus I feel like a road trip, just to get away for a minute and let shit die down." Slump said but little did Tee know, Slump had been thinking about Young Black since the day he saw fear in the little nigga's eyes and before he let Black run his mouth about what happened, he was gonna put the little nigga to sleep forever.

After hanging the phone up with Tee, he called Ridah, who had been watching Black since 3 Kings when he called him.

Slumped

"Hello."

"What's good my nigga."

"Not shit, just sitting on this young egg."

"Well, you're done sitting. I need you to grab that egg and meet me down in the delta off Old Twin Cities in about an hour...and Ridah...nobody but you and him."

"Alright Slump. I got you."

Ridah was known for keeping bitches around him when he did his thing, to show off his gangsta. But Tee and Slump told him that one of them hoes was gonna tell or get him killed. But he never listened. That was Ridah. Mr. Look Whose Flawsing. And even though Slump loved him like a brother, he spoke out loud, all good things must come to a bad end.

Chapter 6

"Where we going?" Black asked looking out th[e] window of Ridah's black on black 87 Capri[ce] Classic.

"I gotta make a quick run. Don't worry. I'll have y[ou] back home before the street lights come on." Ridah sa[id] passing him the blunt.

"It don't even look like nobody even lives all the way o[ut] here. Shit, I think my grandpa used to bring us fishing o[ut] here."

"Hit the weed lil' nigga and relax. We only going to me[et] Slump cop some work and he said he had something for y[ou] too. That's the only reason I'm even riding aoround with yo[u] young square ass." Ridah said. The thought of going to me[et] Slump had made Black nervous and excited at the same tim[e] because he couldn't lie to himself, the nigga Slump scared t[he] shit out of him. And he hadn't heard from Tee so he wa[s] hoping Slump was going to him a cut of the money they g[ot] from Munch's crack house.

"Damn!" Black said as Ridah pulled over and parked i[n] front of Slump's new Audi."That motherfucker is wet." H[e] said staring at it. Suddenly, a strange feeling something ju[st] didn't feel right. Why would they come all the way out he[re] to get some work when they could have met at 3 Kings o[r] somewhere closer.

"Come on nigga!" Ridah said getting out the car. Whe[n] Black exited, Slump told him to come here. As he wa[s] walking up to Slump, Ridah hit him in the back of the hea[d]

Slumped

with his Smith and Wesson Bullldog .44 mag, knocking him out cold.

"So what we gonna do with him now?" Ridah asked.

"Grab his legs and help me carry him to the water." Slump said right before shooting Black between the eyes, killing him instantly.

"You are a cold blooded nigga Slump. I hope I never get on your bad side."

The Come Up

Chapter 7

"Flight 916 now boarding." The woman's voice said through the loud speakers in Sacramento International Airport. It had been five months since Slump and Tee robbed Munch's main crack house. Now they were on the way to Houston, Texas to meet with Stone and see if they could push the 10 kilos of pure cocaine they got, thanks to Young Black for getting them in the spot.

"So what you think Tee?" Slump asked.

"I can't really call it yet, Slump. The way Stone made it seem, this might be the come up we both need. Now all we got to do is check the scenery out. If it's as sweet as he says it is, then we going to show these corny ass country niggas how to get money. You feel me?"

"Yeah, I hear what you saying, but what happens after the work is all gone."

"I haven't thought about that."

"Well, I have and I been doing a little bit of information gathering myself on the boy Munch. You know I ain't never liked that nigga anyway. Ol' fake ass kingpin. And I say if everything goes as planned, when we get back, we might as well cut the head off that snake. Besides, I been hearing the boy work with them people. That's why he got ran up out the Bay area."

"Yeah, I been hearing that too." Tee said. "And I like the way what you're saying sounds. If we can pull that off, we won't never have to do anything else."

"Well, lik I said, I been doing my homework and I used to fuck with this bitch that fuck whit him now. And I ran into her a couple weeks back and you know she really feeling me still, so I think I can get her to set it up. All we need to do is kidnap his ass and he going to tell us where everything is. No question about that. But we will talk more about that later. Right now, let's enjoy this flight and see if everything in Texas is big like they say it is." Slump said.

"Yeah, I can dig that. Anyway, so what's it been like between you and ol' girl." Tee asked.

"Well shit, you know after she gone done helping me get my spot together, we been doing us. And I can see myself changing my life and doing right by her. That is once I get my money right."

"Damn, so it's that good huh?" Tee asked with a smirk on his face.

"Yeah, it's that good. And the pussy is outta this world. Shit, she had me calling her name."

"Oh look at this shit. My nigga is in love. Don't let me find out she got you whipped." Tee said as they both started laughing. "No, but seriously Slump, we both know they way this game ends. This ain't something we can do forever."

"I'm way ahead of you Tee, but this ain't the time or place for this kind of talk when ain't neither of us ready to stop. Look, let's get this money and hope after it's all said and done with, God's as forgiving as they say He is."

"I'm with you until the bloddy end, my nigga." Tee said looking Slump in the eyes.

"Let's hope that end don't come too soon." Slump said looking Tee back in the eyes.

Chapter 8

Stone met them at the airport in Houston, Texas and took them back to his house in Houston's 3rd ward projects. It reminded Tee and Slump of a little Oak Park or Del Paso Heights back in California. A little city within a city.

"So did everything make it?" Slump asked Stone.

"I got that, folks. And I didn't open it like you said so it's still the same way you shipped it." A week before Slump and Tee got there, they FedEx two packages, both with two bricks each. The other six were being driven out to them by Porsha and Jazzmine. After their night of freaking with Tee, he had kept the dynamic duo close. They had their own little love triangle going. Slump didn't care too much for the loud mouth hood rats, but Tee seemed to e in heaven. So he kept his dislike for them to himself.

"Here they go." Stone said sitting the two boxes down on his coffee table. Slump opened one, then the other, putting the four kilos on the table. "This is some of the purest coke Cali gots to offer. And there is a lot more where this came from. Now the way I see it is, you told Tee an ounce was going for $1,300 and a whole bird was going for $31,000 and that's not even for some grade A coke. So what we want to do is corner the market. Let's say $1,000 a zip and $26,000 for a whole bird. That should get everyone's attention. Now you been doing your thang out here for a minute Stone, so we shouldn't have to hurt anybody."

"There is some cats out here from DC and they been pretty much supplying all the wards and they think they are some real killas." Stone informed them.

Slumped

"Fuck them!" Slump said looking Stone in this eyes. And for some reason, that look alone told Stone all he needed to know. The big bad Boogieman done finally made it to Texas and he knew Slump was only human so he bled and could die just like everyone else, but Stone knew Slump and the boy's gun game was far from being anything but normal. So he had no doubt in his mind that them DC cats time was no very limited

Chapter 9

Everything was going just as planned. Porsha and Jazzmine made it the day after Slump and Tee. So now they had all ten bricks. Stone had spread the word that his folks from Cali had the best coke at the lowest prices. They went trhough four bricks in two days and four zips, which made them $144,000 in less than a week. Now all around Texas, from Houston to Crockett, niggas was coming to get that Cali price, but still, no one knew who Tee or Slump was. Everybody dealt with Stone.

"Damn, my niggas. I ain't never seen this type of money before and it's like it came overnight. But tell me it's not over yet. We are down to the last six bricks and four of them them are sold tonight when we go to the Hytop in Crockett."

"Don't trip. Slump said. "We are just getting started. Now tell me about this club we going to."

"Well, it's not like a Cali club. Here anything goes and you don't have to worry about not being 21 yet. Like I said, anything goes. The nigga Jack owns the club and he be doing a lot of business with them DC cats, which is why I find it kind of funny he called me about four bricks."

"I don't." Tee said. "He wants to see who the new niggas in town are, but why, they are just curious. I got a plan. Check it out. When we get there, Porsha and Jazzmine are going to get to know the DC niggas if they are up in there.

"We wouldn't be doing this shit just for anyone." Jazzmine said. You lucky we love you nigga."

Slumped

"Bitch, you don't love me. You love money." Tee said laughing.

"And you know you right." Porsha said.

"But look, I need you all to be on your best game, I don't care if you got to suck them nigga's dicks, we need to know where they spot is. Ya'll think ya'll can handle that." Tee said looking at the two, thinking to himself, *if these bitches weren't so money hungry, they could make a nigga happy.* Now why don't y'all go get money while we talk. They both kissed Tee on the cheek saying they would meet him back here after they went back to their hotel room.

As they walked out the door, Slump said, "Do you trust them bitches enough to do what we need them to do? I mean we can't afford to slip on this. We might not get another shot at these niggas."

"Slump, them two bitches love money more than they love anything else, and on top of that, they really are feeling me and this little thing we got going on."

"But do you trust them?"

"About as far as I can throw them, which is why they would want to stick to the plan or they will never leave Texas. Tee said with murder in his eyes.

"That's all I wanted to hear."

Chapter 10

They pulled up to club HyTop around 10:30 p.m. in Stone's candy apple green donked out69 Caprice classic sitting on 30 inch Geovonies. The club was packed. Everybody who was somebody was there. Even the wannabe' were there trying to act like somebody and take home one of the corn fed brick houses who were out trying to catch a baller, even if it was only for the night.

Tee being the oldest of the trio was really getting his "OG" on in his black Calvin Klein jeans with matching jacket and black and gold Jordan dub Zeros. Slump was in his trademark black Coogie jeans, red and black Coogie hoodie, and red and black Jordan 5's.

Stone being a country boy at heart had on blue Nautica jeans, a white T-shirt and blue and white Nike AirMaxx's. But all eyes were on the two women that had just got out the new black Infinity.

Porsha and Jazzmine playing there part to the T, were two of the baddest bitches to grace the doors of HyTop. Porsha in blue Baby Fat jeans and a pink Baby Fat halter top, with her pink 5 inch Jimmy Choo stilettos, looking like she walked off the pages of a Sweet's magazine. Her 5'7", 36-24-40 body had all mouths watering jer jeans looking like they were painted on. Jazzmine, not one to be outdone, had on white Apple Bottom shorts with a red fish net halter top on over a white bra and her 5 inch red thigh high stiletto boots with her

Slumped

5'5", 34-28-42 body driving all the niggas crazy as she walked by, letting them see what an Apple Bottom really was.

They had already talked to Tee and Slump prior to getting in the club, so they acted as they didn't know who they were when they passed them going inside.

"God damn! Tee I know you be having a ball with all that ass them two bitches got." Stone said to Tee.

"Only if you knew, playboy." Tee said looking at Jazzmine's ass. "Only if you knew."

Once inside the club, they made their way to the bar and each bought a bottle. Stone and Tee both with Remy XO and Slump with Grey Goose. After they all had their bottles, they made their way to VIP, where Jack had a table reserved for them. After they sat down, Stone pointed out the two DC cats sitting in the back of the VIP section.

"That's them two niggas right there. The one on the left with the big rose gold chain on was Red. The other one with the Michael Vick jersey on is Money."

Slump looked back at the two flashy dudes thinking, *if them niggas don't know nothing about being real street niggas*, then said aloud to Tee, "This is going to be easier than I thought. Look at them two soft body ass niggas. And all that flashy ass jewelry. Them niggas don't know all that shit does is say, 'Hey, look at me'."

"Yeah I see them." Tee said waving one of the clubs VIP hostesses down and told her to take a bottle of Crystal to them. While she was taking the bottle of bubbly to them, Plies song, "Medicine" came on and Porsha and Jazzmine had the club on stand still as they freaked each other on the dance floor. Catching the attention of Red who quickly pointed them out to Money.

"Look," Tee said to Slump. "Pussy's every man's weakness."

"Shit, not mine." Slump said.

Slumped

"Yeah, well, you ain't normal nigga." Tee said winking at Slump.

"Stone, what's good nigga." An older Creole looking nigga said in a gre and black pinstriped Armani suit

"Not too much Jack. I want you to meet my family. Tee, Slump, this is Jack. He is the one I was telling y'all about."

"What's good." Slump and Tee said.

"Everything as long as the price is right." Jack replied. "Why don't we take care of business first and then enjoy ourselves. Jack continued turning and walking towards the back of the club with Stone, Tee, and Slump not far behind him.

Chapter 11

Once they got inside Jack's office and closed the door, Jack said, "I been hearing a lot about y'all. Well, really you Stone. Word on the street is that you got the best coke since the 80s and the lowest prices. So how can I get my hands on some of that fish scale?"

"Well first it depends on how much you want. And what you are willing to pay." Stone said.

"Well earlier I told you I wanted 4 birds but if the prices are as good as everybody says they are, I might want to get a couple more."

"Well I got six of them thangs left. And I need $27,500 for each one." Adding 1500 to each brick. The whole time, Slump nor Tee said anything.

"So $165,000 for six huh? You make it $160,000 even and we got a deal."

Stone looked over at Slump and Tee to see how they felt about it.

"It's up to you." Slump said knowing they weren't taking any loss.

"It's a deal." Stone said counting the extra $4,000 to pocket for himself. "Bring the money out to my house in the morning."

'Agreed." Jack said before telling them that he had some people he wanted to introduce them to inside the club.

Slumped

Making their way back to the VIP, the first thing they noticed was Porsha and Jazzmine sitting with Red and Money.

"Red, Money." Jack greeted.

"What's up Jack?"

"How y'all doing tonight?"

"A whole lot better now." Money said looking at Jazzmine.

"I would like y'all to meet some business associates of mine. This is Stone and Tee. And the nigga with the cold eyes is...Slump, is that right."

"Yeah." Slump simply said.

"Nice to meet y'all and thanks for the bottle." Red said

"No problem." Tee said

"I don't think I ever saw you two lovely ladies in the club before." Jack said to Porsha and Jazzmine.

"Yeah, we're not from out here.

"We from Cali." Jazzmine said.

"Well, I hope y'all have a good time."

"Oh trust me, we will." Porsha said putting her hand on Red's leg.

"Well, I don't know about you two, but I'm sho trying to find me something to lay up in tonight." Stone said to Tee and Slump.

"I can dig that." Tee said ready to get his mingle on with one of these corn fed bitches.

"Y'all do y'all." Slump said pulling out a pre rolled peach Swisher stuffed with Blu Dragon. "I'm gon' chill and play in the smoke."

"But first, let me hit that so I can get my mind right." Tee said.

The rest of the night went smoothly. Porsha and Jazzmine had Red and Money's noses wide open. After they left the club, they took the girls out to eat at a 24 hour IHOP and them tried to get them to follow them back to their house. Not wanting to seem like hoes, the girls declined and they exchanged numbers agreeing to hook up the next day.

Chapter 12

When they got back to their room, Tee was in the bed watching a porno starring Ms. Super Pussy herself, Pink. Turning the TV down and sitting up, he said, "So!"

"Well, we got them niggas eating out of our hands. They tried to get us to go home with them tonight, but we played it cool and told them we would hook up tomorrow." Jazzmine said.

"That's what I'm talking about." Tee said.

"Why you up in here watching that fuck flick by yourself?" Porsha asked

"I was waiting on y'all so we could make our own fuck flick. So why don't y'all strip down to your birthday suits and show me how much y'all love me." Tee said. He had been waiting to fuck them both since he saw them in those outfits. Doing as they were told, they stripped and got in the bed with him.

"Is this for me? Jazzmine said wrapping her hand around Tee's nine-inch dick.

"No bitch. It's for us." Porsha said leaning over and kissing the head of his dick then tongue kissed Jazzmine.

"I want to see you make her cum." Tee said to Porsha. Jazzmine laid on her back spreading her thick brown thighs. Porsha not wasting any time went to work. She took Jazzmine's clit between her thumb and index finger and pinched it like she knew Jazzmine liked it, causing her clit to swell. Then she licked it in fast little circles while she put two fingers in Jazz's wet pussy causing Jazz to go crazy.

Jazzmine reached out to Tee, taking his rock hard dick in her mouth and deep throating him. She knew how much he liked her head game. Porsha told Tee to turn around in the bed so his feet were up by the headboard so Jazz could give him head while he ate Porsha's pussy.

Tee flicked his tongue rapidly across Porsha's clit while she did the same to Jazz.

"Fuck this. I can't take it no more. I want to feel you inside of me." Jazz said as she got up and straddled Tee, taking his dick deep inside her pussy while he worked Porsha's pussy with his tongue. The whole time, Jazz was riding him with her pussy muscles squeezing down on him every time.

She raised up, "Oh my God. Yeah! Yeah! Fuck me! Fuck me." Jazz said as the first of many orgasms sent chills up her spine.

Porsha feeling left out on the dick told Jazz to lay back so she could get hers.

Tee standing up, told Porsha to turn around so he could hit it from the back, knowing how much of a freak Porsha was. He put his finger inside her asshole.

"Oh yes. Hit that pussy baby. Hit it." She said. They fucked and sucked each other in every way they could think of. Exhausted laying there, each with their own thoughts running through their heads. Porsha thinking of how she could come out of this on top. On the under, she was really digging Red and was having second thoughts about setting him and Money up.

Jazzmine just wanted it to be done with so she could spend all the time she wanted with Tee. She was really getting tired of sharing him with Porsha. She wanted him all to herself, and if setting some nigga up was the way to win him over, then so be it.

Chapter 13

"Hello sexy. What you doing?" Slump said into his phone.

"Nothing. Laying here thinking about you. Wishing you would hurry up and come home. I miss you." Nicki said.

"I miss you too. I should be home in a few days. We just tying up loose ends. So how you been doing."

"I've been fine. Just thinking a lot about you. It seems like forever since I saw you."

"It's just been a lot going on. I ain't really had time to do too much."

"Oh yeah. So you ain't got no time for me." She said with a little bit of attitude.

"No, I ain't said that."

"Well that's what it seems like. I mean, since you took me out, we ain't really seen too much of each other. I feel like you just used me to hook up your little apartment."

"Well, don't think like that. It's just before we started talking, I was kinda in the middle of something."

"What! You got some little hood rat."

"No Nicki, you ain't got to worry about no other bitches."

"Well what then?"

"Look, we can talk about this when I get back."

"Only if you promise to be honest with me about whatever it is."

"I promise. Now go to sleep. I will see you in a few days."

"Alright, but you better not be out there fucking with no country bitches."

"Girl you are crazy." Slump said laughing.

"No Jaylon. I'm serious."

"I am too. Now go to sleep and I will see you in your dreams.

"Can't wait." Nicki said before hanging up her phone.

After getting off the phone with Nicki, Slump thought long and hard about how fast he had to come up. Growing up in the streets and back alleys of Sacramento, he knew at a young age you had to take what you wanted from the game and give nothing back. Never show fear or any weaknesses was rule 15 of the 48 laws of power. Totally annihilate your enemy. Leave no loose ends. He had a bad feeling about involving Porsha and Jazzmine into their business and he always went with his gut. But tonight, he just rolled him a blunt, put Stone's 64 inch flat screen on BET and caught some late night videos, lit the blunt, and thought nothing else about   it.

Chapter 14

Slump awoke to the front door slamming shut and Stone coming in looking like he hadn't slept at all.

"Damn my nigga. Did you have a rough night."

"You don't even want to know. I'm glad I had to get back here to meet Jack. I was with this ol' big booty bitch named Pam. I been trying to fuck for a while now. Do you know what it feels like to fuck two layers of skin of your dick. My shit so raw it hurts when my boxers rub up against it.

"Whoa, too much info. Too much info. So where Tee at?"

"I thought he was with you." Stone said.

"Nah, he probably with his two freaks." Just then, Tee and Jazzmine came through the door and they didn't look any better than Stone did.

"You look almost as bad as I feel." Stone said to them.

"Long night." Tee said slapping Jazz on her ass.

"So how did it go with them DC cats last night, Jazz?" Slump asked.

"Everything is good. They supposed to hook up with me and Porsha later on today."

"Where she at anyway?" Slump asked.

"Back at the room snoring with her mouth open." Tee said. "So what's up with our money. That nigga Jack showed up yet?"

"Naw. Stone was just about to call him and see if he was ready." Slump said.

Slumped

"I called him before I got here. He said he would be here around noon. So in about ten minutes." Tee pulled a Swisher from behind his ear and threw it at Slump.

"What's this for?"

"Nigga don't act dump. It's breakfast time for my lungs." Tee said.

Slump threw the Swisher and a Ziploc bag of Blu Dragon back at Tee and said, "Feed yourself."

He game the weed and blunt to Jazz and told her to put her fingers to work.

"No problem."

Stone's phone rang, "Hello...alright...he outside...alright..."

"Jazz, go in the back room until he leaves. We don't need him telling Red and Money he saw you with us." Slump said.

"Don't smoke all the blunt. I wanna hit it." Jazz said getting up.

"Roll another one. Just do it in the back room and close the door." Slump said.

When she was out of sight, Stone opened the door and told Jack to come in. Jack came in with a black duffle bag saying what's up to everybody.

"Can we make this quick fellas? I got somewhere I need to be."

"No problem!" Stone said and reached behind the couch to grab a bag that looked like the one Jack had. "It's all there." He said handing the bag to Jack.

"I trust you," Jack said giving him the bag he carried. "All $160,000 are in there. Are we straight?"

"As long as all the money is here. If it's not, you will be hearing from me, ASAP!" Stone said.

"C'mon Stone. You know I don't play when it comes to my money."

"In that case, have a nice day." Stone said taking the blunt that was being passed to him by Slump. "If you have any problems with the work, call me." He said as Jack when out the door.

When the door closed, Jazz asked, "Is he gone?"

"Yeah. If he wasn't, you would have just fucked it all up." Tee said.

Slump was pulling bundles of money from the bag.

"Is it all there," Tee asked.

"Yeah! All $160,000." He counted out $20,000 and gave it to Stone.

"Good looking, kinfolks."

"We couldn't have done it without you. Now all we gotta do is make this other move."

"I've been thinking the same thing. And I think we should hold off and go back home and hit Munch for all he got and come back out here. Think about how much money we made off ten bricks. There is no way we would have seen this much money in Cali.

"Yeah but I'm not trying to make this long term." Slump said.

"I'm not either nigga but we might as well get all we can, right?"

"All profits. No losses."

"Man, I'm not trying to be all up in y'all's business but what do y'all got going on and how can I become a part of it? Stone asked. Slump looked at his cousin for a minute thinking they could use a face that wasn't known.

"I don't think this is your type of get down, cuz." Stone stated.

"Oh I get it. You don't think I'm with the shit right." Stone said with an attitude. "Read the book, nigga. Don't just judge a book by its cover." Stone continued without giving Tee or Slump a chance to respond.

"Well since you put it that way. I got no problem with it. How bout' you Tee?"

"The nigga is family."

"Well, there it is then."

"When we leaving?" Stone asked

"Day after tomorrow. Now Jazz, how would you and Porshea feel about staying and keeping our two new friends company." Slump asked.

"To be honest, I think Porshea would love it. She was really feeling that dude Red...and I mean really feeling him."

"I know she was acting kind of strange last night. But I thought she was just drunk so I didn't really think about it or pay it any attention." Tee said

"Yeah, you were too busy trying to put your dick up in her. Jazz said a little too heatedly causing everyone to look her way.

"Oh shit, I think somebody tired of sharing." Slump said.

"So what." Jazz said looking Tee right in his eyes. "I was only doing it for him anyway. Me and her ain't never been that close. That's Lexas friend anyway."

"Well you sure got a funny way of showing it. Slump said.

"I never said I didn't like fucking her. That bitch pussy sweet as Jolly Ranchers."

"Damn sure is!" Tee said laughing.

"Okay, so what we gon' do about Ms. Sweet Pussy?"

"I say we let her hang herself. I mean after all, she ain't nothing but a sack chaser." Stone said.

"Red ain't trying to wife the bitch. He just want some pussy."

"Yeah, but what if she tells him about out plan?" Slump asked.

"Then we take that bitch out to the country and feed her ass to the hogs. Have you ever seen what them mutherfuckers will do to a body? Stone said looking at Slump with a silly grin on his face and cold eyes.

"I like the sound of that and I'm not worried about them two niggas. They eyes don't lie. Them niggas is soft. And besides, if she tells them she was going to set them up for us, what you think they gonna do with her?" Slump said.

"Nah, she ain't gonna say nothing. The bitch might be grimey but she ain't stupid. All she see is dollar signs. A new nigga with some money she can try to help him spend." Jazz said.

"I pray for her sake that she keeps her mouth closed because I'm not Italian." Slump said.

"What the fuck does that mean?" Tee asked.

"You know how in all them old mob movies we be watching, they always say no women or kids. Well, when it comes down to it, I'm killing the bitch and the baby." Slump answered

"You are a cold-hearted motherfucker kinfolk.

Chapter 15

Jazzmine left the men and went back to the room so her and Porshea could get ready to meet with Money and Red. The whole ride back, all she could think about was what Slump said. She promised herself she would do all she had to stay off his 'hit list'. Just thinking about how cold his eyes were when he said it brought goose bumps to her flesh. Not to mention all the rumors about him being a cold blooded killer. The first night she met him and Tee and 3 Kings with her cousin Lexas and Porshea, she thought couldn't be the person that heard all the stories about, but one look into his eyes and she knew it was the Boogie Man himself.

When she walked into the room, Porshea laid on the bed in her black thong with matching bra talking on the phone.

"Bitch, who you on the phone with?" She asked.

"Red. They want to know what time they can come get us?"

"Tell them I'm bout' to get in the shower, do my hair, and we will meet with them." And just to play her part, she added, "Tell Money he might get lucky." Then headed to the shower as Porshea relayed the message before hanging up to join Jazz in the shower, where she planned to do more than just rubbing soap on her back.

"What you doing?"

"What it look like I'm doing? I'm taking a shower." Porshea said taking the peach and cream body wash from Jazz's hand and telling her to turn around. Doing as told, Jazz turned around but instead of washing her back, Porshea cupped her breasts and played with her nipples until they were the size of two Hershey's kisses. Then, she let one of her hands make its way down to Jazz's flat stomach to the low patch of her pubic hair. The moans escaping Jazz's mouth let Porshea know that she was getting aroused.

"We ain't never gonna make it out of here if you keep doing that. Jazz said as she grinded her pussy on Porshea's hand.

"We got more than enough time." Porshea said turning her back around and shoving her tongue into Jazz's mouth. Now pussy to pussy, they rubbed and grinded on each other until they climaxed. Once they finished in the shower, they got dressed, and called Money and Red, who they agreed to meet in Crockett at Aim's Fried Chicken.

The whole ride out there, Jazz picked Porshea's brain. Trying to see what she had planned.

"You really feeling this Red nigga, ain't you?"

"A little. Why?"

"Because we are supposed to be handling business and I ain't trying to get killed."

"I ain't either, but who says we can't get ours too before we do what they asked? Shit, to tell you the truth, I'm gonna get mine and I don't care who don't like it."

"Yeah, well bitch, don't get me mixed up in your bullshit." Jazz said thinking about what Slump said earlier.

Chapter 16

Meanwhile, back at Stone's house, Slump and Tee discussed what would happen once they returned to Cali.

"Like I told you the day we flew out here, I used to fuck with this older bitch named Alicia."

"Big booty Alicia?" Tee asked.

"Yeah! Anyway, she used to fuck with ya boy Munch but she still got love for a nigga like me and I was thinking about using her to get ol' boy."

"How you gonna do that?"

"You know that bitch can't stop talking once she got some weed in her. So I figure, I will kick it with her, get her to feel comfortable, and slide in a few questions. If that don't work, we can just follow her ass because she stay with him out in Elk Grove."

"What's an Elk Grove?" Stone asked coming in the front door.

"Well, once you left to make that run, we talked about how much more we could make once we got back in Cali. And Elk Grove is a town in Sacramento. The city where the nigga we gonna strip stay at. So sit down and pay attention. We got one shot at doing this and it's got to be done right." Slump said as they went on about how they were going to make their move just as Porshea and Jazz were meeting with Red and Money at the town's only hot stop besides Hytop, Aims Fried Chicken.

Chapter 17

Porshea pulled in and parked next to Money's root beer colored 1972 Cutless Supreme sitting on 26 inch chrome blades. Money sitting on the hood of his car, eyes Jazzmine with lust filled eyes as she got out of the rented Infiniti they drove to Cali.

"How you doing?" Money asked.

"Fine!"

"Naw! Not how you looking, how you doing?" Money said smiling, showing off his iced out grill.

Corny ass nigga. Jazz thought but said instead, "I feel almost as good as I look."

Porshea being the hood rat she was, was all over Red not caring who was watching.

"Dang, can't you at least wait til' all these people gone before you start raping the man?" Jazz asked.

"You can't rape the willing." Red said before Porshea could respond.

This is gonna be a long day. Jazz thought.

"Come on! Let's go in and find a table." Money said putting his arm around Jazz.

Once inside, they found a table in the back, ordered drinks, and looked over the menu.

"Why you way over there? I ain't gonna bite you." Money asked Jazz.

"And how I know that? I barely even know you."

Slumped

"C'mon now ma. Don't be like that. Do I look like I would hurt you?"

"Naw. You look harmless." Jazz said sliding closer to him.

Porshea and Red couldn't keep their hands off each other.

This bitch better stop acting funny. Porshea thought cutting her eyes at Jazz.

"So what we gonna do when we leave here?" Porshea asked Red

"I don't know what they gon' do, but I can think of a few things we could do."

"I like the sound of that." Porshea said before they ordered their food. A million things were running through Jazz's head and there was no way she was giving this nigga any pussy. The truth was she didn't even want to be there. All she wanted was Tee. They finished their food and had a few more drinks then decided to return to Money and Red's house in the new projects. The 'new projects' was what they called a bunch of low income houses and apartments in the north part of Crockett. Although Jazz didn't want to, she rode with Red while Money rode with Porshea. They pulled up to the house a few minutes later. Once inside, Money asked what the ladies wanted to drink and poured them both a glass of XO Remy Martin with a twist. He crushed two ex pills and put them in their drinks. Giving them the drinks, he caught Red's eyes and gave him the nod letting him know the party would be starting shortly. He sat next to Jazz with a drink of his own in his hand and made small talk with her. Jazz not knowing he slipped the pill, wanted to hurry and finish her drink, then say she didn't feel well and make an excuse to leave.

Porshea already halfway done with hers stated she was feeling good as she rubbed Red's dick through his jeans. Jazz feeling the effects of the ex, wanted to get up and leave, but Money started to kiss her neck. Before she knew it, her shirt and bra were off and he was sucking on her nipples.

Slumped

Porshea was so far under the control of the ex that she was giving Red head, deep throating all his eleven inches. Money now had Jazz completely naked as he ate her pussy as Jazz was oblivious to her surroundings but loving every moment of it. Money then pulled her off the couch and laid her on the ground where she caught sight of Porshea's pussy. She pushed Money away and crawled towards Porshea's pussy.

"That's what I'm talking about. I knew you bitches were freaks." Money said with a condom in his hand, but put it down and got behind Jazz and pushed himself inside her causing her to gasp out in pain before pleasure. Money and Red fucked Porshea and Jazz for hours while switching partners. When they were done, they took pictures of the girls freaking each other and left them naked in the living room. When the girls came to the next day, they didn't know what happened, but they knew every hole on their bodies hurt and they were naked and alone. Once dressed and about to leave, they found a note on the door.

Ladies,

It was fun. Had a great time. See you around and tell them niggas using you that was an old trick in a new game.

Money and Red

After reading the note, Jazz turned to Porshea. "Tell me you didn't say nothing to Red about Tee and Slump."

Porshea not sure if she let something slip about them when they were drinking said, "I didn't say nothing to him about them."

"Bitch, do you think I'm crazy. I hope not because Slump is crazy and I don't' want to be on his shit list. I heard a lot of shit I would rather not say about that boy."

"Yeah, well I hope like hell he kills those two niggas." Porshea said meaning every word of it. "I can't believe they did this to us."

"Nah, I can't believe we didn't see the shit coming. Come on. Let's get the hell outta here so we can tell Tee what happened." Once they were in the car, headed back to Houston; Jazz called Tee and told him all she could remember.

Chapter 18

"**F**uck!" Tee said hanging up the phone. "So them niggas think they on top of they shit. I got something for them bitch ass niggas."

"What you talking bout'?" Slump asked.

"Them DC niggas slipped Porshea and Jazz something in their drinks, fucked them, and left a note telling us we used an old trick to a new game."

"How the fuck they even know we know them bitches?"

"I don't know and they both swear they ain't said nothing."

"Well, them niggas will be at the Hytop tonight and since we are about to take this trip tomorrow, why don't we give them and everybody else something to think about why we gone." Stone said speaking for the first time.

"Shit if everything goes as planned, when we come back, we are going to be the niggas with the work so we gone have to handle them anyway, right."

"Yeah, you got a point. But now, ain't the time to kill em." Slump said.

Tee really didn't care about Porshea getting fucked but he was really upset Jazz got taken advantage of. "Fuck that. We going to the club tonight and I'm going to stump the teeth out of them nigga's mouth."

"Well, fuck it. We going to the club tonight." Slump said.

About an hour later, Jazz called Tee and told him they had made it back to the hotel. Slump, Stone, and he jumped in

Slumped

Stone's glass house and went to check on them and get ready for the night.

Chapter 19

They got to the Hytop around 11:30 that night and the only thing on Tee's mind was trying to punch the gold and diamonds out of Money's mouth, but as soon as they walked in, Jack came out of nowhere and asked them to come down to his office. They could tell something was up so Tee and Slump told Stone don't let Red and Money leave.

"Don't trip, kinfolks. I got these niggas. Y'all just go see what old Jack want. I'm going to go buy our partners some drinks." Stone said walking off.

"Let's get this shit done because I'm gon' beat the shit out of that Money nigga, watch." Tee said.

Once in Jack's office, Slump stated, "What's good Jack. You need some more work?"

"Nah, not yet. I just wanted to show you something." Jack threw and envelope on the top of his desk and Slump picked it up.

"Damn, one thing for sure. Them bitches is bad as a muthafucka." Stone said handing Tee the pictures from the envelope.

"So what you want for these because I ain't got nothing for you." Tee stated.

"So do you know these ladies then." Jack asked.

"Yeah, I know them." Tee said looking at Jack with death in his eyes.

Slumped

"I don't want nothing and to be honest, I don't approve of how they did these two. I just wanted to say don't kill them up in my club. This is my place of business."

"Oh, don't worry. We ain't gonna kill them." Slump said.

"Nah, just knock a few teeth out. Come on Slump, I'm through talking." They walked out of Jack's office and to the bar.

"Give me a bottle of Remy XO and a round of drinks for everybody on them." Tee said pointing to Red and Money. Slump walked over to the DJ booth and told the DJ to announce free drinks on Red and Money.

"Alright y'all. I just been told that everybody got a free drink tonight on Red and Money." The DJ said through the speakers. Everyone then rushed to the bar as Red jumped up.

"What the fuck they talking bout'. I ain't paying for that shit."

"Shut your bitch ass up nigga." Tee said walking up to Red. Before Red could say anything, Tee broke the XO bottle across his head. Money reached for his gun only to have Stone put the barrel of his 40 caliber to the back of his head.

"Yeah, go head. Pull it out and give it to me." Stone said.

"What the fuck is this all about."

"Shut up and give me the gun."

"Man we can work this out," Money said in a pleading voice handing Stone the gun. Red tried to get up from where he laid next to Tee's feet. Before he could gain consciousness, Tee kicked him in the head like he was punting a football.

"And as far as your bitch ass, an old trick in a new game huh." Just as money was about to say something, Slump hit him in the mouth with a vicious right jab.

"Shut yo' bitch ass up. Didn't nobody tell you to talk. I want you to listen real carefully to me. You and your girlfriend over there just wore out your welcome."

"No, fuck talking to these niggas. I told you what I was going to do." Tee said. By now, the DJ had stopped the music and everybody was watching the scene unfold in front of them.

"So you think you are a kingpin or something. Nigga you can slip shit in bitches drinks, fuck em, and take pictures. What type of gangsta is you."

Money not wanting to seem like a bitch said, "Nigga, you sent them hoes to set me and Red up and them bitches got what they had coming. Now you think you tough because you got this fat country nigga here holding a gun on me. What you ain't man enough to bust yo' own gun. Fake ass Hollywood gangsta." Before he could say anything else, Tee caught him with two quick left jabs and a right hook, staggering him but not knocking him out and the fight was on. Money threw a right punch that landed solidly but Tee shook it off and threw punch after punch opening a cut over the top of Money's right eye. But Money had more fight in him than Tee expected throwing a series of punches of his on bursting Tee's lip. By this time, Red woke up and was getting to his feet, not seeing Slump standing behind me, he went to rush Tee and met a hard right hook that almost took his head off. Not being ready for it, he fell to his knees and before Slump could hit him again, Stone hit him across the head with his gun and started stumping him until his Jordans were covered in blood. Then he went through his pockets, pulling out a roll of money. "The drinks is on him." He said to Slump.

Tee had been setting an example out of Money, whose right eye was now all the way closed. He had blood coming from his nose and mouth and could barely stand on his feet. Tee caught him with a left hook that would have made Mohammad Ali proud, knocking him out.

"Get yo' ass up nigga. Get up." Tee said standing over Money. Money didn't move. Then he heard someone in the crowd say, "I think that nigga is snoring. Somebody get him a pillow."

Slumped

Slump walked up to Tee. "C'mon bro. Let's get out of here, we got a plane to catch. Get his money too, Stone."

"I'm already ahead of you, kinfolk." Stone said going through Money's pockets. "Here Jack. This is for the drinks and the mess we made." Stone said handing him the money he just took from Red and Money.

"Yeah, good looking out. And when y'all get back in town, holla at me."

"Yeah, when I get back, it's gonna be some better prices than before.

Chapter 20

On the plane back to Cali, everybody was lost in their own thoughts. The only thing on Slump's mind was how everything got to the point it was now. He didn't plan on becoming a d-boy but he was already in too deep and after they moved on Munch, it would only get deeper.

"Pulling him from his thoughts, Tee said, "What about little."

"Not shit, but how your lip over there looking like a busted hot link."

"Yeah, that nigga got me with a cool one. Shit, I didn't think the nigga had it in him. But that's what I get for thinking. Now I'm going to tell you what I know."

"Speak then."

"I know we are about to step into the major league once we knock this nigga Munch off. And I just want to know if you are ready for all this. We had this talk before if I remember it right about you questioning my gangsta."

"I'm not questioning your gangsta. I know you have no problem with pushing a nigga hairline back."

"I'm talking about us getting this money and all the drama that's going to come with it." Tee said.

"Yeah, that's what I was thinking about before I looked at your lip." Slunp said smiling.

"Do it really look that bad. I should have killed that nigga." Tee said poking his bottom lip out.

"Oh don't worry. I think you will get the chance at doing that real soon."

"I been thinking about that too! But I had to show him and the rest of those country niggas watching how the dog get down. You feel me?"

"You know me. I'm with it whichever way the wind blows the leaves my nigga. All profits, no losses. But I'm gonna be up front with you. I don't plan on doing this rest of my life. I'm getting in and out. I've seen too many niggas that thought they would never fall once they got on top only to lose it all and I ain't going out like that. I'm gonna get mine and then I'm out of here. Where I end up, I don't know.

"I got a lot of love for you, Jaylon. Always have. I watched you grow to be the nigga you are right now. You are the brother I never had, so whatever you want to do, I'm with it until the bloody motherfucker end. And until we get there, I'm trying to get money nigga. And who knows, I might get up out of here with you. And I know it goes against every player bone in my body but I'm really feeling Jazzmine."

"I can tell. Because your facial expression turned real cold once you saw her in those pictures. And I get the feeling she only did all that shit to prove she was down for you. But that other bitch Porshea ain't shit but a gold digging hood rat with a bomb ass body."

"She got some good pussy too. But I ain't fucking with her like that no more. Once they get here and drop the rental off, I'm done with that bitch. And while we are on this topic, what's up with you and Ms. Superwoman."

"We cool. We kicked it a few times after she helped me hook my spot up but I want to be done with all this before shit gets too serious because I don't know the outcome of it all and I would hate to break her heart. She is a good girl. You feel me. The kind a nigga could spend his forever and a day with."

"Yeah, I feel that. And I'm gonna do all I can to make sure we come out on top. All profits. No losses."

"All profits. No losses. Now what you gon' tell Vicky about that hot link you got stuck on your mouth."

"There you go again with that shit." Tee said laughing. The plane landed at Sac International around 3:15p.m. Tee went to his spot he shared with is baby momma while Stone went with Slump to his apartment.

"Say kinfolk. It's been a minute since I seen Auntie Kay and my little cousins. And I'm hungry as a motherfucker for some of that fried chicken she been making."

"Nigga you always hungry. After my lady friend gets here, we can ride out."

"Do she got some friends?"

"She might. But these bitches on they grown woman so you might have to step your game up."

"What you trying to say. I ain't got no game."

"No, I'm not saying that. I'm just saying that country shit might not work for you." Slump said smiling. Before Stone could respond, the front door opened and Nicki walked in.

"Hey sexy. How you doing?" Slump said walking up to her and giving her a long, lust filled hug and kiss.

"Damn Jaylon, did you miss me?" She said blushing.

"More than you will ever know. Nicki, this is my cousin Stone. Stone this is my girl."

"Woman!" Nicki said.

"Yeah, this is my woman Nicki."

"How you doing?" Stone said.

"I'm doing better now that Jaylon is back. So Stone, is that the name your mama gave you?"

"Naw, my name is Michael but everybody just calls me Stone."

"Well Michael, it's nice to meet you. So what did y'all have planned?" She asked Slump.

"Well I thought we would have dinner with my mom and little brother and sister."

"Well what we waiting for. I would love to meet your mom." After Slump and Stone took a shower, they went to mama Kay house.

"Damn kinfolk. This motherfucker is clean. Ain't this the brand new Audi A8."

"Yeah I got it before I came out to Texas."

"Shit, I need to get me something like this."

"Nicki, look in the glove box and see if I still got some blunts in there." Slump said.

"Yeah, you got one. Why?"

"Give it to Stone." She handed the swisher to Stone who pulled out some Blu Dragon that Slump had given him before he left the house and rolled the blunt. Lighting it and taking a long pull of some of Cali's finest, he hit the blunt a few more times and passed it to Slump. And to his and Slump's surprise, Nicki took it and hit it a few times as Slump looked at her."

"Slump, what?"

"Nothing. I just didn't think you smoked."

"I keep telling you Jaylon, stop thinking and start knowing."

"Yeah, alright Ms. Smart Ass. Pass the weed."

Chapter 21

"Jaylon!" Little Lee said jumping off the couch and rushing his big brother. "Where you been and who is that? She hella fine." He asked looking at Nicki

"Boy watch your mouth!" Mama Kay said coming into the living room.

"Mama Kay, this is my lady Nicki. And Nicki that's my mother. And the little nigga that keeps on smiling at you is my little brother Lee. Ms. Thang back there on the phone is my little sister Shawanna."

"Nice to meet you baby girl." Mama Kay said. And then as it hit her who Stone was, "Michael. Boy come here and give me a hug."

"How you doing Auntie!" Michael said embracing Mama Kay.

"When you get here?"

"I get here earlier today with Slump...I mean Jaylon."

"What you mean with Jaylon? You went to Texas and didn't tell me you were going."

"It was a spare of the moment thing Ma." Slump said.

"Well, how long you staying, Michael?"

"I don't know. I guess until you get tired of me."

"Well shit, I know y'all hungry, let me make something."

"Is there anything I can do to help?" Nicki asked.

"Yeah, come on in here and let me get to know you, Ms. Nicki. You gotta be special because Jaylon ain't never brought no girl home before." After they went into the kitchen, little Lee said, "You hitting that bro. She fine as a motherfucker."

"Boy you better watch your mouth."

"Shut up fat boy." Lee said to Stone.

"Every time I see your ass, you always talking shit." Stone said putting Lee in a headlock.

"And everything I see you, you getting fatter and fatter." Lee said laughing.

"Shawanna, who you on the phone with." Slump said.

"None of your business."

"She on the phone with that pussy ass nigga Eddie." Lee said.

"Why don't you mind your business. Always running your mouth."

"So what. That nigga's a punk."

"I'm gon' call you back, Eddie!" Shawanna said into the phone. "My brother is tripping."

"Naw, her brother ain't tripping. But if you want me to start I will." Slump said loud enough for Eddie to hear.

"I hate you two niggas." Shawanna said hanging up the phone.

"No you don't. Now come give your big brother a hug." She came and gave him one, saying, "Ain't nothing going on between me and him anyway. He just my friend. And besides, he know you my brother.

"So he know he will get fucked up then." Slump said.

"He better!" Lee said.

"Shut up boy!" Shawanna said. "Anyway, I thought you said you were gonna look out for some new gear for me."

"I had some things I needed to take care of but tomorrow I'll have Nicki take you shopping."

"For real Jaylon!"

"I promise sis."

"Alright, I'ma go help them in the kitchen."

"What about me?" Lee said.

"I got you too bro!"

"I wanna go with them." Stone started laughing.

"You better watch out, kinfolk. I think the little nigga trying to get your girl."

"Naw, she too old. But do she got a little sister?"

"I don't think so," Slump said laughing at his little brother.

"Oh yeah, guess what!"

"What!"

"You know that kid Black that be selling Munch's work?"

"I think I heard of him but I ain't never met him. Why?"

"Word on the street is that Munch had something done to him because ain't nobody heard from him Munch's spot got robbed and Fat Mack got killed."

"Is that right." Slump said looking at his little brother.

"Yep!"

"How you hear about all that? I thought I told you not to be running around in them streets."

"I wasn't. I heard about it at the pool hall last weekend."

"What was your ass doing up in the pool hall little nigga.'

"C'mon Slump. When you was my age, you used to go there."

"So what, you ain't me, Lee. I keep telling you about that shit. Don't make me fuck you up. And I better not hear about you out there trying to hustle for nobody either."

"I got you big bro. Don't trip."

"I'm serious Lee. I keep you gear up and with a little money in your pocket."

"I know Slump. Trust me. I ain't gonna do nothing that's gonna put me in jail."

"You better not!" Slump said.

"What y'all talking about?" Mama Kay said coming from the kitchen.

"About how good that food smell." Stone said

"Hope y'all hungry."

Slumped

"C'mon momma, look at him. Everything about him say hungry." Lee said.

"Shut up boy before he kick your little ass."

"Shoot. I think I can take the butterball!" Lee said causing Slump and Stone to start laughing.

Chapter 22

They ate dinner and talked to Mama Kay for a while before leaving, but not before Shawanna reminded Slump about going shopping. After promising her that Nicki would take her, she made Nicki promise to not let him forget.

Once in the car, Nicki said, "Jaylon, you really are loved by your mom. And I can tell your brother and sister love you too and they mean a lot to you as well."

"Yeah, they are all I got and it's been that way since Pop died."

"Well now you got me and I got you."

"And ain't that cute." Stone said from the backseat.

"Shut up fat boy!" Slump said laughing.

"I ain't gon' keep telling you and your nappy headed brother, I ain't fat nigga. I'm just big boned."

"And got a helluva appetite." Nicki said laughing.

"Well, since my cousin seem to be all in love and shit, I'm gonna let that one slide." Stone said laughing too. "But y'all gon' get enough of calling me fat."

"So what do you two got planned now." Nicki asked.

"Not shit. Probably stop and get a bottle of Grey Goose, some blunts, and call it a night." Slump said.

"Yeah that sounds about right." Stone said.

They stopped at the liquor store, then went to the house. Once they got there, sipped and smoked a few blunts, Stone passed out and Slunp took Nicki into the room.

Slumped

"I didn't think he would ever go to sleep. I been trying to get you in this room all night."

"Is that right." Nicki said pushing him down on the bed. "And what makes you think I'm gonna give you some."

"Because it's mine." Slump said pulling Nicki down on top of him and kissing her. "Damn girl, I missed you so much."

"Show me how much." Nicki said. And he did.

As they both laid in bed exhausted, soaked in each other's sweat. Nicki said, "Be honest with me Jaylon. What are you doing?"

"What do you mean?"

"I mean what are you doing in the streets. You riding around in an $80,000 car and you ain't working. So where does the money come from?"

"Why do we gotta talk about this now. The night was perfect."

"I gotta know what I'm getting myself into. I'm feeling you a lot and I don't want to get hurt in the end. I need to know I can trust you."

"Nicki, you don't ever have to worry about me hurting you in no type of way. And if you need to in order for me to, I'll tell you."

"I'm listening."

"Alright. I been selling coke."

"But Jaylon, I..."

"Don't interrupt me. Let me finish. I been selling coke but I don't plan to much longer. I'm only in it for the money. I've been taking care of my family making sure they have everything they need. My goal is to save enough money to get them away from here. Somewhere I can be a different person. Where my brother don't have to worry about turning out like me or my sister don't have to get pregnant before getting out of high school. Somewhere my mother can sleep easier knowing I'm not dead or locked up. Somewhere I can start a family of my own. Maybe start a small business. Now

Slumped

I know you ain't into the street life, and I planned on being down with this move before we talked about something like this. I've been in love with you since the first time I laid eyes on you and I knew I had to be on my grown man game before I stepped to you. Now I'm almost done with what I have to do."

"Which is?"

"I can't tell you all that, baby girl. And I think it's better that way. I hope this doesn't change anything between us because I would hate to lose you."

"Jaylon, can I trust you."

"Yes, you…"

"Wait a minute. Let me finish. Can I trust you to never lie to me, never cheat, or cause me any type of pain?"

"Girl, you can trust me with your life and I know I would give my own to make you happy."

"Can you promise me that after you do whatever it is you have to do, it's over?"

"Yes, I promise Nicki."

"Alright, I won't bring this up again. You just make sure you stand by your word. Because before I let you hurt me, you will lose me."

"I got you baby girl. Now go to sleep."

"Jaylon."

"Yeah!"

"I love you too."

That night, Jaylon laid in bed holding Nicki thinking about his future and how he would let no one or nothing stand in his way. After they moved on Munch, for him, it was over. Or so he thought.

Chapter 23

"Hello? Oh what's up Tee. Yeah I'm up. Alright I'll see you when you get here."

"About time you got up." Nicki said coming out of the bathroom wrapped in a towel.

"I was tired girl. You wore my ass out last night." Slump said getting out the bed.

"So who was that on the phone."

"Just Tee telling me he was on his way over here."

"Oh yeah. What ya'll got planned for the day."

"Shit. Just gon' take Lil' Lee to get him some shoes and a few outfits. After that, it's whatever. What about you?"

"Well, since you told Shawanna I was gonna take her shopping, I was gonna do that. Maybe go get my nails done, then go home and study. I got my finals coming up. But other than that, I ain't got no plans."

"Well, how bout' we go out to eat. I know you can hook Stone up with one of your girlfriends." Slump said, pulling the duffle bag out the closet.

"Oh I gotta play matchmaker huh?"

"Naw, I'm just saying, bring one of your friends and whatever happens, happens."

"Well I guess." Nicki said looking at what Slump was pulling out the duffle bag.

"Here, take that. Get my sister a few things, then buy yourself something nice."

After taking quick count, she said, "Jaylon, this is $5,000. I don't need all this."

"Like I said, buy yourself something nice. Get your hair done or something. Shit, I don't know. But have fun."

"Well since you put it that way, I guess I do need a few things."

"And I need you." Slump said pulling at the towel.

"Boy stop it. Every time I get out the shower, you always trying to get me naked."

"I can't help it. I'm hooked on your goodies." Slump said pinching her on her butt.

"Boy stop! Let me get dressed." Just then, they heard knocking at the front door.

"Stone, get that. It's Tee." Slump called from the room.

"What's up kinfolks." Stone said as Tee came into the house.

"Not shit. Another day, another dollar." Tee said. "Where Slump at?"

"He in the room with his future."

"Yeah nigga, my future." Slump said coming down the hallway.

"What's up baby boy." Tee said giving him a pound.

"Not shit bro. Bout to hop my ass in this shower, go get little Lee and hit a few shoe stores."

"I like the way that sound." Tee said. "I've been arguing with Vicki dumb ass all night. That shit is nerve wrecking. I need a blunt and a drink right now, shit."

"Well I can't help you with the drink. But the blunt, I got you."

"Well for right now, that's gonna have to do."

"What's up Tee," Nicki said.

"Oh shit. What's up girl."

"Well, I'm about to leave, but I'll call you later." Nicki said to Slump as she kissed him and said bye to Stone and Tee.

Slumped

When she walked out the door, Tee said, "Your future, huh."

"Yep and it sure do look good." Slump said laughing.

"Yeah, you right about that, kinfolks." Stone said.

"Y'all go head. Roll up. I'm bout to go wash my ass, then we can get up out of here."

Chapter 24

 "So when the ladies supposed to be getting back?" Slump asked Tee. As he, Lil Lee, and Stone walked through Arden Fair Mall.

"If not later on tonight, they will be here first thing in the morning and I can't wait. I couldn't even fuck Vicki last night because I was so stuck in thought about Jazzmine."

"Damn, it's like that huh."

"Yeah, that girl got a nigga's nose wide open. It's just something about that bitch that drive me crazy. But enough about that, have you got in touch with ol' girl yet?" Tee asked.

"No, but don't trip. We will be seeing her, real soon. She work up here at the bath and body store."

"Say kinfolk. This place is live as motherfucker. I ain't never seen this many bitches in one place before. And they got all shapes and sizes." Stone said looking like a fat kid in a candy store. "I most definitely gotta get out here more."

"Naw, nigga. You just gotta get out of them trees, country boy and get in the city. Where the kitties are shaved and pretty." Tee said.

"You two niggas are straight freaks." Slump said laughing.

"Hey bro. Let's go into Foot Locker." Lil' Lee said.

"It's your day, baby boy. I'm following you."

"Can I get the new Jordans?"

"I told you, you can get any two pair of shoes you want."

Slumped

"Three!" Said Tee. "I'll buy you one too."

They spend the rest of the day in and out of different shoe and clothing stores. They then headed to Bath and Body. Walking in, Lee said, "I don't need nothing out of here."

"You sure you don't need no soap to wash your dirty ass?" Stone said laughing.

"Oh, you got jokes huh. Fatter than me." Lil' Lee said back.

"C'mon y'all. Chill out. Matter of fact. Why don't y'all go to the food court and I will meet y'all over there in a few minutes." Stone, Tee, and Lil' Lee left for the food court just as Alicia was walking up to Slump.

Alicia was 5'6" and had the smoothest milk chocolate colored skin. 34-27-40. A dime piece with hair all the way down her back. Hers too and not because she bought it.

"Hey sexy."

"What's been up with you." Slump said as she walked up and hugged him.

"Not too much, just working and doing me. How about yourself.?"

"I'm good. Was just taking my little brother to pick up a few things for school."

"Yeah, I saw his little crazy butt when y'all first came in."

"Oh him and my cousin Tee went to get something to eat."

"So what brought you in here today?" She asked.

"You did. And the fact that I been thinking a lot about you since the last time I saw you." Slump said looking her in the eyes.

"Jaylon you know I got a man already."

"So it's like that now, huh. You ain't got no time for me."

"I didn't say that. All I said was I have a man."

"So what you saying, we can't kick it?"

"I don't know Jaylon. But let's not get into that now. I'm supposed to be working."

Slumped

"Alright. But I need to see you. Do you still got my number?"

"Yes!"

"Good then. Why don't you call me when you can get away and talk."

"Alright, I'll do that. I promise."

"Well then. I'm gonna let you get back to work." Slump said, kissed her on the cheek and walked out the store.

"So what did she say?" Tee asked before Slump even sat down.

"She ain't said shit nigga. I ain't just gon' come out and say what's up girl. How you been. By the way, I want to rob your nigga and I need your help."

"Well shit, you the one that said the bitch still love you and shit. I thought y'all had something going on."

"Check it out Tee. I know you older than me and everything, but why you always gotta question me. Is you in a rush to do it or something. I mean because shit, if you got a better idea, spit it out nigga. I'm all ears."

"You right Slump. You right. I'm just ready to get this money, my nigga." Tee said.

"Well, don't trip. It's coming. Ol' girl gonna get at me later in the week and I'm gonna put shit all in motion. I know you ain't hurting for no doe, are you?"

"Naw, it ain't nothing like that. I just been wanting to get this nigga for so long. I'm a little impatient. My bad."

"Now you sound like I did the first time I got down with you. So I'm gon' tell you like you told me. We take our time, do it right, and leave no loose ends."

"Speaking of loose ends, you heard about Black." Tee said.

"Yeah, Lil' Lee was telling me something about that." Slump said like he had no idea what had really happened to Black.

"Yeah that's what I heard. I hope the lil' nigga alright."

Slumped

"Yeah, he probably laying around here somewhere. Man, I don't believe this shit." Slump said.

"What!" Said Tee looking around, spotting what Slump was seeing.

"Ain't that that one bitch that you fucked and sent her in the room with me?"

"Yeah, that's her. I sure hope Stone know what he getting himself into. And where the fuck is Lil' Lee ass at."

"I gave him a hundred and he went to the hat store. You know you gotta have a fitted to match the shoes.

"Well shit. C'mon, let's go get his lil' ass and get up outta here.

Back in Texas

Chapter 25

"There ain't no way I'm letting this shit slide." Money said to Red. "Them niggas got shit fucked up."

"Yeah, I feel you. Them niggas don't know who they fucking with." Red and Money used to be them niggas back in DC until Money's temper got them in trouble with a local detective they used to pay when they sold drugs. The detective got greedy and threatened to lock them up unless they paid him more money. Instead of paying him, Money killed him, and they had been in Texas ever since.

If Tee, Stone, and Slump would have known that these two were in fact DC's infamous Murder Money and Dirty Red, they would have killed them both that night at the Hytop. Something they might live to regret later, who knows, but one thing was for sure, Red and Money were not the type to let anything slide without bloodshed and they had a whole squad of young killas that would take God to war just for the recreation because their gods were Murder Money and Dirty Red. Not to mention they already had something that belonged to them.

In the backroom of the warehouse where they called "The Vault," Porshea and Jazzmine sat naked, tied to some chairs. The night Tee, Slump, and Stone robbed and beat Money and Red, a local hustler named Skip told Money had had seen the two girls at the Super 8 off the Highway 10. So Red and he rushed there and just as Porshea and Jazz were leaving, Money, Red, and Skip pulled in and forced them into the trunk of their rental, took them back to the vault, and did any and everything that came to mind to the two women, from fucking them to letting a few other people fuck them, and forcing them to fuck each other. At first, they tried resisting and fighting back, but after being beaten, burned with blunts, spit on, and kicked, they just wanted to live and were willing to do whatever they were told.

"Jazz! Jazz! C'mon girl. Say something." Porshea said looking over at Jazz whose head hung over limply. She was bleeding badly from a gash over her left eye. Skip had just left out the room. He had been their tormentor for the last two days, but today, out of anger, Jazz had told him when Tee found out what they were doing to them, he would surely kill everyone who had a part in it. And he savagely fucked her in the ass until she passed out from the pain, and him thinking she was faking, kicked her in the face, bursting her eye open.

"C'mon Jazz. Answer me!" Porshea said through tears, but Jazz wasn't moving or responding. Porshea could see she was breathing from the slow rise and fall of her chest. "Please God, help us!" Porshea said aloud.

"Ohhh." Jazz said coming to.

"Oh thank God."

"Jazz!"

"Porshea?"

"Yeah girl. I'm here. How do you feel?"

"Like my asshole got kicked." Jazz said trying to smile but it hurt too much.

"Yeah, you should have seen the look in that crackhead motherfucker's face when you told him Tee would kill him. He was scared but tried to hide it."

"If I get loose, these niggas ain't gonna have to worry about Tee because I'm gonna kill them myself. I swear I'm gonna bite the next dick off that gets anywhere near me.

"Please don't do nothing crazy Jazzmine." Porshea said.

"What the fuck you mean don't do nothing crazy bitch. Look at us. We got to do something. They ain't gonna keep us here forever."

Slumped

"What the fuck is you tramps in here talking about? How was your nap?" Skip said looking at Jazz.

"Fuck you nigga!" Jazz said as he punched her in the mouth, knocking her over in the chair.

"I see you still ain't learned your lesson yet. I got something else for you bitch." He said unbuttoning his pants.

"No please. Leave her alone. Please! I'll do whatever you want me to." Porshea said.

"You gon' do that anyway. But if you play nice, I'll let you slide this time." Skip said.

"I'll do whatever you want. Just please don't hit her no more."

Chapter 26

"Hey gorgeous!" Slump said walking into the kitchen with Mama Kay as she did what she always did when she had the house to herself...bake.

"Hey baby, when you get here?"

"I just walked into the door bringing lil' Lee back."

"Oh, I hope you didn't spend all your money on his ass."

"Nah. I'm cool. What you baking?"

"Brownies for the bake sale at the church. I know you gonna come this Sunday right? And bring that pretty little girl with you. Speaking of her, you like her, don't you son?"

"Yeah I do. She is real special to me."

"I could tell. When she is around, you got life back in those big brown eyes."

"Yeah, she makes me really want to live. You know what I mean?"

"Yeah I know what you mean. So what you gonna do about it? Momma Kay asked him looking into his eyes.

"What do you mean what am I gonna do?"

"Boy, don't play stupid with me. You know what the hell I'm talking about. I know what you are out there doing and I just want you to know you will never forgive yourself if you hurt that girl. And you will never find another one like her. When you love someone Jaylon, you gotta be willing to make changes. Make sacrifices. Because it's no longer just about you. You have to think about how what you do will affect her. I mean that is if you are serious and she ain't just some good pussy that got you sprung."

"Momma!"

"What boy. You act like I always been this old. I had my fair share of niggas just like you running behind me."

"Alright ma, that's a little too much information. But to answer your question, I'm serious. I'm just in the middle of something right now."

"Yeah, and a year from now, you are still gonna be in the middle of it." Before he could respond, he heard Shawanna's big mouth.

"Momma! Come look at what I got."

"Do you gotta scream?" Lil' Lee said from the couch where him and Stone sat with a PS3 controller in hand playing the new Madden.

"Shut up boy. Look at my stuff Momma!" Shawanna said pulling shirts, pants, skirts, and different colored halter tops.

"Damn girl, what you do, buy the whole store." Mama K asked.

"It looks like it. And I didn't even get a thank you." Slump said.

"THANK YOU !!!" Shawanna said giving Slump a big, wet kiss on the cheek.

"We got something for you too." Nicki said handing Mama K a Krest Jewelry bag.

"What's this?"

"Open it and find out." Shawanna said. Mama K pulled the box out the bag and opened it.

"Oh it's so beautiful." She said holding up the 18 karat gold chain with the diamond and gold heart locket on it. "Put it on for me baby." She asked Nicki as she looked over her shoulder and continued. "You are such a special girl." Slump knowing full well what she meant by the statement. Clearing his throat, he told Stone and Tee it was time to go. He gave Mama K and Shawanna both a big hug and popped Lil' Lee upside his head. "I love y'all." Kissing Nicki, he said, "I'll see you at the house."

"Alright babe." She said before walking out the door.

"Auntie, can I get some of that cake you baked in there?" Stone asked.

"I ain't even baked no cake Michael. It's some brownies and yes, you can get a few to take with you."

"Don't eat all the brownies fat boy." Lil' Lee said.

"Shut up chump!" Stone said rushing into the kitchen.

Once they were in the car, Tee said, "Slump, you still got some of that weed left?"

"I got a few zips left. Why?"

"I need like a quarter. You know Vicki ass is a pothead and if I'm bout to be in there with her ass tonight I need her to be high. Shit she don't bitch as much when she high."

"It's good. I got you bro. So what are y'all gon' get into tonight."

"We are gonna go out and eat with Nicki and one of her girls."

"Oh word. You trying to hook Stone up, huh."

"Something like that. He damn sure don't need to be fucking with that bitch he was talking to at the mall."

"Oh shit. I forgot about her." Stone said from the backseat.

"Good!" Slump and Tee said together.

"Aw shit. Don't let me find out y'all hating on the country boy."

"Naw cousin. We ain't hating. We saving. That bitch ain't no good. She real disrespectful."

"Oh you know her?"

"Yeah, I fucked a while back."

"And he scared the hell outta the bitch." Tee said laughing.

"Ain't her and Jazz related?" Slump asked.

"Yeah. Speaking of Jazz. They should have been back by now."

"You ain't heard from them?" Slump asked.

"Naw, I ain't talked to them since they dropped us off at the airport."

"I thought you said you did."

"Naw, I said I thought they would be back tonight or first thing in the morning."

"You tried to call them?"

"Yeah, but I ain't getting no answer."

"Them two freaks is probably pulled over fucking each other. But I'm sure they're alright." Stone said.

"Yeah, they're good." Tee said.

"So who your girl gonna bring for me tonight, kinfolk?" Stone asked.

"I don't know but all the bitches she fuck with are for sure bad ones."

"Yeah, I can vouch for that." Tee said.

Once they got back to the house, Slump gave Tee some tree and got in the shower. For some reason he had a funny feeling but put it off and thought about what Mama K said.

Around 7:30, Nicki got there with her friend Angel, a soft spoken, big boned chocolate girl. A little chubby but far from ugly. And to everyone's delight, her and Stone hit it off instantly. They went to Joe's Crab Shack where they had the best lobster and strongest Long Island Iced Teas.

"So Michael, where are you from?" Angel asked.

"I'm an old country boy. I'm from Texas. How about you?"

"I'm also a country girl coming from the big boot state of Louisiana. But I've been living out here in Cali since I was about fifteen. So how do you like it out here so far?"

"I like it a lot better now that I've met you."

"Aww, ain't that cute." Nicki said.

"Leave him alone." Slump said.

"I'm just playing with him." Nicki said sipping her Long Island. "But y'all do look good together."

"So Mike. You don't mind if I call you Mike, do you?" Angel asked.

"He shouldn't."

"Why."

"Because Jaylon calls him Stone and he calls Jaylon Slump"

"Stone huh. I like that." Angel said. "I need a rock in my life."

With that, Slump damn near choked to death trying to swallow and laugh at the same time.

"What's so funny?" Stone asked.

"Nothing. I'm just happy for you two cornballs. Ya'll both country as hell." Slump said.

"Leave em' alone." Nicki said punching him in the arm.

They had a great time and for the first time in his life, Slump was at peace not worried about anything but keeping his beautiful woman happy and with a smile on her face. But still, something wasn't right. He just didn't know what it was.

Chapter 27

"**D**amn Skip. What you been doing to this bitch." Money said looking at the battered Jazzmine. Her eye was completely swollen shut and she had cake up blood on the left side of her face and hair.

"That one has a real bad attitude but I done almost broke her. Ain't that right." Skip said reaching out to touch her, causing her to jump like she was slapped. Money laughed like he was just told the world's funniest joke.

"Damn these bitches stink." Red said walking into the room. "Damn Skip. You done fucked her pretty little face up." Jazzmine sat there with a blank look on her face mumbling incoherently to herself.

Yeah, you bitch ass niggas think what you want to. But if you don't kill me, I'm gonna make sure all of you pay with your lives. She thought.

"Please let me clean her up." Porshea said.

"Untie them and let them clean their asses up." Money said.

"You sure." Skip asked.

"What I say nigga. Ain't no windows in there for them to get out and even if they could, ain't nowhere for them to go."

Once untied, Porshea went to Jazzmine's side to help her up.

"C'mon Jazz. I got you." She said with silent tears running down her face. Once they made it in the bathroom, Jazz came out of her fake trance and hugged Porshea.

"Shh…Listen to me. We gotta get out of here."

"How we gonna do that?"

"Easy. All that crackhead motherfucker wanna do is get high and fuck. So the next time it's just us and him in here, we are gonna give him the best fuck he ever had but we both got to be untied."

"That nigga is crazy Jazz."

"Porshea we got to or these niggas gonna kill us. Alright."

"Alright, Jazz."

"What the fuck is you two bitches talking about?" Money said kicking the door open. "Wash your pussies and get the fuck outta the shower."

"Look at her face Money and all the blood in her hair. Even you can't be this heartless." Porshea said.

"You don't know me too well, bitch. Now hurry up before I drag you out by your hair. And don't close this door again. You bitches ain't got nothing I ain't seen before." Money said walking off.

"I hate that nigga." Porshea said under he breath.

"He gonna get his. I promise you." Jazz said.

Chapter 28

"Man I don't know what the fuck is going on. I been calling both of their cell phones and neither one of them pick up. Something ain't right. I don't know what, but something ain't right."

"I've been having that same feeling for a few days now but what you think it could be." Slump said.

"To tell the truth. I don't know why ya'll sweating them boppers anyway. The same way you meet a bitch, you lose a bitch. And them two could be doing anything or anyone for that matter. I say fuck em. If they show up, they show up. If they don't, they don't." Stone said.

"Yeah, well who asked you?" Tee said.

"I'ma act like I didn't hear that because you are my kinfolk people but don't' let the smooth taste fool you, playboy. I'm out here on business. Don't make this personal."

"Ya'll both need to chill the fuck out." Slump said before it went any further. "Smoke some weed and chill out. Tee, ain't nothing we can do but hope they are alright. I got some good news though. I talked to ol' girl and I'm gonna hook up with her later so I can see how she feels about helping us out and I don't need you two trying to kill each other because someone's emotions got in the way. So we straight?"

"Yeah we straight." Stone and Tee said.

"I'm serious ya'll. We got a lot of shit about to happen. Some life changing shit. And after we make this move, we have to be able to trust each other with our lives." Slump said looking from Tee to Stone.

"It's good man." Tee said.

"Yeah kinfolk. We tight." Stone said.

"Good, now let's go see if I still got a smooth tongue and a sweet dick because even though I don't want to, I know I'm gonna have to fuck her to get all the way in her head." Slump said as he walked out the door to meet Alicia.

"Hey what's up love?" Slump said as Alicia walked up to his car. He pulled up to the apartments where she lived in Mathomas. She had been out there waiting for him.

"Not too much. And before I get in this car with you, tell whose it is or who you stole it from."

"Oh I see you got jokes and shit huh. Well it ain't stolen and it belongs to me. Anything else you need to know. "

"Naw, not right now."

"Well get your ass in then." Slump said.

"Wait a minute Jaylon. You ain't said nothing about us going nowhere. You said you needed to talk to me about something."

"What you scared of being alone with me or something?"

"No! I just wasn't expecting to be going anywhere."

"Get in the car Alicia and stop laying with me."

"What if I don't' want to."

"Well then we ain't doing shit but wasting time and I'm out of here." Slump said looking her dead in her eyes.

"I hate it when you look at me like that." Alicia said getting in the car.

"Well, why you always got to make shit so difficult."

"Why you always come around when you need something or want some pussy." She countered.

"Look you been knowing me since we was kids and you know how I live and what I do to get my money so I'm gonna skip all the bullshit and just get straight to the point. I know you fuck with the nigga Munch."

Slumped

"What a minute. So this is about him? I should have known it. I ain't seen you in seven months and all of a sudden, you want to talk."

"Naw, it ain't nothing like that Alicia. I been trying to see you. This just gave me a real reason."

"What you want Jaylon cuz I ain't got time for this shit."

"Oh so you ain't got time for me after all I've done for you. After what I did for you, this is how you're gonna repay me?"

"So I owe you now."

"You fucking right you owe me. How many niggas you know what have done what I did?"

"None." She said under her breath, tears now falling freely down her cheeks as memories she tried to forget rushed back.

When she was sixteen, her uncle raped her almost every night since she had been forced to live with him after her mother died two years earlier. Her uncle Shawn, her mother's brother, was her only living relative and he vowed that if anyone ever found out about them, he would kill her. Alicia had become pregnant a few weeks after her sixteenth birthday, not for the first time, but for the third. She had no one to turn to but Jaylon, her high school boyfriend. She bared all to him hoping that he wouldn't see her differently after she revealed her secret. Jaylon was far from your average sixteen year old. Most guys her age would have seen her as a freak and didn't want any more to do with her. But not him, he felt a deeper connection with her and wanted to free her from this pain. From the monster that abused her. One night he broke in and caught her uncle in the act of raping her. Planning to just get her out of there, the scene drove him mad and before he knew it, he shot her uncle in the back of the head as he thrusted in and out of Alicia. Once the police came, she told them what had been happening for years. The police arrested Jaylon and charged him with first-degree murder, which he beat but still ended up in the

California Youth Authority for being on probation and having a gun.

"What do you want me to do Jaylon."

"First tell me if you love him or not?"

"No I don't love him. Not like that but I do love what he does for me."

"So then, it's only about the money?"

"Something like that."

"What if I told you I'll take care of you."

"Just tell me what you need me to do, Jaylon."

"I need you to find out where he keeps all his money and drugs and that's it. I will take care of the rest."

She sat there and thought about it for a minute, then said, "I'll do it but after you do whatever it si your planning on, I want some and your word that he will never know I told you."

"You got all the information I need and I will make sure you get the money and he will never know we had this talk."

"Well it might take some time because a few months ago, his number one spot was robbed and his man Fat Mack was killed. Wait a minute, you didn't have anything to do with that, did you?"

"Ask me no questions and I'll tell you no lies." Slump said simply.

"So that's how you coped this car." She said without expecting a response. Instead, he changed the subject. Already getting what he wanted, hating the fact that he threw their past in her face knowing the pain it caused her, but thinking all is fair in love and war.

"So what you want to do now?" he asked.

"Nothing. I got to work in the morning and it's getting kinda late. We been riding around for an hour and a half. Just take me home and I'll call you when I have what you need." After dropping her off, he headed back to Stone and Tee to tell them the play was in motion.

Chapter 29

Now that things were destined to happen, they decided to hit 3 Kings and get their drink on. And as usual, Big Sam was working the door.

"What's up Jaylon...Tee."

"Aw you know Big Sam?" Tee asked.

"Same shit, different toilet." Slump said.

"Big Sam, this old country nigga right here is my cousin Mike from Texas. He's gonna be out here for a while so get used to seeing him."

"Alright then fellas. Y'all have a good time. And Jaylon, you know I gotta ask."

"Don't trip Sam. I left it in the car." Slump said with a smile on his face. Once inside the club, Stone said, "We should have here, shit. This my type of place as bad as I need some pussy." Slump and Tee both started laughing. They all ordered some drinks and found them a table.

"So what was Alicia talking about?" Tee asked.

"She down for it, but she wants to get paid."

"Oh yeah."

"Yep, she said she wants fifty stacks. How ya'll feel about that?"

"We ain't got no problem with it." They both said in unison. Just then, Ridah came up to their table. "What's up my niggas." He said to Tee and Slump.

"What's up." They said as Slump introduced Stone.

Slumped

"I've been trying to catch up to you but you been MIA" Ridah said to Slump.

"Yeah, I've been out of town, but what's up." Thinking this nigga better not ask for money. He had already gave him ten stacks for the role he played in offing Young Black.

"I just need to holler at you about that thing."

"What thing?" Tee asked.

"Oh it ain't nothing. I'm gon' let ya'll get back to doing ya'll. Nice to meet you Stone." Ridah said.

As Ridah walked off, Tee said, "What the fuck is that fly ass nigga talking about Slump.

"I will tell you later." Slump said looking across the club and Ridah.

"So now we got secrets and shit huh."

"Naw, it ain't nothing like that. Matter of fact, let's get up outta here."

"What! C'mon kinfolk. We just got here." Stone said.

"Yeah but something just came up." Slump said and the look on his face spoke a thousand words.

Once they got outside and into Tee's truck, Slump told them how he had Ridah follow Young Black and then bring him out to the old roads where Slump killed him. After he told them the story, Tee said, "So you knew the whole time Black was dead when I told you he was missing. I should have known you had something to do with it. After all, I know how you feel about loose ends. So now what are you going to do about him?"

Before Slump could answer, Stone said, "Let me deal with that nigga. I don't like how he tried to play you. He was on some slick shit putting your business out there like that. And I need to show you and Tee how I get down. That fuck nigga just gave me a reason so I'm gonna give ya'll an example." Neither Tee nor Slump said anything because the look Stone gave them said it all.

Chapter 30

"Oh shit...yes...yes...oohhh fuck me...yes right there...." Porshea said as Skip thrust in and out of her.

"You like this dick, don't you bitch." Skip said on the verge of coming.

"Yes daddy!" Porshea said thinking, this little dick motherfucker gonna get his.

"Oh yeah bitch. I'm bout to come." Skip said stroking Porshea.

"Wait don't' come yet. I want to taste you." Jazzmine said from the chair she was tied naked to.

"Oh do you want Big Daddy Skip to put all this dick in you."

"Yes! Please untie me. I've been over here watching long enough."

"Yeah I knew you would come around. Can't no bitch resist this dick." He said feeling cocky while untying her. Even though her eye was still swollen shut, Jazzmine was still a bad bitch. Standing up and kissing Skip, while stroking his five in erection. She told him, "Lay down big daddy, so I can take all this dick up in this pussy, while grabbing his hand and placing it on her pussy. "Look how wet you got me."

"Come on back to the bed." Porshea said. Skip was so caught up in the moment, he never say her grab the big glass ashtray that sat on the floor by the bed.

Slumped

Jazzmine pushed him back toward the bed as he sat down. While playing her part, she got down on her knees and gave him the best head he ever had. She was sucking his dick like her life depended it, which it did. And before he knew what happened, Porshea smashed the ashtray in the back of his head with everything she had repeatedly. He yelled out as he tried to push Jazzmine off him but she had bitten down on his dick like she was part pitbull. Almost biting it off, he fell to the floor trying to cover up, but Porshea and Jazzmine only started kicking and stomping him until he was unconscious.

"What are we gonna do with him now?" Porshea asked.

"We are gonna tie his ass up and get the fuck outta here. Now come up." They tied Skip to the chair the same way he did them. They found their clothes and looked for the keys to the rental car. Once they found them in Skip's jeans along with a couple hundred dollars, they got out of there. They drove all night trying to get as far away from Money and Red as possible before they stopped at a gas station to call Tee.

"Please pick up!" Jazzmine said.

"Hello?"

"Tee!" Jazzmine said breaking down crying.

"Jazzmine. Where the hell ya'll been. I been calling ya'll phone and ya'll ain't been answering. What the fuck is going on."

"They kidnapped us and had up in some warehouse in a back room where they did all kinds of things to us."

"Wait a minute girl. Slow down. Who kidnapped you?"

"Money, Red, and this crazy nigga named Skip, who beat me and Porshea on a regular if we didn't do what we wanted him to.

"Where's Porshea. Is she with you?"

"Yeah, she right here."

"Are ya'll alright? Where are ya'll?"

"We're at some gas station in El Paso."

"Do ya'll got some money."

"Only about $170 we took for Skip when we got away."

Slumped

"Alright, look. Find a Western Union and call me from there. I'll wire ya'll some money so ya'll can get back here. Don't stop for nothing. Now go find one, I'll tell ya'll what to do after that. Remember don't stop for nobody. Now hurry up."

When Jazzmine hung the phone up, Porshea asked, "What did he say."

"He told us to find a Western Union so he can wire us some money and not to stop for nobody." After Tee hung up, he called Slump and told him what happened. Slump told him to keep him posted and asked if he needed any money.

"Naw, I got it. But when we get back out there, you know we gonna have to deal with them niggas, right?"

"Yeah! But we ain't about to talk about it over the phone. So come to the house or I'll come over there."

"Naw, I'll come over there after I send them the money."

"Alright then. In a minute." Slump hung up and told Stone what he'd just heard. Afterwards, Stone said, "I know how Skip is. He used to get money in Houston until he started getting high. Now he does whatever to support his habits. I heard he supposed to be working for Money and Red. I guess it's true. I knew we should have killed them niggas."

"Yeah I'm starting to feel like that too." Slump said lighting a blunt.

Tee got there about an hour later. "Man, I'm gonna murder them bitch ass niggas. I can't believe they had the nuts to ever try some shit like that." He said pacing back in forth in Slump's living room. Slump had never seen Tee so upset before and they had been through a lot together.

"I know you got feelings for them and I can understand how you fee. But let's not get sidetracked from the big picture. They knew what they were getting into when they agreed to help us get them niggas. But now we got something bigger and I need you focused. When the time comes, believe me, I'll help you make them niggas pay with their lives."

Slumped

"Yeah, I got you on that too. But ain't nothing we can do right now." Stone said.

Out of nowhere, Tee started laughing.

"What's so funny?" Slump asked. Tee told him how Jazzmine said she damn near bit Skip's dick off.

"What type of stupid motherfucker is gonna put his dick in the mouth of somebody he kidnapped? That nigga must have been high or something?" Stone said.

"You know what they say, crack kills. I'm just glad they're alright. So how long before they get back." Slump asked.

"Well they were in El Paso when I sent them the money so they should be back tomorrow. I told them not to stop for nothing. Just thinking about what they went through is driving me crazy, Slump. I mean yeah, we all knew it was a chance they chose to take but I can't stop blaming myself and I won't until I get them niggas heads hung up on a wall." Tee said.

"Yeah, I feel your pain. But we can't change what happened so all we can do is get even. And trust me, get even we will.

Chapter 30

Later that night, Ridah sat in his car getting his dick sucked by a local ripnutt named Candy. He had been parked in the back of 3 Kings too caught up in Candy's head game and never saw Stone creeping up on the side of his car until it was too late. The big Smith and Wesson bulldog 44 magnum roared once taking most of the left side3 of his face off before Candy could get his dick out of her mouth. The big gun roared again blowing blood and brain matter all over the inside of Ridah's Caprice Classic. Stone ran back to the car where Slump and Tee waited for him.

"That was one hell of a blow job." He said laughing.

"I always knew his dick would be the death of him." Tee said.

Slump didn't say anything. He just looked at Stone through the rearview mirror and nodded his head. He felt no words were needed. His cousin showed him when it came down to it, he was down, he was down for whatever. Whichever way the wind blew the leaves and that's all Slump needed to know. Instead of leaving the scene, Slump parked in the front, they got out, and went inside to have a drink. The first person they saw was Munch and a few of his goons.

"Look at him. Sitting there like his shit don't stank. Like he can't be touched. I can't wait to wipe that look off his face for good." Tee said. Once Munch saw them, he waved them over to his table in VIP.

"What's up Tee. Young Slump?" He said as they walked up to the table.

"Just another day." Slump said.

"Yeah you know how it is. Just trying to make a dollar out of ten pennies." Tee said.

Not paying Tee any attention, he looked over to Slump, "When you gon' come fuck with me Slump. I could really use a nigga like you. Could put a lotta money in your pockets too."

"No disrespect to you Munch but I ain't never been for sale."

"Yeah, well when you get tired of being broke, come holler at me." Munch said causing his little entourage to laugh.

"I didn't get the joke." Stone said to the big black nigga with dreads standing in front of Munch. Stone hit dread head with a hard right hook putting him to sleep before he even hit the ground. Before it could get any further, Big Sean and two of 3 King's bouncers just as big grabbed Stone and tried to calm everyone down.

"Jaylon, I got a lot of love for you but I'm gonna ask you and your people to get up out of here." Big Sean stated.

"It's all good Sam. We were just leaving."

"I"ma kill you nigga." Dread head yelled as his boys held him back.

"What's wrong? He can't take a joke." Slump said as they were walking away. They could still hear the big dread head yelling. They made it as far as the bar before three cops walked through the door. The owner of the club, an OG named King, was now talking to the cops, but Slump, Tee and Stone kept their cool and walked out the club. They could see cops all over the back parking lot and yellow tape around the car, which they all knew was Ridah's. They got in Slump's Audi and drove off.

"What made you hit him?" Tee asked Stone.

Slumped

"He looked a little sleepy. Besides I didn't like the way that other nigga was trying to play my kinfolk. Who was he anyway?" Stone said.

"That's the nigga we been telling you about?" Slump said.

"So that's Mr. Money Bags, huh?"

"Yeah that was him."

"Yeah well fuck him. His time on earth ain't long now anyway." Stone said.

"Nigga you need some pussy." Tee said laughing. They dropped Tee off at his truck.

"When Jazzmine and Porshea get here, call us." Slump said.

"Alright. You niggas be safe. I'll call you in the a.m." Tee responded.

Chapter 31

At the time Tee was getting out of the car with Slump and Stone; in Texas, Red and Money were pulling up to the warehouse.

"I hope this crazy nigga ain't kill these bitches yet. I want to fuck that Porshea bitch one more time." Red said.

"That bitch do got some good pussy, don't she." Money said laughing. The first thing they noticed they noticed when they got out the car was the smell.

"Damn, you smell that shit. It smells like a dead body around this motherfucker." Money said. The smell only grew stronger the closer they got to the door. When they got to the door, the smell was so strong Red threw up all over his shoes.

"Skip! C'mon Red. Something ain't right." Money called out, getting no reply. He pulled out his 40 caliber.

"Shit nigga. The smell says something ain't right. They got to the back room where Jazzmine and Porshea were supposed to be and found Skip tied to the chair naked.

"Oh shit. What the fuck them bitches do to him. Look at his dick. They damn near cut it off." Red said.

"I knew we should have killed them two bitches. Let's go check the safe."

They went to the room where they kept all the dope and money. "Nothing's missing from here." Red said.

Money grabbed one of the big duffle bags and threw the other to Red. "C'mon. Let's get this shit and get up outta here."

Slumped

"But what we gon' do about Skip?"

"Fuck Skip. I'm gonna burn this bitch up with his body in it. Ain't no telling if them bitches went to the police or not and we don't need nothing linking us to this shit."

They got their drugs, money, and the few guns they kept stored in the vault. They poured gas on everything and set fire to the warehouse.

"I'm really starting to hate these niggas." Red said as Money drove away.

Chapter 32

Porshea and Jazzmine made it back to Sacramento at 6:35a.m. the next morning.

"How you feeling?" Porshea asked Jazz who hadn't been all that talkative.

"Girl, I don't' know what I'm supposed to be feeling, let alone how. I mean I'm glad to still be alive and I hope that dirty motherfucker bleeds to death, but as far as what I'm feeling, I don't know."

"Yeah, I know what you mean. I just want to get in the bathtub and soak. But I don't feel like I will ever be clean again. I can still feel his hands on me. I've never been more scared in my life. And we didn't get shit out of the deal."

All this bitch think about is money. Fuck the fact that we were beat and raped for a whole week. Jazz thought.

"What do we do now," Porshea asked pulling Jazz from her thoughts.

"Let's go to my cousin's house before we call Tee."

"I know that nigga betta have some money for us."

"Aight bitch. Is that all you think about, some motherfucking money. Them niggas was gonna kill us and all you think about is money this and money that."

"I'm just saying. I needs mine. You the stupid one who thinks this nigga Tee cares about you. And after all we went through, if you think he is gonna still want you, you're even crazier than that nigga who did this shit to us."

Slumped

Maybe Porshea was right. She had been raped over and over by three different men. Maybe Tee wasn't feeling her no more but she wouldn't let Porshea know how close her words struck to home. They made it to Lexas house and one look at Jazz's face sent Lexas on a rampage.

"What the fuck happened to you. Where you been. It was them two niggas. I knew I shouldn't have let you fuck with them." Jazz got her calm and told her all about her trip to Texas and how they were kidnapped the day they were coming back. After they were cleaned up and smoked a blunt of Cali's finest, they called Tee, who seemed more excited about her being back than she was.

"Where ya'll at?" Tee asked.

"We're at my cousin's house."

"How do I get there?"

"You know where Point Natomas apartments are off Northgate Blvd. and San Juan?"

"Yeah, I know where they at. Give me twenty minutes and I'll be there." Before she could answer. He hung up.

"Hello." Slump said.

"What's up my nigga." Tee said walking out of Vicki's house.

"Not much, just getting up. What's good with you?"

"I just got off the phone with Jazz. I'm on my way to see her and Porshea right now."

"Oh yeah. They back. That's what's up. So you want me and Stone to ride with you or what?"

"Naw I'm good. I just wanted to let you know they were back. Besides, they are at her cousin's spot and I know you ain't trying to see that bitch. So I'mma go check them out and holla back at you and stone later."

"Alright. And if they need anything, let me know. Shit we owe them that much."

"Yeah for sure. I'm gonna hit you later."

"Alright my nigga."

"Who was that?" Nicki asked.

"Nobody but Tee. Go back to sleep." Slump answered.

"Why you planning on sneaking out."

"Naw, I ain't going nowhere." He said laying back, pulling Nicki into his arms. Trying not to think about if it were her who had been done like Porshea and Jazz were. He kissed her on the forehead and held her until she fell back asleep.

Chapter 33

"**D**amn baby girl." Tee said looking at Jazz's face.

"I'm alright. It don't hurt no more."

"This was never supposed to happen. I promise them niggas will pay with their lives for what they did to you." Lexas wanted to talk shit to Tee but looking at him, she saw the pain in his eyes and more than that, she saw the love.

"Hello. What about me and what I need. I was there too." Porshea said.

"Yeah but your face ain't all fucked up." Tee said.

"That's because I kept my mouth closed."

"Yeah, well you need to try to do that shit now."

"Nigga you got your nerve. We drove your dope out there, got kidnapped and raped by some niggas and you go the nerve to come at me sideways."

"Look. I'm sorry all this shit happened to ya'll."

"Well sorry ain't put no money into my pocket."

"So that's all you want is some money." Tee said pulling a fat roll out his pocket. "Here bitch, take this shit. And forget your ass ever met me." He said throwing the roll at Porshea.

"Jazz. Let me take you to a hospital or something." Tee said.

"I'm alright. I just need to relax and get my thoughts together."

"Well let me take care of you baby girl. Can I do that?"

"If that's what you really wanna do." She said looking him in his eyes for the first time.

"Yeah that's what I wanna do. For as long as you let me. Let me make this up to you. Just tell me what you need me to do." *Damn, I'm crazy about this girl.* All of a sudden, Slump's plan to make this move seemed like the best thing going. He was tired of Vicki anyway. "Yeah girl. Let me make you happy." He said to Jazzmine.

Chapter 34

"What's good." Slump said as Alicia got in the car.

"Not too much. You know. Just doing me. But let's cut to the chase. You don't care about how I'm doing. All you want to know is if I got anything to tell you yet. And don't try to bullshit me. And I heard about what happened at 3 Kings with your boy Snake Tiny..."

"Who the fuck is Tiny?"

"Don't play stupid Jaylon. I'm talking about that shit you probably set up."

"First off, get your facts straight. Your man tried to play me and my cousin didn't find the shit funny so he knocked Tiny on his big ass. And if you think you're about to sit and my car and play me because your nigga likes to pillow talk. Then you got me fucked up. Matter of fact. If all you want to do is bitch about them bitch ass niggas, you can get out." Slump said pulling over.

Instead of answering him, she grabbed the blunt he had pre-rolled out the ashtray and hit it. Inhaling deeply, she said, "Damn. This is some good weed. And I don't know what crawled up your ass and got you so sensitive but you need to drive off before the police pull up behind your ass."

"I ain't got time for your games Alicia." He said pulling off.

"But you are so cute when you are mad." She said as the weed took effect.

"Pass the weed." Slump said knowing that at any time, she would be running off at the mouth. Weed made most people chill, sit back, and relax. But with Alicia, it was like it amped her up. She would talk nonstop for hours.

As if on cue, she said, "I ain't been able to find too much out yet. He'd been playing his cards close to his chest since Fat Mack got killed. But he do got another spot on North Highlands off Madison and on a street called Renick. And his so-called brother J Wood is running it. He's a little fat nigga that think he's all that."

"Oh yeah. So he be the only one up in there or what." Slump said passing him the blunt back.

"No, I think Tiny be there with him. Or at least he was. You know it's been almost a year."

"Almost a year for what."

"Almost a year since you gave me some. You know weed makes my pussy wet." Alicia said putting her hand on his lap.

"It ain't the weed girl. You just a freak." Slump said trying not to think about how good the sex was between them.

"You never seemed to have a problem with it."

"I don't think my lady would be happy with me sleeping with you."

"I didn't ask you to sleep with me. I just want you to fuck me. Don't tell me Ms. Thang got you pussy whipped, or better yet, I know you ain't scared of pussy." She knew he hated being told he was scared of anything.

"I ain't never been scared of anything."

"I can't tell."

"Who's at your apartment right now?" He said getting off the freeway.

"Nobody. And Munch always calls before he comes."

Back at her apartment, her legs were over his shoulders while he tried to knock the bottom out of her pussy.

"That's what I'm talking about. Fuck this pussy." She said. He always like the way he talked when they had sex.

Slumped

"Oh shit. Yeah...yeah...yeah...don't stop. I'm coming. Oh God, I'm coming." And right before her orgasm took control, he stopped, pulling all the way out of her.

"Put it back in. Please!" she begged.

"What you gonna do for me?"

"I'll do whatever you want me to. Just put it back in."

"Whatever?"

"Yes. Anything."

"Would you lie for me?"

"You know I will. Now fuck me and stop teasing me." She said looking Slump in his eyes as she thrusted her hips towards him, putting all nine inches back inside her pussy. Slump stroked her until her body shook uncontrollably. Watching her as he laid there, he tried to tell himself it was only business but he couldn't help but feel like he betrayed Nicki's trust. Going into the bathroom and washing his dick in the sink, he came out, dressed, and left.

"I need you to start digging a little deeper into the nigga's business."

"I'll do my part. You just better have my money when it's done."

Chapter 35

It had been two weeks since Porshea and Jazzmine had been back. Tee had been by Jazzmine's side the whole time. Tonight, he wanted to do something. He was tired of just being stuck up in the house. He had brought Jazzmine to the townhouse he had rented in Antalope. Not even his baby mama, Vickui could say she had been there. Looking at Jazzmine, Tee asked, "What you want to do tonight, gorgeous."

Her face had healed and even though her bruised eye hadn't completely faded, it wasn't that noticeable.

"I don't know. Why what do you wanna do?"

"I was thinking we can go out to eat. Maybe call Stone and Slump and have them and their chicks meet us somewhere."

"I don't know Tee. My eye is still kind of black."

"You barely even notice it. Besides, who cares, you still look better than 99% of the women walking around today anyway."

"Only 99%?"

"Hell baby, ain't nobody perfect. So what do you say?" Tee said causing her to start laughing.

"Why not."

"That's what I'm talking about." Tee said picking up the phone to call Slump.

Chapter 36

"Who was that?" Nicki asked once he hung up the phone.

"Tee wanting to know if we wanna go out to dinner with him and Jazzmine tonight."

"What you say?"

"I told him yeah, we could do that. Why you got something you have to do."

"No but I don't got nothing to wear."

"Here." He said handing her five crispy hundred dollar bills.

"I don't need all of this."

"Just take it and get something sexy. Hey Stone!" Slump yelled toward the living room.

"What's up." Stone yelled where Angel and he was hanging.

"Ya'll want to go out to eat?"

"Hell yeah!" The couple said in unison.

"Good. I just told Tee we would meet him at the Olive Garden tonight. Him and Jazz are finally about to come out the damn house."

"Oh yeah. How ol' girl doing anyway?

"Well shit, if we are gonna be meeting them for dinner, she gotta be doing alright."

"C'mon Angel. Ride with me to find something to wear." Nicki said.

Slumped

"Okay, I need to go by my house too so I can get me something." Angel stated.

"Naw. Here! Just buy you something." Stone said handing her three hundred dollars.

"Boy you are going to spoil me. You know that."

"That's what I'm trying to do. Now go on. Hurry and come back." Stone said slapping her ass.

Once the ladies left, Stone and Slump got deep into conversation.

"You know I've been thinking about what ol' girl said about the spot ol' boy had. And I don't see why we don't' hit that one while we waiting around doing nothing."

"Yeah, I been thinking about that too. And if we get a chance tonight, I'm gonna run it by Tee and see how he feels about it because it's way past time we started making shit happen."

"Now you talking my language."

"You know you crazy right?"

"It must run in the family because you ain't wrapped too tight your damn self." Stone said laughing.

Chapter 37

Jazzmine stood in front of the full-length mirror in a black dress made by Nicole Miller. Turning towards Tee, she said, "99% huh."

"Hell naw. Baby you are perfect now." Tee said meaning every word of it. He got off the bed where he'd been sitting, watching her dress. He wrapped her up in his arms. "I will never let anyone or anything hurt you again. You know that right?" He said looking in her eyes. Now once had he tried to have sex with her since she'd been back. He could sense she wasn't ready for that yet. No matter how bad he wanted her.

"Yeah. I know." Jazzmine said kissing him on the lips.

"Careful. Don't start nothing you can't finish. Now go ahead and get yourself ready. I told them we would meet them at 8p.m. I ain't trying to hear Slump's mouth. Knowing him, he'll be there at eight on the dot."

"Alright." She said after stealing another kiss.

"Alright girl. You keep doing that, you're gonna get yourself in trouble."

When they got to the Olive Garden, just as he suspected, they were already there.

"See. That little nigga got a problem with being precise." Tee said laughing.

"We look a little too dressed up." Stone said as they made their way into the restaurant; him in black Gucci slacks, a red button up shirt and leather Gucci driving shoes. Angel in a red Chanel suit and Jean and David heels. Slump was wearing a leather Versace with brown gators to match Nicki in her cream Dolce and Gabbana body suit and brown stilettos. Tee, being the OG out the group, was rocking a black with grey pin striped three piece Armani with black gators and Jazzmine in her black Nicole Miller.

"All eyes on us." Stone stated.

"Naw, all eyes on them." Slump said pointing to the ladies. They were seated and ordered drinks. They introduced Nicki and Angel to Jazzmine and asked how she was doing, noticing she was back to her sexy self.

"I'm cool. Tee been spoiling me."

"There seems to be a lot of that going around." Angel said.

"Tell me about it." Nicki stated as the girls laughed.

"Damn, I ain't never heard no woman complain about being taken care of." Slump said, sipping his Long Island Iced Tea. "So what's been up Tee?"

"Not too much. Just laying back with my future. You know."

"Yeah, I can dig that. Speaking of futures, I got something I need to holler at you about. Well, we got something we wanna run by you."

"Oh yeah."

"Yeah, but it can wait." They ordered their food and for the first time since they'd been back, they relaxed and enjoyed themselves; not worried about anything other than the women sitting next to them. After they ate, the decided to the night was still young so they decided to go to the Red Lion to have a few more drinks and listen to some music. When the ladies left to use the restroom, Slump and Stone put Tee up on robbing Munch's spot on Renick.

"The way I see it. We watch it for a few days, get a feel of how they are running it and bust that motherfucker wide open." Slump stated.

"That sounds like a plan to me but what about the real money. I know that nigga sitting on something cool."

"Yeah, Alicia is still trying to find out more on exactly where it's at but once she does, it's a go. But until then, I don't see why we can't hit the nigga's pockets. After all, when I got tired of being broke, I would holler at him."

"Holler at who?" Nicki asked.

"Holler at the person who came up with that bodysuit you got on and thank him." Slump said kissing her on the cheek. By 11:30 they all had their fair share of drinks and had different plans on how they would end their night. Stone decided to get a room so he could lay down his dick game. Angel had been hinting on giving him some pussy all night.

"So are you going to stay here?" Slump asked him.

"Yeah, I'm gonna call you in the morning."

"Be nice to him girl." Nicki said laughing.

"Oh I'm gonna be real nice. Bye Jazzmine. Nice to meet you." Angel said.

"All right then. Until the next time. And we definitely got to do this again." Jazzmine stated.

Slump and Tee agreed to hook up the next morning after picking up Stone so they could discuss how to move on the dope house.

"You think I'm stupid, don't you Jaylon?" Nicki said on the way back home.

"What are you talking about?"

"I'm talking about ya'll sitting there planning to do God knows what when we came back to the table."

"Look, I told you I had some things to take care of."

"Yeah, well I don't know how long I can sit around and wait on you to take care of these things. What if something happens to you. You get shot o wind up in jail. What am I supposed to do then? Who's gonna take care of me? Who is going to help me with the baby?"

"Wait? What baby are you talking about?" The alcohol made her slip. She didn't' want to tell him like that.

"The baby I'm pregnant with."

"How long have you known?"

Slumped

"I went to the doctor about a week ago for my check up and found out I am six weeks."

"So what you wanna do?" Slump said after a long moment of silence.

"What do you mean what I wanna do. Just like a nigga. You can lay down with me and fuck me without a rubber but when a bitch end up pregnant, it's what I wanna do. No nigga, it's what we gonna do. I didn't get pregnant by myself and I damn sure ain't going to raise no baby my myself. So now what you gonna do."

"I told you to give me one year. Just one and I would be done with this little thing I had going on."

"Well news flash nigga. You got eight months."

Slump took Nicki home and once they pulled into the apartment, he said, "I'll be back in a few hours."

"Where you going?"

"I don't know. Just ride around and get my thoughts together." Instead of arguing with him, she just got out the car and slammed the door.

When Slump made it back to the house, the sun had already started to come up. He had thought long and hard about everything and he was too close and in way too deep to turn back now. Nicki would just have to get with the program. Staring at Nicki in the doorway of the living room, all he could say was, "Damn…a baby."

Chapter 38

"**L**ook at that nigga. He think he Big Willie or somebody. Look how he got them niggas shook. I say we run up on him right now and lay his bitch ass down." Stone said. Slump and he had been watching J-Wood for about twenty minutes.

"Naw. We gonna just watch him and peep his moves for right now. Look. Ain't that big funny man right there?"

"Yeah, that's his big nice ass."

"Let's get out of here before somebody notices us."

"Yeah, whatever." Stone said looking at Slump.

"What's the matter with you?"

"I was gonna ask you the same thing kinfolk because for the last few days, it seems like you got something heavy on your mind."

"Only if you knew Mike."

"Aw shit. I gotta be something because you ain't called me Mike since we were kids. So tell me something. Who do we gotta kill."

"Naw, it ain't nothing like that. I just found out Nicki was pregnant and with all that's going on, I'm not sure if it's a good time to be having a baby."

"Yeah, I feel you. But you making it sound like what we're doing is forever."

"C'mon Stone. Think about it. This shit don't stop for niggas like us. Our souls have sold."

"Naw. Fuck that nigga. Speak for yourself. I ain't sold shit to nobody. I do what I gotta do to get by. I don't take pussy or touch on little kids. And I only get at niggas who get at me or my family. The way I see it; you got niggas like us and you got niggas that get in the way. But all that 'I sold my soul' shit; you can save that shit."

Slump didn't say anything. He just looked at his cousin.

"Besides nigga. I think you would be one helluva father anyway. Shit, you been taking care of Lee and Shawanna since your pops been dead so it's not like you don't know what to do. We gonna handle this business, get this money, and ain't nothing gonna stop you from being a daddy. So get your mind together. We can't afford to slip up now."

Chapter 39

Sitting in the Hytop, Red told Money, "I think it's time we turned up the head around this motherfucker. Look at how these niggas is acting all brand new and shit since we had that problem with them Cali niggas and that fat country boy. I mean I know we need to keep a low profile, but we are a long way from DC."

Money had been thinking the same thing. Ever since the fight with Tee, some of the niggas working for them had all been coming up short and acting like it wasn't a problem.

"Yeah I feel that. And I say we start right here." Money said.

"What you mean?"

"I mean that nigga Jack and how he acting like he don't need us anymore."

"So that's the plan?"

"I don't know yet. Give me a couple of days and I'm sure I'll come up with something. These country motherfuckers ain't never seen before." Money said with death in his eyes."

Chapter 40

Almost two weeks had went by from the day Slump and Stone sat watching J-Wood. Tee, Stone, and he sat in a black Astro van they had stolen earlier that day.

"So tonight's the night.." Tee said putting on a pair of murder ones.

"And it's about time too. I'm damn near broke." Stone said.

"Alright, we know the big nigga with the dreadlocks is up in there with him and there might even be a bitch or two. So this is how it's gonna go down. Once we get in there, we get the dope and the money. I don't care about the nigga with the dreads or the bitches, but we need J-Wood. I think he may know about Munch's operation. After all, he came out here with Munch from the Bay area and I think they are related somehow. Maybe his brother or something. So he comes with us. In and out…and Stone, don't shoot nobody unless you have to."

"I got you kinfolk. But if that nigga so much as breaths wrong, I'm gonna push the memories out the back of his head."

"Alright. Mask up and let's get this money."

"Damn girl this pussy is good. Where you been all my life?" J-Wood said as he stroked Porshea's pussy.

Slumped

"I've been here the whole time. You just ain't been looking in the right places." She said tightening her pussy down on J-Wood's dick. "Come here Big Daddy." She said to Tiny who had been watching his boy Wood beat her pussy up.

"Oh so you into dread heads too." He said stepping in front of her and pulling his dick out. Just then, the front door was kicked in and three masked men ran in with guns. One of them had two and he was the one doing the talking.

"Don't even think about. Just put your dick away and put your hands where I can see them." Slump said. "You! Step out the pussy and pull your pants up real slow." He said to J-Wood as he stepped back. They all noticed Porshea.

"You don't move bitch." Tee said to her. Stone tied Tiny's hands behind his back with the Playstation controller. He was glaring at Stone with hate-filled eyes and then he started to laugh.

"What the fuck you find so funny." Stone said hitting him on the head with the big Bulldog .44 caliber.

"Yeah, I thought that was you." Tiny said looking up at him.

"Now I'm really gonna kill you."

"Shut up Tiny. Can't you see this shit is for real." J-Wood said. "Look! The money and the dope is in the safe. If you let us go, I'll tell you the code. Just don't kill me."

"Get up! Now open your mouth." Slump said.

"C'mon man!" He started to plead as he got up.

"Shut the fuck up and open your mouth." Pointing one of the Ruggers in his face. As Wood opened his mouth, Slump put the barrel inside of it.

"Since you want to play let's make a deal, check this out. I'm gonna give this one chance to keep your life. Man, shut that bitch up!" Slump said to Tee who had been standing over Porshea. Without saying anything, he placed the 12 gauge to her head. She shut up instantly.

"Now, like I said. When I take this gun out of your mouth, we are going to the safe. You are going to open it and put everything inside of it in this duffel bag." They walked to a wall safe behind a big Scarface picture. When he opened it, Slump saw all the little bundles of money and what looked to be fifteen keys of coke. "Now slowly put all that shit in the bag." J-Money did as he was told.

"Alright man. You got what you wanted. Now let me and my people go."

"I ain't done with you yet. And as far as that bitch and nigga go, my guns are pointed at you." And on that note, the house seemed to explode with gunfire as both Tee and Stone pulled the triggers of the two big guns.

"Walk nigga!" Slump said pushing J-Wood out the door and the van. Tee jumped in the driver seat and Stone got in the back with Slump and J-Wood, who was begging for his life.

"Aw shit!" he said as Tee pulled off his mask and drove away. Slump and Stone had both taken theirs off as well. J-Wood knew the only way he would make it out alive is to give them whatever they asked for...or so he thought.

They drove J-Wood out to a house in Elk Grove that was owned by Stone and Slump's uncle Tony, also known as Tony T throughout Sacramento. He was a country boy himshelf who had come out to Cali from Texas when Slump was a kid. He drove diesels for JB Hunt nationwide and this was one of those times he was on the road. Not that he would have tripped much if he had been home. This wouldn't have been the first time something like this happened.

"Tee, pull up to the back of the barn." Slump said. Once Tee put the van in park, they got out and took J-Wood and the duffel into the barn. Once inside, they tied J-Wood to a chair.

"Alright. We are going to start this with a few simple questions. First, how much money is in that bag?" Slump said.

"A little over $90,000."

"How many bricks?"

"17."

"Alright, now this is where it's gonna get a little harder." Slump said as J watched Tee who was standing behind Slump with a blow torch in his hand.

"What's he going to do with that?"

"Oh you don't got to worry about him as long as you tell us what we need to hear." J-Wood broke out in a cold sweat and started stuttering.

"Ma...ma...man I wi...will...tell you whatever you wan. Just don't let him do nothing to me."

"Like I said, don't worry about him. Tell me about your brother."

"My who?"

"See I can't help you if you don't help me."

"Yeah. Maybe you need your memory warmed up. Tee said lighting the torch.

"I ain't got no brother out here."

"So you think we're playing. Stone, take his shoes off."

"Man c'mon. what you doing?" J-Wood asked struggling against the ropes.

Once his shoes were off, Tee asked. "Which one?"

"Which one what?"

"Which toe do you want to lose first. You know you can't walk without the big one."

"C'mon ya'll please. I don't know who ya'll talking about. You got all the money and the dope. Please don't do this."

"How about this one." Tee said pointing the flame to his small toe. As soon as the flame touch it, the smell of burnt flesh and shit filled the room.

"He shitting on himself!" Tee said as J-Wood passed out.

"Yeah, it's going to be a long night." Slump said.

"The fuck if it is." Tee said walking over to a bucket.

"What you gonna do with that, hit him with it until he wakes up?" Stone asked.

"No country boy. I'm gonna fill it up with water and throw it on him until he wakes up."

"Look at that nigga's toe or what's left of it. That motherfucker look like some burnt bacon or something."

"Damn Stone. Why everything gotta look like some food to you." Slump asked with a smile on his face.

"Cause a fat nigga like to eat."

"Oh shit. What the fuck. Please man. Don't hurt me." J-wood screamed, coming to as the water hit him.

"If you tell us what we need to know, I promise you won't get burned again." Slump told him.

"I don't know if you noticed or not but you're knee deep in shit." Tee said.

"Naw. He sitting in shit right now." Stone said laughing.

"Aww man, c'mon. At least let me clean myself up."

"Man, fuck playing with this nigga." Stone said punching him in the mouth.

"Now nigga, you are about to start talking or losing more body parts."

"I already told you..." J-Wood couldn't finish his sentence before Stone punched him again, knocking him out of his chair.

"Please! I gave you everything." J-Wood said spitting out blood and teeth.

"Not everything. Now tell us about your brother." J-Wood may have been a lot of things, but he would die before telling him anything about his brother. Munch was more like a father than a brother to him and he knew if they found out what they were doing to him, he would have all of them killed. Just the thought caused him to start laughing hysterically.

"Oh you think we playing. This shit is funny to you huh." Slump asked.

"No but what my brother is going to do to you is more than enough to make me smile even if I die today." J-Wood said looking Slump straight in the eyes. Slump looked down at him, smiled, and shot him straight in the head.

"Now what the fuck are we supposed to do?" Stone and Tee asked.

"He wasn't going to tell us anything." Slump said still looking down at J-Wood.

"And what makes you so sure about that?" Tee asked.

"His eyes." Tee called Jazzmine and told her how to get to Tony T's house. When she got there, they loaded the dope and money in Tee's trunk. Then her and Tee followed Slump and Stone to the middle of nowhere. They set the van and J-Wood on fire.

"I thought you told him that he wouldn't get burned anymore." Stone said lighting a blunt as Jazzmine drove away.

Chapter 41

"Hello…Jaylon?"

"What's up momma?"

"You need to come get your brother before I kill his ass."

"Who Lee. What he do?"

"This little motherfucker done got caught with some weed at school and now they talking about kicking him out. I swear I did everything I could to make sure ya'll grew up right. I slaved my ass off to keep a roof over ya'll head and food on the table. And this little black motherfucker wanna pull some shit like this.

"Calm down momma. It ain't that bad. It was just some weed."

"Yeah, it was just some weed this time. What next. And you don't make it no better doing whatever it is you doing. He looks up to you and want to be like his big brother, Slump. That's all I hear. Slump this…Slump that."

"Look momma, I'll be there in a minute. I'll talk to you when I get there. *As if I ain't got enough shit to be worried about already. Nicki is due any day now and since we killed J-Wood, Munch done pulled a Houdini.* Fuck!

"What's the matter?" Nicki asked.

"My brother got caught with some weed at school and now Momma K all bent out of shape and shit. Talking like it's my fault he doing what he doing. I'm bout to go holler at him. I'll be back later." Slump said grabbing his keys and walking out the door.

It had been eight months since they had robbed Munch's spot and killed J-Wood, Tiny, and Porshea. the shit was crazy. He didn't know how but he was one of the known d-boys in Sacramento that was really getting money. Him and Stone, who had decided to extend his stay in Cali and Tee had a handful of young niggas moving coke, weed and meth. But something happened he didn't expect. He started to like the lifestyle. The lifestyle he no longer thought about getting out of. Just taking the game over. And because of that, him and Nicki always seemed to be fighting and he had been seeing more and more of Alicia. Once he got in his car, he called Stone, who had moved in with Angel.

"What's up kinfolks?"

"Not shit. Just on my way to Momma K house because Lil' Lee done got caught with some weed at school."

"Ohh shit. I know she talking hella shit."

"How do you guess. She's saying it's my fault and shit like that."

"You know she don't mean that. She just mad right now. So what's up after you leave from over there?"

"I don't know. Why?"

"Shit. Stop by here and pick me up on your way over there."

"Alright bet. I'll see you in a minute." Slump said.

Chapter 42

"Jaylon, I don't know what to do with this boy anymore. He done got so disrespectful. And I know his ass be smoking weed. He come home from school with his eyes all red and shit and don't say nothing to nobody. He go straight to the icebox and start eating up shit. And don't let me ask his black ass to do something. It take him forever to do it. I just don't know what to do anymore." Momma K said looking at Slump.

"Where is he at momma?"

"He's in his room. You need to go talk to him or something. Shit, take his ass with you."

"How long is he suspended for?"

"Five days, why?"

"Because I'm gonna let him come stay with me. Give you some time to cool off and see if I can talk some sense into him. But other than this, how you doing momma?"

"I'm alright and the money you be giving me help out a lot."

"I wish you would quit your job and let me move you out of here."

"And then what Jaylon. What am I going to do when the police take you to jail or worse, when you get killed in those streets it seems like you love so much now. Huh, then what?" she said with tears in her eyes. "Just take your brother for a few days. Take him and talk to him. You too Mike. And when are you going home?" She said getting off the couch.

Slumped

"I don't know. I been thinking about moving out here permanently."

"What happened to ya'll. Ya'll used to be some of the sweetest little boys."

"Nice guys finish last. Auntie K."

"Yeah but they live long lives." After she said that, she went into her room.

"Stone, go tell that lil' nigga to come on. I'm gonna be in the car. If I go back there right now, I might knock his little ass out."

"Shit, he still might get his little ass fucked up." Stone said.

"What's up big bro!" Lee said getting into the car.

"I ain't got nothing to say to you right now. So just sit back and shut the fuck up." Lee knowing his brother's temper decided it would be best to just keep quiet. Stone had already told him he was lucky he wasn't getting fucked up. So he just sat back and tried to act like he wasn't scared. He looked up and noticed Slump looking at him in the rearview.

"Man what's up with you Lee. I mean seriously. I keep you in all the flyest shit. The newest Jordans or Lebron's, whatever you ask for. And all I ask is that you do right at school."

"I do be doing right at school. I do all my work and get good grades."

"Then why you smoking weed and shit." Stone asked.

"I wasn't smoking no weed."

"Then what the fuck was you doing with it? And I don't want to hear that you found it shit either. And on top of all that, you disrespecting Momma K by not doing what she tells you." Slump said.

"Alright. I'm gonna be real with you. Yeah I smoke a little tree sometime. But that's not what I was doing with that today. I'm tired of always having to ask you to do shit for me like I can't take care of myself. So I been selling bags at school and I wouldn't have even gotten caught but the bitch

Slumped

ass school cop always expect me to give him free sacks and when I told him today that he's gonna have to start paying for his shit like everybody else, he got mad and shit and took me to the office and said he caught me smoking in the bathroom. So the principal searched my locker and found the last ten sacks I had. And momma just be tripping. She always talking about how she know what you be doing in the streets and how she would kick me out if she found out I was selling and drugs. If I don't take out the trash or something, she always go off the deep end like she crazy. I'm fifteen almost sixteen but she still treat me like I'm a little ass kid. If a chick call the house for me, I gotta go through a thousand questions. But she don't say nothing if a nigga call for Shawanna. So I been getting my hustle on so I can get me a cellphone."

"Man. You could've came and asked me to get you a phone."

"See that's what I'm talking about right there. I ain't no baby. I can get my own shit."

"you don't know shit about hustling lil' nigga." Stone said.

"Oh yeah fat boy. Then how I got this." Lil' Lee said pulling out a fat roll of money

"I started selling weed two weeks ago with $50. Now I got $3,400. I went from an eighth to a half pound in two weeks." All Stone could do was smile.

"So that's why you asked for the $50."

"Yep. And here. I told you I would pay you back." Lil' Lee said trying to hand him two twenties and a ten.

"Naw, you go ahead and keep it. But now what you gon' do. Momma K said they were talking about expelling you."

"I don't think they will. This my first time ever getting in trouble. It's not like I'm a fuck up or something. But the coach might kick me off the basketball team. I ain't really sweating that shit because I've been ready to quit anyway. I only got two years left until I graduate anyhow."

Slumped

"Well it seems like you got your mind made up. Well the first thing we're gonna do is get you a phone. And you ain't gonna sell no more weed at school, right."

"Then how am I gonna get my money?"

"I don't give a fuck what you do away from the school and that punk ass rent-a-cop. Besides, what you think the phone is phone. And you better not let Momma K find out because she is going to kick both of our ass."

"Shit, mine too." Stone said.

"And before you try to sell anything else, give me your word that you will come to me first or you ain't selling shit period. And if I find out you doing it behind my back, I'm gonna fuck you up. You hear me?"

"Yeah I hear you and I give you my word on that." Lil' Lee said.

"Well now that we got that out the way. You got some weed right now, lil' nigga? I ain't smoked all day." Stone said.

I got some of that hardball purple if you got ten dollars fat boy." Lil' Lee said causing Slump to start laughing.

Sitting at the light on Hillsdale and Palm Ave., grabbing for the lit blunt he just dropped between his legs, Tee never saw the blue Chrysler 300 that pulled next to him or the gunman until it was too late.

"That as for J-Wood and Tiny." Snake said jumping back into the car and driving off.

Chapter 43

"What! Oh shit. Alright. I'm on my way." Slump said into his phone.

"What's wrong?" Seeing the panicked look and the way he started driving.

"Nicki is having the baby. That was Momma K saying they were on the way to the hospital."

"Well don't be driving all crazy and shit. We do got guns in this motherfucker. So just calm down nigga. Damn!" Stone said laughing.

"What's so funny nigga?"

"I ain't never seen you this nervous before. That's all and it's funny. And on top of that, I'm high as hell. Damn Lil' Lee, where you get his weed from. This shit is fire."

"I got this white boy that's growing it. I met him through a friend. So you can just say he's a friend of a friend."

Fifteen minutes later, they pulled inot Kaiser South and went into the room Nicki was being prepared to have the baby. Both her and Slump said they didn't want to know the sex of the baby. But Slump was hoping for a girl and Nicki wanted a boy.

"Hey baby. How you feeling?" Slump asked.

"Like a basketball is trying to come out of my ass." She said as a heavy contraction hit her.

"Come hold my hand. Jaylon."

"I love you to death but ain't about to crush my fingers."

"Where's the doctor? I need some drugs. Oh shit, I think it's coming."

The doctor entered the room. "Oh yeah, I think the baby is ready to come out of there. They took her into the delivery room. Three and a half hours later, they were the proud parents of a 8 pound 7 ounce baby girl, who they named Jadda Lashay Lewis. While Slump was in the nursery, Stone's phone rang.

"Hello...alright calm down Jazzmine. I can't understand you."

"I said Tee's been shot and it don't look like he's going to make it. They life flighted him to UC Davis."

"What! When did it happen? Who did it?" Stone fired question after question to Jazzmine, which she had no answers for. He told her that they were at the hospital. That Slump just had his baby and they would be there as soon as they could. Once he got off the phone, he went to Slump. "Kinfolk, they done got Tee."

"What do you mean they got him?"

"I mean somebody done put lead in him and now they don't know if he's going to live. Jazzmine said they took him to UC Davis.

"Fuck. This is not how it was supposed to be."

"What do you mean?"

"I mean we had a plan and we didn't stick to it. We got greedy and now my homie might pay for it with his life."

"Yeah well plans change but no matter what, I got you, whichever way the wind blows the leaves."

Slump looked down at the bundle of love he held in his arms, kissed his baby girl and said, "Daddy will always be here for you whenever you need me." And as if Jadda understood what he was saying, he swore that she smiled at him.

Meanwhile, Jazzmine paced the UC Davis floor stopping any and everyone who looked like a doctor. She learned he suffered a gunshot wound to the head and two in the back and they were doing all they could to save his life.

"Who do you think it was?" Stone asked Slump leaving one hospital to another.

"I don't know. I've been asking myself that ever since that phone call. What did Jazzmine say."

"She couldn't tell me shit. All she knew was he got shot. The cops called her because she was the last number in his phone.

"I wonder if his BM knows yet."

"Do you think we should call her?"

"Yeah but let's wait until we know more. Besides, I don't want to be all up in the middle of no bullshit at the hospital. And that's just what's it's going to be with her and Jazzmine in the same room. You know she still mad at how he left her and Lil' Tee to be with Jazz.

When they got to UC Davis, Jazz was a hot mess. Her eyes were red and swollen from crying. When she say them, she ran up to Slump and broke down some more. He hugged her and tried to think of something to say to her. But what do you tell someone when the person they loved might be dying. What would make them feel better. Instead, he just held her and let her cry. When she calmed down, he talked to her.

"What has the doctor said." She repeated what she told Stone.

"I can't lose him now Jaylon."

"It's gonna be alright. He's a strong nigga. He's going to pull through." He said not believing the words himself. It was 5a.m. when the doctor came out to talk to them.

"The shot to his head was luckily only a graze. But the two shots to his back did a lot of damage to his spinal cord. He may never walk again, but it's still too soon to tell. We did everything we could to patch him. He lost a lot of blood and still haven't regained consciousness yet. However he is stable. We did all we could do. The rest will be up to him." Dr Jenkins said.

"Can we go see him?" Jazz asked.

"Yes follow me." When they got to the room, just seeing Tee with tubes and shit coming out everywhere was more than Jazz could handle. She had to be sedated.

"Damn, this is some fucked up shit man? And look at her. She been through all kinds of shit in the last year and took that shit all on the chin. But seeing him like this is fucking her up more than anything. I guess she really do love this nigga."

"Yeah, she loves him. C'mon let's get outta here."

"Naw, I'm gonna stay here with them. You go check on your chick and that new baby girl. When Jazz wakes up, I'm gonna put her in a cab if she will leave. Then I'll catch up to you later."

"Alright. If he wakes up, call me." Slump said giving Stone a pound.

"I got you kinfolk. If he comes to, I'll hit you."

Slump walked out the hospital to his car and just sat there thinking about everything. They hadn't got into it with anyone except the local block boys, but nothing serious. He was confused about anyone who could have had Tee shot. And the last lick had been the one on J-Wood. With that, he called Alicia.

"What's up love. How you doing?"

"I'm good. Why you ain't been to see me lately?"

"Shit, it's been a lot going on. But I've been thinking about you."

"Oh yeah. What you been thinking about?"

"That look you be getting on your face when I be hitting that spot."

"Boy you so nasty. But what's really been keeping you away. Let me guess…your baby momma."

"Naw, it ain't been that. Like I said, shit just been happening. You know business. Besides, I'm a daddy now. She had the baby girl last night."

"Well congratulations."

"Thank you."

"So what you doing right now. On your way back to the hospital?"

"No leaving one. Like I said a lot has been going on. While I was watching my baby being born, somebody tried to kill Tee."

"What! Is he alright?" Alicia said sitting up in her bed.

"He was hit three times. He is still unconscious and they don't know if he'll be able to walk again. Got to wait until he wakes up to run some test."

"Do they know who did it?"

"That's one of the reasons I called you. When is the last time you heard from ol' boy?"

"I saw him last weekend."

"Oh yeah. What was he talking about?"

"Nothing really. He stopped by for a minute, then he left."

"What did he want?"

"Some pussy. Like every other nigga wants."

"Did he get some?"

"Why you jealous?"

"For what. It's yours. Give it to who you want to."

"That's the only reason you called? To see who I was giving my pussy to." Alicia asked with attitude.

"Naw, I thought I was calling an old friend. I just felt like talking. I just had a baby and one of the few people I call family is laying in a hospital bed and we don't even know if he's going to wake up. I guess what they say is true."

"What's that?"

"When he gives life…he takes life." Slump said.

Chapter 44

Yeah I caught that bitch ass nigga slipping. He was at the light reaching for something and the way he was moving around, it looked like his ass was on fire." Snake said into his phone.

"What about them other two niggas?" The person on the other end of the phone asked.

"Naw, they wasn't with him. He was by himself. But don't trip. I'm on them too. One down…two to go.

"Nah, this is personal. Just get the fat nigga. I got something special planned for Slump and that bitch Alicia." Munch said hanging up.

3 days later

"How you feeling my nigga?" Slump asked Tee.

"I've never felt this helpless in my life dog. I lay here and think it's all a bad dream and I'll wake up soon, then a nurse or Jazz comes in here to see if I shitted or pissed on myself. And I get so fucking mad. But who do I blame? The nigga that did this to me or myself for how I've lived my life. Yeah the money, the bitches…all that shit was cool.

"Hold on. I mean I can't say I know what it is you are going through but you talk like it's over. Like you already dead or something."

"Yeah, well that's what I been feeling like since I woke up in this bitch. These motherfuckers always poking me and shit asking if I feel this or did I feel that. Try to move your legs and wiggle your toes"

"Man, they just doing their job." Stone said from across the room.

"Yeah nigga. I been meaning to say something to you anyway." Tee said.

"C'mon Tee. Don't say something stupid." Slump said thinking back to when Stone and Tee had words.

"Nah, it ain't nothing like that. I just wanted him to know that I appreciated him being there for Jazz. She told me how he kept her on the positive track while I was in a coma."

"I thought you would do the same for me. Besides, we family now. And family stands by each other. Now all we need to do is get you back on your feet. And I been doing some thinking. I had Angel do a little research on the internet and she found this specialist in Texas that we may need to look into. I called and checked him out. He said all the cases he had where the doctor said they had a chance, he could make them walk again. So what do you think?"

"How much?"

"It don't matter. If you are willing to do it, then we will pay whatever." Slump said.

"Well when do we leave?"

"Once you are healed enough to travel. Besides, until we find out who is gunning for us, we need to lay low. Make them think they got you." Slump said.

Chapter 45

"What do you mean you're going to take a trip? We just had a baby. I'm not gonna be raising no kid by myself." Nicki stated.

"You act like I'm not coming back. I said I would only been gone for a few months."

"Yeah, just like you said you would be done with a lifestyle in a year."

"Look Nicki. I'm not trying to argue with you. It is what it is. We gotta take Tee out there to the specialist and hopefully he helps him back on his feet."

"I know he's like a brother to you but you got responsibilities as a father now."

"You keep saying it like I'm leaving and never coming back. I tell you what Nicki. Why don't you come with us if it will make you happy."

"You are what makes me happy. Why don't you understand that Jaylon? You know what. Fuck it. Go ahead and run behind your little friend but I'm telling you now, this shit is getting old and you are going to have to make a choice. The streets or me and Jadda because you ain't about to put my daughter in harm's way all because you and your fucking friends want to be Tony Montana or Neno Brown. Think about that while you're on your little trip." Nicki said walking out the room.

"You ain't got no problem spending none of the fucking money though. Do you?" In response, all he heard was the front door slamming. "Fuck!" He screamed, punching a hole in the closet. The pressure of fatherhood and his best friend in a hospital was getting to him. He just wanted to relax without looking over his shoulder wandering if he was next. He didn't think it stopped with Tee. And until they got whoever was after them, he couldn't relax. He wouldn't relax. And going back to Texas wasn't any better. They had unfinished business out there as well.

"What's up kinfolk." Stone said pulling Slump back from his thoughts.

"Not much cousin. Just thinking."

"Yeah I could tell. I saw Nicki and lil' momma leaving when I pulled up. She seemed like she was mad about something."

"Yeah, she mad at me for leaving but she'll get over it. Anyway, what's up with you."

"It's not what's up so much as what we gonna do when we get back there."

"I say we get it over with."

"I was thinking the same thing. So what do you have planned.

Chapter 46

"What do you mean we are going back."

"I didn't say 'we' Jazz. I said me. I couldn't ask you to go back there after what happened to you." Tee said.

"So you must think I'm some kind of weak bitch or something. Like I'm scared to face them niggas. Well I'm not and if you are going back, then it is a 'we' because you need me now just as much as I need you. Until you're back on your feet. I'm gonna be your legs." Jazz said causing Tee to start crying. "Just promise me one thing."

"Anything you want baby girl."

"Just promise when you get those niggas, they will die slowly and I get to watch. For me and Porshea."

"I promise." Tee said thinking about the way Porshea looked before he killed her. *Oh well. shit happens.*

Little did he know, Slump and Stone planned to move on Red and Money a.s.a.p. It was an old problem and they felt enough time had passed already.

"Stop crying baby. It's gonna be alright. I know my son and you and Jadda mean the world to him." Momma K told Nicki.

"But you don't understand Momma K. He told me he was gonna be done with this shit. And it seems like he's only getting deeper and deeper involved in whatever it is they got going on. And now that Tee has been shot, it seems like he has become another person. I mean seriously. I don't know how to explain it to you. But his eyes, they are just so cold." Knowing exactly what she was talking about, Momma K said a silent prayer for her son and whoever it was that crossed him. She knew if they didn't kill him, he definitely was going to kill them.

"Momma K, I just don't know what to do. I love him and don't want to be with no other man but him..."

"Baby look. I can't say I know how you feel but I do understand and sometimes you have to let a man handle his business because men set their mind something and the more we stand in their way of whatever it is they are planning to do, the more we become the enemy. When all we are trying to do is help."

"I hope you are right because I'm not going to allow him to place me and my daughter in harm's way and I'm not going to wait on him forever."

"Well baby. I pray you don't have to."

Chapter 47

"You sure you ready for this trip?" Slump asked Tee.

"I'm as ready as I'm ever gonna be. I know I'm tired of sitting in this bitch. The doctors said my wounds are healed up enough and the sooner I start my rehabilitation, the better. And to tell you the truth, I can't wait to burn something." Tee said laughing.

"I heard that shit. And you will never guess who got the best weed around right now." Stone said.

"Oh yeah. Who?"

"Your little partner. And I should be kicking his ass." Slump said.

"C'mon kinfolks. Don't hate the hustler. Hate the game."

"Wait a minute. I know ya'll ain't talking about my lil' nigga Lee."

"None other. And that motherfucker really got fire. And he won't give a nigga shit. Always walking about I love you bro, but I need my money." Slump said.

"Who he getting his weed from?"

"I can't believe this nigga." Stone said.

"What!" Tee said laughing.

"Your ass can't even walk and you're thinking about robbing somebody. Let's get you back on your feet. Besides, we ain't hurting for no money."

"Yeah you right. The little nigga getting his cake up. Well at least he won't be needing nobody to buy his Jordans. I got something I need to tell ya'll too. Well something I need to ask."

"Anything." Slump and Stone said in unison.

"I know you have been thinking about our problem out there."

"Yeah, we was talking about that before we came here tonight." Stone said.

"I need your word that nothing will happen to them niggas until I'm back on my feet.

"Why wait?" Slump asked.

"Yeah. It's been long enough." Stone said.

"I promised Jazz they would pay for what they did and it would be slow and painful."

"Alright, we will do it your way." Stone said.

"But if they so much as think they got us shook I'm gonna burn their asses down with or without you. We should have never left them niggas alive in the first place." Slump said.

"So is that your word." Tee asked looking at Slump.

"Yeah, that's my word."

"Stone, how about you?"

"Shit, whichever way the wind blows the leaves. But like my kinfolk said, if they do anything. It's on and popping like hot chicken grease."

"That's good enough for me. Now when do we leave.

Part Two

Chapter 48

The flight to Texas didn't go as smooth as they thought it would. First they had the problem with security because Tee kept setting off the metal detector. He still had bullet fragments near his spine. Then, once they were in the air, all Tee did was complain about how much pain he was in. the truth was, they were all nervous about coming back. To keep a low profile, they decided to rent an apartment in Beaumaunt, close to the rehabilitation center Tee would be attending. Dr. Winston Brown had a 90% success rate. They had their hopes up but it had been almost a month now since Tee had been in his care and he still had no feeling in his legs.

"What's up bro?" Slump said walking into Tee's room.

"Not shit man. Just thinking. It's not like I can get up and walk away.

"I just got through talking to the doc and he said the test shows signs of progress. But as long as you keep being negative and not doing your part, he can only do so much."

"So what's this. A pep talk?"

"Nah, it ain't nothing like that. Because no matter what I say, it won't matter. I mean shit, if you like pissing and shitting on yourself and being stuck in a fucking bed, that's on you dawg. And I know you miss fucking Jazz. But hey, if you like it, I love it. But I will keep it 100 with you bro, this shit ain't free and I wish you would stop feeling sorry for yourself and get it together."

Slumped

"What the fuck am I supposed to do?" Tee yelled.

"Stop feeling sorry for your motherfucking self. Do whatever the fuck you have to. I don't know. Man fuck it. If you just wanna give up, give up then. I'm outta here." And with that, Slump turned and walked out the room.

"Slump! Slump! Jaylon, don't just walk away from me nigga. Come here!" Tee yelled. The last thing he heard Slump say was "Get your punk ass up." A week and a half later, he woke up in the middle of the night screaming that his legs were on fire.

"Do something!" He yelled once Dr. Brown got there.

"Calm down. Calm down and tell me exactly what you're feeling."

"It's like my legs are on fire or something."

"So you can actually feel your legs."

"Hell yeah, I feel them. I'm not imagining the pain."

"Good! Good!"

"What the fuck do you mean good. Help me motherfucker. Ain't that what you're getting paid to do."

"Yes, that's what I'm getting paid to do and I'm doing it. Now shut up and tell me if you feel this." He said lifting Tee's left leg and bending it at the knee.

"Yes! Yes! I can feel it. I can feel my legs." Tee said excitedly. From that night, Tee's recovery had been rapid. They started with water exercise building the strength back into his muscles. He felt he was ready to get back on his feet but Dr. Brown didn't want him to rush anything. So kept him on water rehabilitation. But at night, he would lift his legs until they couldn't lift anymore. Five months into his stay, the doctor asked if he was ready to finally get on his feet. He was more than ready. Jazz and Stone knew about his recovery on his feet but they didn't tell Slump who he hadn't seen since he walked out of his room.

"So doc, how much longer do you think I'll be here?"

"I don't think I can do too much more for you. You have already surpassed my expectations and a lot faster than I've ever seen. To be frank, I don't know why you chose to stay this long." Dr Brown said as he watched Tee run on the treadmill.

"I had my reasons, but I'm ready now."

"Well, I'll go fill out the necessary paperwork and you call a ride." Tee called Jazz who had Stone and Slump come to the hospital. Stone thought Tee had a relapse. But once she explained everything was all good, that Tee just wanted to surprise Slump, he told her they would be there.

"Man I ain't trying to go up there. I'm done feeling sorry for that nigga."

"Well kinfolk. He said he really needed to see you and what he had to say was for your ears only."

"This shit better be good."

"I'm sure it is."

When they got there, Jazz and Tee were waiting in the outside visiting area. Tee sitting in a wheelchair.

"I hope you ain't wasting my time."

"I don't know. You tell me." Tee said standing.

"My nigga. It's about time." Slump said on the verge of tears.

"Now that I got all of you together. I just want to thank you for putting up with my complaining and not turning your back on me. I don't think I'll ever be able to repay you." He said with tears running down his face.

"You already have."

That night, they went to a Texas steakhouse to celebrate. Each lost in their own thoughts about what were to happen next, trying to enjoy the night although they all knew what was coming. The shit was about to hit the fan in Texas.

Chapter 49

"So you sure you ready for this?" Slump asked Tee. The two of them and Stone were sitting in the parking lot of Hytop Club for twenty minutes before they saw Red and Money pull up and go in.

"Yeah, I'm ready. I been waiting a long time for this." Tee said putting on a pair of black leather murder ones. "I ain't never been in this good of shape. Not even when I got out of prison."

"Yeah kinfolk. You do look like some type of action figure." Stone said trying to lighten the mood.

"So you sure this is how you want to do it because I still say we follow these niggas home and make them kiss the fucking baby."

"Nah Slump. I really want to punch on this nigga again. Besides, when he dies, I told Jazz she would be there to watch."

"Well fuck it then. Let's get ready to rumble." Slump said smiling.

"Yeah! Round two!" Stone said as they got out of the rental. "Only this time. It ain't none of that one on one shit." The three of them made their way to the door.

"Oh shit. It can't be." Jack said looking at the tv monitor as Slump, Stone, and Tee came into the club. It had been three years since he last saw them but he still remembered the ass whooping they gave Red and Money and with that thought, he knew what they were here for. Rushing out of his

Slumped

office, he tried to talk them out of doing anything crazy in the club tonight.

"Hey fellas. Long time no see." He said walking up to them.

"What's good Jack." Slump said.

"I don't know. You tell me."

"We just came to talk to some old friends."

"Well from the way he's looking. It can't be no good news." Jack said pointing to Tee.

"Don't play stupid. You know why we are here."

"Look man. Don't do this up in my club. Here, come on. Let me buy ya'll a drink."

"Fuck your club and drink nigga. Now you can do one thing and one thing only" Tee said.

"What's that?"

"Go to fucking sleep." Tee said hitting Jack with one of the hardest right hooks he ever felt. He was sleep before he ever hit the ground. Red and Money not missing any of it made a break to the back door of the club.

"They are running out the back door!" Slump said trying to make his way through the crowd.

"Let them run. They know we are here now." Tee said grabbing Slump.

"What about him?" Stone said pointing to Jack who was trying to pick himself up.

"Help him up. He's gonna tell us how to find them niggas."

"C'mon Jack man. Shake that shit off." Tee said helping him to his feet.

"What happened? Who hit me?"

"That ain't what's important. But how do we find your boys? Let's go on back to that office of yours and have a little talk."

"I don't feel safe going back there by myself with him." Jack said pointing to Tee.

Slumped

"You won't be alone with him. We will be back there too."

"That don't make me feel any better. All you niggas look like you are here to kill somebody. And what the fuck ya'll been feeding that nigga since the last time I saw ya'll. He look like one big fucking muscle."

"You keep trying to be cute nigga and I'm going to eat you. Now c'mon." Tee said pushing Jack toward his office.

"Damn nigga. You done came up in the world huh. Got cameras all over the place and shit huh." Stone said as they got into the office.

"Yeah, I gotta keep my eyes on my money."

"Enough with the chit chat. Now tell me where I can find them two bitch ass niggas." Tee said.

"I told them boys they had fucked up doing them girls like that but they didn't want to listen. I just want ya'll to know I didn't have anything to do with it then and I don't now.

"So help yourself then Jack and quit stalling. How do we find them niggas."

"It's not that easy. Those two move around so much it's hard to say where they will be. But I've been hearing they got a little trap house in the new projects at least that's what everybody has been saying. But now that ya'll back, it ain't no telling how far them two going to run now. But I should warn ya'll. They got a couple of young boys who be with them sometime. They ain't from out here either and they are some crazy looking motherfuckers too."

"Oh yeah. How long they been coming around."

"I just started seeing them these last couple of months and since they been around, everybody who has had words with Red and Money for one thing or another seem to come up missing, if you get what I'm saying."

"So you seen these cats before?" Tee asked.

Slumped

"Yeah, I seen them a few times. Hell they almost fucked my club up worst than your big muscle bound ass did and matter of fact, I think I still got the tape. let me look."

A few minutes later, they all sat there looking at the monitor watching the two unknown niggas beat the shit out of an unlucky drunk nigga.

"And you say you don't know their names."

"They call themselves Pain and Able or some biblical shit like that. I just know them two boys are crazy as hell. Look at em. They almost killed that nigga that night. And they was laughing like kids in a toy store the whole time they did it."

"Yeah well fuck them. And you tell them other two faggots, the next time you see them, they can run but they can't hide." Slump said.

"I was wondering when we was going to see them niggas again." Money said to Red as they drove out the back of the club.

"Man, fuck them niggas. And I still don't know why we ran away like this. I ain't no bitch ass nigga and now we look like we scared of those three pussy ass niggas."

"Shut the fuck up nigga. That's your motherfucking problem. You don't think. You always quick to do some dumb shit. We would have been on America's Most Wanted if we would have set shit off back there. Besides, what's the use of having brought our young wolves out here if we ain't going to let them howl at the moon."

"Yeah whatever. I think you scared of that nigga after he whooped your ass."

"Fuck you. That big muscle bound nigga don't' pump no fucking fear."

"Oh so you noticed that nigga is a whole lot bigger than he was last time we saw him. Did you see how hard he hit Jack's ass. Had that nigga sleep before he even hit the ground."

Slumped

"Man fuck them niggas. What's up with them chicken heads from the other day."

"You talk about me not thinking. Nigga all you care about is pussy. And that's how we got in this shit in the first place."

"Yeah well I care about one other thing too, my nigga."

"Oh yeah, what's that."

"Money nigga. Those motherfucking C-Notes." Money said laughing.

"Yeah but the fact is we got problems and we need to take care of them before they take care of us."

Chapter 50

"**S**o what you think about them two young niggas?" Tee asked Slump when they got back to the room.

"I think we need to get t his shit over with so I can get back to my baby girl. That's what I think. I mean them niggas ain't no different from any other niggas. They bleed and die the same. Why? How you feel about them?"

"I wasn't expecting it, but I don't really care. I just know I want them other two bitch ass niggas and if them two young punks got to be had then they just got to be got."

"What you two in here talking about? And where is Stone?" Jazz asked with some food from Sonic.

"Well, we were talking about nothing important. And Stone said he was going for a ride to clear his mind and check on his house and cars since he hadn't been by there since he'd been out here."

"Yeah I bet he went to check on his shit. More like some big booty country girl." Jazz said laughing. "Here Jaylon. it's a double cheeseburger and some fries. And I know you don't like mayo."

"Good looking out sis."

"Here baby. I got you the same thing with everything on it."

"That's what I'm talking about." Tee said taking a bite of his burger.

"Jaylon. have you talked to Nicki since you got here? How is the baby doing?"

Slumped

"They are cool. Nicki kinda mad so I ain't got too much to say to her. But my baby girl, she doing good. Getting bigger. I was just telling this muscle head we need to wrap this shit up and get back so I can do my daddy thing."

"Oh look at you. Trying to grow up on me. That's what I'm talking bout'. Do your thing bro." Jazz said seriously.

Chapter 51

Stone sat in the front seat of the rental car watching the spot in the new projects that Money and Red's two young goons were supposed to be running. He felt bad for not telling Slump and Tee where he was really going but fuck it. He rocked better alone. Besides, it wasn't like he was gonna rob the spot. Just shut it down. He had already sent a couple of base heads up to the door so he knew they were inside. Before he came, he stopped by his house and got his bulletproof vest and his Hekor and Kotch 50 caliber desert eagle. Now all he needed was a way in. he thought about just walking up to the door and opening it, but then he might only get one of them. The longer he sat there, the more impatient he got.

"Fuck it. I might as well get it over with." He said getting out to car to no one particular. He walked to the front door after putting on the hood to his sweatshirt. He knocked on the door.

"Ya'll know the rules." He heard through the door before it opened.

"It's after 1a.m. so you better be spending a hundred dollars or better." A cocky dread head boy said.

"I got something better." Stone said pulling out the p89's. "How much will you give me for this?

"Oh shit. Come in and close the door. Yo Trey. Come check it out." Another dread head a little taller than the first entered followed by a skinny base head bitch.

Slumped

"Check what out nigga. I was back there trying to get sucked so it better be good."

"Look." The first one said handing the gun to his friend.

"Damn nigga, this shit clean as fuck. Ay man. How much you want for it."

"Just give me something cool." Stone said his right hand never coming out of his pocket.

"I got something for you." Trey said walking back toward the room. Just then, Stone shot the first one in his stomach through the pocket of his hoodie. Then he pulled out the 50 caliber and shot him in the head.

The base head started screaming and Trey spun around and pointed the Rugger at Stone. He pulled the trigger.

"C'mon now stupid. You didn't' think it was loaded did you?" Then he shot Trey through the middle of his head. "Now look here bitch. You can have whatever they got in here and live as long as you keep your mouth closed. Never say shit about what you just saw or you can leave with nothing." He said picking up the Rugger.

"You mean you ain't about to rob them because I know where all the dope and money at."

"I did what I came to do so why don't you just take what you want and leave. But remember what I said. If I hear anything, I'll find you and make you hate the day you were born."

"I won't say nothing. I swear I won't."

"You would not want to." Stone said walking out the front door.

Chapter 52

"Man what is them two little niggas doing?" Red said hanging up the phone. "I've been calling them for the last hour and a half and ain't neither of them answering."

"They probably got some fucking chicken head up in there."

"Naw, knowing Trey, he probably got some bitch with no teeth blowing smoke on his dick. I keep telling him about having them base head bitches in there. In fact, come on Red, let's just slide up over there."

"Man leave them little niggas alone. Let them get their freak on. You act like when we was coming up, you never got your dick sucked by a crackhead or didn't pick up the phone when the big homies called. So sit down and quit tripping. We will go holler at them in the morning and why we at it, move the money in the safe to the vault.

Chapter 53

It was after three in the morning by the time Stone made it back to the room him and Slump shared. Tee and Jazz stayed in the one next door. When he got in, he thought Slump was sleep because the tv was off and it was dark.

"What's up Mike?" Slump asked.

"Not shit. Had to clear my head and check on some things." Stone and Slump grew up together. Although they were cousins, they were close like brothers. So from the tone in Stone's voice, he knew he was hiding something. Instead of letting it go, he decided to call him on it.

"We been straight with each other our whole lives. I know you and I know when something's on your mind."

"Naw, it's a dead issue." Stone said reaching over and switching on the light.

"What's a dead issue." With the light now on, he noticed Stone had a vest on. "And why you got a vest on if you was only checking on some shit or taking a ride to clear your head."

"Well if you know me so well, kinfolks, then you know like I said, it's a dead issue."

"Quit speaking in riddles nigga and tell me what's up. Well…"

"Alright!" Stone said and told Slump about killing the two niggas from the video they watched at Jack's office.

When he was finished with the story, Slump said, "Why you always got to do shit by yourself. What if something happened to you. We wouldn't know shit. You could be laying up somewhere with your ass all shot up dead. Then what nigga. Explain that to me."

"Well, I'm not so calm the fuck down."

"Why you always got to do shit by yourself. What if something happened to you. We wouldn't know shit. You could be laying up somewhere with your ass all shot up dead. Then what nigga. Explain that to me."

"Well, I'm not so calm the fuck down. I know how to handle mines and that's what the fuck I did."

"But that ain't the point. Look Mike, man you are like a brother to me. Always have been and I ain't trying to lose you to no bullshit. All I'm saying is."

"I know what you saying." Stone said cutting him off. "And it won't happen again. Now can we move past this shit. It's a dead issue."

"Man you know you're fucking crazy right."

"If I'm crazy. Then what does that make you?"

Chapter 54

"Oh shit. This pussy is good." Munch said pushing his dick in Alicia from behind. "Almost makes me feel sorry for what I got to do."

"What you talking about?" Alicia said trying not to sound scared. Instead of answering her, he pulled his dick out of her pussy and shoved it up her ass.

"Oh stop Munch. You know I don't get down like this." She said trying to pull away from him, but he had murder on his mind and had pinned her body down ass up on the mattress with his own.

"Alright ya'll!" He said loudly and two niggas Alicia knew as neighborhood junkies came in her room. Munch got off her and she tried to cover up.

"Munch what the fuck is going on and who in the fuck is these niggas?"

"Bitch don't play stupid with me and try to act like you all innocent and shit. I know you ain't nothing but a hoe."

"No for real Munch. You and these niggas need to get up out of my house. I'm serious. Niggas leave."

"Or what bitch. You gonna call that wanna be killa Slump. And what the fuck are you two niggas just standing there looking for. You better earn your fucking money."

"Shit, I ain't got no problem with that." The older of the two junkies, Slim said walking toward the bed. "I don't remember the last time I had some pussy from someone this fine." Flashbacks of what her uncle did to her paralyzed her with fear. She blacked out and when she came to, she was in the room on the floor. Her whole body ached. She had blood and semen coming out of her ass and her pussy felt like someone shoved a baseball bat inside of it. All she could do was ball up in the fetal position and cry. Upset at herself for not fighting back. She wished Jaylon was there for her like he was with her uncle. She knew she needed to get up and clean herself up. She needed to go to the hospital. What if they had something. She needed to call somebody. The cops maybe. No sooner than the thought crossed her mind, her phone started ringing. Without looking at the caller ID, she answered it.

"Jaylon! Please tell me it's you." She said crying.

"Naw bitch. It ain't. and if you know what's good for you, you will keep your mouth closed." Munch said laughing.

"Fuck you, you bitch ass nigga. When he finds out what you did to me, he's gonna kill you."

"Yeah, well you make sure to tell him. But if you call the cops, I'm willing to bet you won't live to tell that nigga anything." He said before hanging up.

Slowly she stood up and walked naked into her bathroom where she turned on the shower as hot as she could stand it. She got in and tried to scrub off the filth from what they did to her. And even then, she felt dirty. *He is going to get his...even if I have to kill him myself.*

Chapter 55

It had been two weeks since Money and Red found Trey and Rock dead in their trap house and it had them shook.

"I still don't' know how they found out about them?" Red said. "And why did they take all the work and not the cash."

"I don't know. That's what's got me confused and Jack swears he didn't tell them shit."

"So what the fuck is we gonna do Master thinker? Because all this ducking and hiding shit is for pussies and I ain't no pussy nigga." Red said sarcastically.

"So what you think we should do Red. Go riding around killing motherfuckers until we find them. Shit we don't even know where to start looking."

"All I'm saying is that if we ain't going to take it to them niggas then I think it's about time to relocate. Shake this dry ass town." Money had been thinking that ever since the night they ran out of the Hytop. They way he saw it, they had already had enough money out of the big ol' state of Texas. But he didn't want Red to think he'd turned into a coward.

"Self preservation my nigga. Self preservation."

"And what the fuck do you mean?" Red asked knowing full well what Money meant. He just wanted to hear him say it.

"I'm just saying, we done about drained this well dry. Maybe we should relocate."

"So you saying we should run?"

"No, I'm saying, we relocate, plan and redeem."

"Yeah, whatever nigga. Where you wanna go now. Cali?"

"What" He had just been thinking Money had turned soft.

"You heard me nigga. I said CALIFORNIA. Don't you got some family out there."

"Yeah, I got some cousins from Oakland. Anthony and James. And they been trying to get us to come fuck with them but that was before we had to get up out of DC."

"Well then, I think it's time we pay the fam a visit. And this whole time, I thought you were getting soft nigga. But I'm starting to like the way you think." Red said.

Chapter 56

"**M**an something ain't right. It's like these niggas done fell off the fucking planet. It's like no one has heard from him and it's like Jack's ass is too scared to lie to us. I'm starting to feel like this trip was a waste of time." Tee said.

"A waste of time. Did you forget the real reason we came here? Killing them niggas would have just been a bonus." Slump said. But I guess that don't matter to you."

"Man you know what I meant. I was just saying, I wanted them to pay for what they did to Jazz.

"And Porshea. We can't forget about her." Jazz added.

"Yeah whatever. Her too. But like I was saying. It's like they did what they did and got away with it." Tee said.

"Not really!" Stone said.

"What you mean not really? Yeah we fucked them up over that picture shit but they got away with kidnapping them and now them two little crazy niggas somewhere laughing at us."

"You mean he don't' know." Stone asked looking at Slump.

"I don't know what?"

"Well kinfolks. I had a talk with them two young cats, and let's just say, where they at, they ain't doing no laughing." Stone said calmly.

"What! Where! When!" Tee said.

Slumped

"All that shit is irrelevant. We are family now and family takes care of each other."

"Let me guess. That's how you went and cleared your head." Slump started laughing at that.

"I guess he got you figured out." Tee wanted to be mad but he couldn't.

"I hope one day I get to repay you both for all you've done." Jazz being the only woman around the three men started to cry. It was a different kind of love the three of them shared but it was a love nonetheless. A bulletproof love.

Chapter 57

They had been home a little over a week and like clockwork, things were still the same. The only difference being Tee. He was a lot more ruthless and unforgiving. He was taking no loses. The team of young goons had put together to move all the work the three were taking compensation. They were known all throughout Sacramento and was feared by most niggas their age and some a little older than them.

"There was the hot head of the crew, Flip, who just happened to be the youngest of the five boys. Then there was Ro, Lil' Man, Junebug, and Spazz, the pretty boy of the crew. All of them had grew up in the streets and had no problem busting their guns. Especially when it came to Slump, Tee, and Stone who they all considered their big brothers. Because of them, they had money to spend and all the fly shit they could spend it on. And a place to stay. The whole time the guys had been in Texas, they kept the spot running like they had never left. Even after Tee got shot and no one was there to make sure they weren't fucking up. Because of that reason, they did something special and bought the boys and 73 Cutlass Oldsmobile station wagon. It was licorice black, with 26 inch blades, with the words 'Go Gettas' on the back window.

Chapter 58

"Look ya'll. We told ya'll to meet us here because we got some shit we need to talk to ya'll about." Tee said to the little niggas with a serious look on his face. Slump and Stone stood next to him.

Each one tried to think of what they had done that brought this talk on.

"Now we been fucking with ya'll for a while now. We don't' be sweating ya'll or tell ya'll how to do ya'll thang. We treat you niggas all like grown men."

"Hey man. Where is all this shit coming from. We ain't did nothing." Flip asked.

"Well if your little hot head ass would shut up and listen, he's about to tell you."

"My bad Slump."

"It's good lil' bro. now like I was saying. We show you niggas much love and loyalty. On top of bulletproof respect. And all we ask is that you show us the same love, loyalty and respect."

"But we do." Spazz said.

"Yeah!" Said Junebug and Lil' Man.

"Why don't ya'll just shut the fuck up and listen. Ya'll act like we did something wrong." Ro said.

"Yeah, why don't ya'll listen to Ro. Unless ya'll done something we need to know about." Slump said.

"I ain't done shit." Said Flip.

"Me neither." The other ones said.

Slumped

"Well…is this about that three hundred dollars." Spazz said.

"What three hundred dollars." Slump asked.

"I didn't think no one would noticed. I already put it back. But my mom was short on her rent and I couldn't let her get put out."

"Man, just because niggas wanna talk to ya'll don't mean ya'll did something wrong. Man fuck it. Just come to the garage." Tee said walking, opening the door. "All I was trying to say was we got ya'll a little something to show that we appreciate the way you been handling your business. And since Lil' Man is the only one who got his L's, he does the driving until ya'll get yours."

"So this is our shit."

"Yeah, but like I said. No one drives but Lil' Man until you got your L's."

"Man that's fucked up because I can't get my L's for another year since I'm only fifteen." Flip said.

"But you can get a permit." Slump told him.

"But then that means you're gonna read a book."

"Aww, that's fucked up Slump."

"I'm just fucking with you, lil' nigga." Slump said laughing.

"Why don't ya'll go ahead and get up outta here. Lil' Man, don't let us here that you let one of them drive. Cause all of you will be back walking. Now get up out of here, and don't do nothing stupid, Flip."

"Man, why it always gotta be me."

"Because 9 times out of 10, it always is lil' nigga."

"But it always be one of them who starts something. I just finish it."

"Yeah whatever lil' nigga. You niggas go have some fun." Stone said laughing.

"We going to get all the bitches now. I mean it ain't like I don't get them all already." Spazz said.

Slumped

"Man get your pretty boy ass in the car before we leave you." Lil' Man said.

"What, you jealous." Spazz said getting in the car.

"They going to kill themselves for sure." Tee said watching them pull off.

"Or somebody." Stone said.

"Nah, they will be alright." Slump said with a smile on his   face.

Chapter 59

"Hello." Slump said into the phone.

"So you wasn't going to call me and tell me you were back." Alicia said with an attitude.

"Yeah I was. I just hadn't got around to it. But now that you called, how you been doing?"

"I've been better. How about you?"

"I'm good. You know my boy back on his feet again."

"Yeah, that's what I heard. That's what's up. But listen, where are you?"

"Why?"

"Because I gotta talk to you."

"Oh yeah. About what?"

"I'd rather not do it over the phone. So can you please come over? I mean, you still remember where I stay right." She said sarcastically.

"Yeah but I don't know. I mean, after all. How would your man feel?"

"Look Jaylon. I really need to talk to you but if you want to be an asshole, then fuck you."

"Alright. Alright. Calm the fuck down. I'll be over there in about an hour, alright."

"Alright. I'll see you then."

"Alright." Slump said hanging up.

Now all she could do was wait until he got there. Ever since the day it happened, she felt like somebody was always watching over her. She felt weak and helpless, but now that

Slumped

Jaylon was back in town, all she felt was rage. She knew what she wanted to do. She just didn't' know how to go about doing it. But once she told him what happened, she knew Jaylon would come up with something. Her phone rang startling her out of her thoughts.

"Come open the gate for me." Slump said.

"Here I come." Once she opened the gate and they got back to her apartment, Slump noticed her.

"Damn girl. What's wrong. You look like shit and this motherfucker look like a hurricane blew through it. Instead of answering him, she started crying. All of the emotion and pain she felt, all the fear, it all came out.

"Whoa! What's wrong Alicia. What happened?" Slump said grabbing her and pulling her to his chest.

After she got all the crying out, she told him what Munch done to her and how he kept calling and tormenting her. She told him how she still felt dirty no matter how many times she scrubbed her skin. How she felt helpless and wished he was there to save her.

"I'm here now baby girl and he won't hurt you again. I promise. Now I need you to snap out of this shit. Pull yourself back together. I know you are stronger than this. You know you are stronger than this."

"Can you do something for me please." She asked him.

"Anything. Just say the words."

"Make love to me Jaylon. Show me that I'm special. That I do mean something to somebody. That I am not just a dirty bitch."

"It would be easy for me to have sex with you, but I don't think that's what you really want or need right now. So why don't you lay right here and let me hold you."

"See that's why I've always loved you because you've always known what I really needed." She said crying again.

Pulling her close to his chest and squeezing her tight, he told her everything would be alright. That he would take care of it for her. That night, he stayed with her; turning off his phone and just held her thinking if it wasn't one thing it was another. No matter what he had to do or who he had to kill, he was not going to lose. The streets would not beat him like it had so many before him.

Chapter 60

"So now you turning off your phone." Nicki asked when Slump walked into the house.

"Man c'mon Nicki. Not right now. Please."

"What you mean not right now. You ain't been home in months and now when you finally do come home, you stay out all night and turn your phone off. Who is she Jaylon? Who is it that's more important to you than me and your child."

"You tripping Nicki. It ain't even nothing like that."

"No I ain't tripping nigga, you tripping. Do you realize your daughter is almost a year old and she barely knows you. Being as how you put everybody else before her."

"Don't I take care of ya'll. Don't she got more shit than she can use. Shit she got stuff she ain't even old enough to play with yet."

"Yeah, but she ain't got you. And your ass is too fucking caught up in the streets to notice or too busy running behind Tee and Stone and whatever raggedy ass bitch you been spending your nights with and I'm tired Jaylon. Tired of coming last to everybody else. Tired of worrying about if something done happened to you or if you're in jail. I told you I didn't want to do this."

"So what is you saying Nicki? That you done. You don't' want to be with me anymore."

"See that's what I'm talking about. Every time I try to talk to you, you either run off or be quick to ask me if I'm done. Is that what you want? You don't want to be with me anymore because if it is, nigga, just say the words and me and my daughter will get the fuck up outta here."

"You got me fucked up, bitch. You ain't taking my daughter no motherfucking where."

"Jaylon, you may have these niggas scared of you but you don't scare me nigga. And I'm not your bitch." Nicki yelled causing Jadda to start crying.

"See you need to calm the fuck down with all that yelling," Slump said going to pick Jadda up which only caused her to cry more.

"See that's what I'm talking about Jaylon. Look at her. She don't even know who you are." Hurt by the way his daughter reacted to him, he grabbed his car keys and walked out the door before Nicki could see the tears that ran down his face.

Slump had been staying nights at the spot with his young goon, even Spazz when he wasn't off somewhere with some young chicken head. But his mind had been on the way Jadda looked at him like he was a stranger. He thought of his original plan and how he was only going to stay in the game long enough to get his money right. Then he was gone. But a lot had changed since they robbed and killed Fat Mack.

"What's up kinfolk? You been acting like you got some heavy shit on your mind these last few days." Stone said pulling him away from his thoughts.

"I do but you might not understand."

"Well, I ain't about to press you.; if you want to talk, spit that shit out and if somebody needs to die, give me a name and you know I got you."

"Nah, it ain't nothing like that. Just going through it with my better half. And thinking about my future."

"Well I said I wasn't going to press you but it seems like you want to talk so why don't you run it by me, cousin." And that's just what he did. For the next hour, he told Stone everything that had been on his mind and when he got to how

Jadda had reacted to him, Stone said, "Well then you know what you gotta do as far as little cuz goes. Start spending more time with her. That's the only way you're going to fix that. As far as what you and Nicki going through, as long as you're in the game, ya'll gon' have ya'll problems."

"I know. That's why I really been thinking. I mean I could probably live alright off the change I got tucked but I just ain't ready to walk away yet."

"So you want the cake and ice cream too."

"Yeah, something like that."

"Well we both know that ain't gonna happen. Not with Nicki. So you got a choice to make."

"Yeah but I ain't in no rush to make it."

"Oh shit. There went the neighborhood." Stone said as the five little niggas come in the front door having what seemed like an argument.

"Man I'm telling you. You need to calm your stupid ass down." Ru said.

"Man fuck that punk ass nigga. Just because you a pussy don't mean I gotta be. Shit. Letting that nigga Rick talk like he all hard and shit. Talking about we can't sell no work on that block, like he own it or something."

"What the fuck is ya'll talking about?" Slump asked.

"Well we were over on Renick fucking with some bitches Spazz had hooked up with and somebody needed a dub so I got the money and then this nigga named Rick, who used to hustle for J-Wood came up acting like he all tough and shit. Saying we need to know where we at and who run shit over here. So I told that punk ass nigga, we run shit and was about to do my thang but Ru scary ass gon' tell me I need to be cool. Like he scared of that nigga or something." Flip said.

"Like I was trying to tell this stupid ass lil' nigga. Being scared ain't got nothing to do with it. The nigga Rick was being all loud and shit causing a scene and hella people was out there. So I thought it was best if we let him think he was running and left. I mean what was we gonna do. Get on him out there and have motherfuckers telling on us." Ru said.

"Man fuck that. You was scared."

"Why don't you shut your little ass up, Flip. Because if I remember right, it was Ru that saved your ass when them niggas tried to rob you at that dice game. He wasn't scared then, was he?" Stone said.

"Man how come everybody wanna get at me?"

"Because lil' nigga, it's always you doing something stupid. Look Flip, all we saying is stop reacting so fast and star thinking. Now tell me about this Rick nigga." Slump said.

"He is a nobody ass nigga. Light skinned. About 23 years old, tall with dreads. He used to be one of J-Wood's runners but since somebody knocked that nigga's top off he been running the spot and now he think he all that." Ru said.

The young bucks had no idea who killed J-Wood.

"The nigga is a sucker though. I got into it with him one day at the liquor store but he didn't want it." Lil' Man said.

"Yeah but he will bust his gun. He the one that shot that nigga Big Al." Junebug said.

"Oh yeah, I heard about that. So that was him." Slump said.

"Yep, that was him."

"See that's what I'm talking about. Like he's all that." Flip said.

"Sounds like you got something to prove, lil' nigga." Slump said.

"I'm just saying. I know I'm the youngest and I might not have downed nobody but I will."

"So what you saying Flip. And before you can answer, think about what you're going to say." Stone said.

"I don't need to think about shit." Flip said and from the look in his eyes, Stone knew that little nigga was truly capable of murder. The eyes never lie.

Slumped

"We say your brother today Slump." Spazz said changing the subject.

"Oh yeah, where you see him?"

"In traffic. We bought a half of the good from him. You know he got the best weed."

"Yeah that nigga keep some fire. And he told us to tell you to hit his line." Lil' Man said.

"Alright. Good looking. Now roll something up."

Chapter 61

"Come here Sweet Pea. Ain't you just too cute. Looking like your daddy. I'm gonna have to kick your mom's butt if she don't start bringing you around here more. You hear that Ms. Nicki." Momma K said.

"I'm sorry Momma K. I just be so tired with school and then coming home having to do everything by myself."

"Well whenever you feel like you need some time to yourself or just don't want to be bothered, you can bring my grandbaby over here anytime. Now how you been doing lately and where is that son of mine?"

"I'm doing fine like I said. I'm just tired but I'm a be okay. As far as that son of yours, he ain't been home in almost a week. Ain't called to tell me to kiss is ass or nothing. He ain't even called to check up on his child."

"What's going on with ya'll. You fighting or something."

"No, he just act like we don't matter to him. And he would rather run the streets with his so called boys doing God knows what and I'm tired of it. I love him to death momma, I really do. But me and my baby girl deserve better. And I refuse to let him keep treating us like we don't matter to him. And he don't even try to be a part of her life. It's like he don't care.

"I can tell you one thing. The boy cares. I can see it in his eyes whenever he looks at you. And I know he loves you and this precious little girl."

Slumped

"Well he sure don't act like it."

"I don't happened to my first born. When he was a child, he was so sweet and loveable. But something changed him and I wish I knew what it was. I really do. But don't think for one minute he don't love ya'll because he do. He just don't know how to show it. Have you tried to call him."

"NO!" His ass needs to be calling me."

"Child, if it's one thing I do know is that men are stupid when it comes to love. They are too damn prideful. They don't want to seem weak.

"So what you think I should do Momma K?"

"I say call him and tell him to bring his ass home and talk to him. Tell him how you really feel. My son ain't stupid and he knows he would be a fool to let you get away. But you got to remember baby. You fell in love with a thug." Momma K said with a little chuckle.

"I know Momma K and that's a thing I told him I didn't want. No man in the streets. But truthfully, all I want is to know that I come first. That me and Jadda matter to him. That's all I really want. I could care less about him and the streets as long as he comes home to me and me only."

"Well then child you need tell him that."

"Oh hey girl. I didn't know you and my niece was here." Shawanna said.

"Yeah, we were in here talking to Momma K about that crazy brother of yours."

"Oh yeah. Which one because they both crazy as hell."

"You better watch your damn mouth."

"Oops, my bad momma. But you know it's true. Ain't neither one of them got no sense. Anyway I'm glad you here, big sis."

"You begging for something." Momma K said.

"I wasn't even going to beg for nothing for your information. I wanted to show her my prom dress."

"You call that little thing a dress. Huh, more like a half dress."

Slumped

"You must ain't got no style momma."

"No I got style. I just wouldn't' be running around showing off all my goodies."

"It ain't showing nothing."

"It ain't covering up nothing either."

"Anyway, come on sis. Let me show you."

Chapter 62

"**M**an, you know that nigga." Slump asked Tee, looking at Snake.

"Nah, I don't know him but he sure keep looking like he know us or something."

"Man fuck that nigga. What we dranking?" Stone said.

"Let's get on that Gorilla Piss." Slump said.

"Man last time I we drunk that shit, I blacked out." Tee said.

"Damn that was the last time we drunk that, wasn't it." Slump said.

"What the fuck is Gorilla Piss?" Stone asked.

"It's Colosrassi Gin and pineapple juice. It guaranteed to have you fucked up."

"Well in that case, let's get that shit. I'm trying to get fucked up." Not paying Snake any attention, they got their drink and left the liquor store and headed to the spot.

As soon as Snake got in his car, he called Munch.

"Who dis?"

"It's Snake."

"Oh what's up killa."

"Not shit. Just seen a motherfucking ghost."

"A ghost. What you talking about?"

"I just seen them niggas at the store."

"What niggas?"

"Your three best friends?"

"You talking about that punk Slump."

Slumped

"Like I said all three of them niggas. I thought you said they were down to two."

"I did but I guess that nigga had God on his side because I just saw him."

"Did they see you?"

"Yeah they saw me but they don't' know who I am."

"That's good. I tell you what. Meet me at the spot on Renick in about an hour. I gotta pick up my cousin and his boy from the airport. They flying in today from Texas, then I'm going to drop them off at the hotel and come meet you."

"Alright." Snake said closing his phone.

Chapter 63

"We made it!" Money said to Red as they walked through Sac International.

"I told you we would. Now I just hope my cousin ass is here on time. I told him we landed at 9:45p.m."

"Damn, look at all these white bitches. Hey there gorgeous." Money said to a tall blonde.

"Hi!" She responded and kept walking.

"They friendly too."

"Look at you. Always chasing pussy."

"And don't forget the money my nigga. Always remember the dough." Money said laughing.

"What's up killa!" Munch said hugging Red.

"Not shit big cousin. And yo, check it out. This right here is my boy Money. Money this is my cousin Anthony."

"Munch." Munch said correcting him and giving Money a dap.

"Nice to meet you. I heard a lot about you. And sorry to hear about your brother."

"Yeah, well all dogs go to heaven. But come on. Let's get out of here. I gotta go and meet my boy so I gotta drop all ya'll off at the room."

"What you gotta drop us off for?" Red asked.

"I just figured ya'll were tired and didn't want to sit around waiting on me. But if ya'll wanna ride, it's cool."

"Shit we sure ain't trying to be trapped in no room with no transportation."

"Yeah, about that. I got something for ya'll to push until ya'll get on your feet. But like I said, this move I gotta make is very important. So if ya'll coming, then let's be out. We can talk in the car." Without going into detail, Munch told him a little about what was going on.

"Oh yeah, I tried to put these cats on and they turned me down. And we been funking ever since and my gut tells me they had a lot to do with James being killed...if they didn't kill him themselves.

"You say it's three of them?" Money asked.

"Yeah, but they ain't shit."

"Well, now that here, we got you." Red said.

"Yeah. We rocking with you."

Chapter 64

"**M**an I ain't fucking with ya'll and that never again. I still don't know how I made it home last night. Shit I don't even remember driving." Stone said.

"I told you to slow down. But you were all Billy Bad Ass and shit. Talking about you could handle your drink." Slump said.

"Yeah but you done mixed gin and some wine and that shi is unreal. That's like gas and oil nigga. I still ain't stopped seeing double yet."

"Shit. I can't speak for ya'll but I went home and stood up in the pussy like I was on ex or something." Catching the look on Slump's face, Tee said, "Stop being an asshole and take your ass home. Spend some time with your girl and my God-daughter."

"Yeah, get your ass up out of here. I'm tired of looking at you all sad and shit. Go home nigga." Stone added.

"Man fuck both of ya'll." Slump said laughing, getting up off the couch.

"I'm tired of looking at ya'll and listening to these little niggas argue all day about who did what and how many bitches Spazz done fucked. So I'm going home." For a minute, Stone and Tee looked at him and then they fell out laughing.

Chapter 65

Munch introduced Snake and Rick to his cousin Red and Money and listened while Snake told him about seeing Stone, Slump and Tee. When he started to describe Tee, Red interrupted him.

"Hold on. Hold on. These niggas sound real fucking familiar. Don't they Money." Red said.

"Yeah I was thinking the same shit. The big buff one. Do he got a scar on his lip."

"You know I never really paid too much attention, but now that I think about, I did see a scar like someone punched his big ass in the mouth or something." Snake said.

Then there's the fat country boy and the little skinny nigga. I think they called him Slim or something." Money said.

"No his name is Jaylon. but they call him Slump."

"Yeah, Slump." Red said.

"I can't believe this shit. I mean, I knew they were Cali niggas but I never thought they would be here." Money said.

"Well it's a small fucking world." Red said.

"Alright now. It's time for ya'll to do some talking and tell me how ya'll know these niggas." Munch said.

"Why don't you tell him Money." Red said. So Money told him how they hooked up with Jazz and Porshea. drugged them, fucked them, and took pictures, and how they left the note talking shit to the men. They told him about the fight.

"Wait a minute." Munch said cutting him off.

"Nah, hold up cuz. Let him finish. The story is about to get good."

"So yeah, we caught them hoes and had them locked up in this warehouse. We had this ol' knock ass nigga watching them but somehow they fucked ol' boy over and got away. Then about a month or so ago, they popped up on us at a club and we had to get out of there."

"Hey Munch, wasn't ol' girl that was found dead at the spot named Porshea?"

"Yeah it was."

"I know it. They are the ones that got Wood. I should have got out the car and made sure the niggas was dead when I hit his ass up."

"Oh shit. You got one of them niggas." Red said.

"Yeah I caught that nigga Tee slipping and aired his shit out a little over a year ago."

"Yeah and we thought he was dead until yesterday when we say him in the store." Munch said.

"Yeah well now we are here so it's four against three."

"Five!" Rick said. He had been listening to everything and decided to tell Munch about the words he had with Flip.

"They got these five lil' niggas who be selling they work."

"Oh yeah." Munch said.

"Yep and the other day I told the little one about busting knocks on the block and he got all loud and shit but the other niggas got him in the car and they left."

"Yeah, well I'll let you deal with that. In the meantime, just keep your eyes open. I'll let ya'll know when we are going to move. So cousin. You niggas feel like going out."

"Hell yeah. But all we brought with us is money." Red and Money said together.

"Wait a minute. So the only thing in those suitcases are cash."

Slumped

"Big faces. Dead presidents. C-Notes. All motherfucking money." Money said.

"You too got to be the dumbest niggas I know. Flying with all that cash."

"What! It was three suitcases."

"Four and don't ask how much." Red said.

"I always knew you was a dummy. But you, I thought you was kinda sharp Money."

"Fuck you. You'll see the only thing sharp on this nigga is his tongue when he eating pussy." Red said laughing as he put his hand on Money's shoulder.

"Well it's a whole lot of that out here for him to chew on. C'mon. Let's go. And Rick stay on your toes. I know if you told me. They told them. So keep your eyes open and don't be laying up in here with no bitches."

"Alright Munch. I got you."

"Now you two come on so you can get this money out my car before the feds have us all under the jail.

Chapter 66

"**S**o you finally decided to come home."

"I shouldn't have left in the first place."

"Look Jaylon, we need to talk about what we gon' do. Because if you don't want to be with me, I can't make you stay." Nicki said.

"Why do it always gotta be about who is staying and who is leaving?"

"Because it seems like your friends are more important than me and your daughter."

"Do I make you happy Nicki?"

"I'm in love with Jaylon and I love him so damn much. But I can't stand Slump. He don't care about nothing but himself and his fucking reputation. It's like it's two niggas in one damn body and that's just who you are. And I'm willing to take the good with the bad because I really do love you. But I will not keep letting you walk all over me and our child. She is almost one and she barely knows you because you are never here. You promised me I would never have to raise a baby by myself but that's exactly what I've been doing and I'm tired of it. Well don't just stand there looking at me. Say something!"

Slump walked over to the couch and sat next to Nicki. He took her hand into his. "Baby, you have no idea how much you and Jadda mean to me or how much I need you both in my life. Love to me has always been just a four letter word like fuck or shit. These feelings are all new to me. I know I

want to spend my life with you. Which I why I bought this."
He said pulling a little black box out of his pocket.

"I know that's not what I think it is, Jaylon." Instead of answering her, he got down on his knees.

"Nicki, I might not be your prince in shining armor or the kind of man that wakes up every day and goes to work. I know I have issues. I know you don't like what I do out in the streets and I can tell you now, I'm not gonna be in the streets forever. But I'm not gonna lie and say I'm done right now because I'm not. But I can promise you and Jadda are in no danger. And none of what I do in the streets will ever come home with me. I know I love you because I feel it every time I look into your eyes or hear your voice. The way your smile lights the world up makes everything seem like it will be alright. I'm asking you to marry me. Be my wife. My Bonnie. Be my forever and a day. Love and know I will always take care of you and our family. So what do you say Nicki. Will you marry me?"

"Yes! Yes! I will. But you have to promise me that whatever it is you're doing will never come back on me and Jadda."

"I promise to always protect and love you and Jadda. I promise I will die before anything will ever happen to the two of you."

"And no more running off if I'm gonna be your wife. You will be home with me, even if we are mad at each other."

"Alright Nicki. You got that. So is that a yes."

"Yes it's a yes. You crazy man." Nicki said kissing him. "Now let me see the ring."

The ring was sterling silver with a three and a half carat princess cut diamond on top. With forever and a day love engraved on the inside.

"I know you are allergic to gold. That's why I picked silver."

"I love it. I can't wait to show Momma K, Angel, and Shawanna."

Slumped

"Forget them right now. Why don't you come in the room with me so I can show you how much I missed you."

"Boy you so nasty." Nicki said getting up and running toward the room laughing.

Chapter 67

"I still can't believe you two niggas flew out here with all that money." Munch said.

"Shit, what was we supposed to do. Leave it?" Red said.

"We done hustled too hard and killed too many niggas for this dough. Wasn't no way we was leaving it. But now that it's here. It's time to enjoy some of it. So what's up with this club you were talking about." Money said.

"3 Kings is the best thing going out here right now. Everybody who is somebody be up there. The bitches be outrageous, be ready to fuck and suck the first nigga worth something."

"Well shit then. What the fuck is we waiting on. I'm sure trying to see what some of this Cali pussy feel like." Money said.

"Pussy is pussy nigga. Some better than others but it all gets wet the same." Red said.

"You two niggas are crazy. Let's go hit one of these malls and get fitted." Munch said.

They went to Arden Fair Mall and while they were there, Munch thought it would be funny to drop in on Alicia. So they went into bath and body and as soon as they came through the door, Munch made eye contact with her. She was scared but tried not to show it.

"What's up Alicia. How you been doing." Munch said with a smirk on his face.

Slumped

"I was doing fine until I saw you."

"Bitch don't make me hurt you up in here in front of all these people." He said after pulling her close.

"Why are you doing this to me. I never did anything to you to have you do that to me."

"Don't play like you're all innocent and shit. You know what you did. I was just stopping by since I was in here with my family and shit."

"Well it was nice of you to stop by, but if you ain't buying nothing, I got paying customers to help."

"Yeah, well I'm gonna let you get back to work but do me a favor. Tell your boy Slump I'm coming for him." With that said, all three men left.

"Who was that sexy thing." Money asked once they walked away.

"That bitch is a serpent. Stay away from her and anything that has to do with her if you know what's good for you."

"It's like that. Damn. It's only two things that make a nigga feel like that when it comes to a bitch. One, either she gave him something. Or two, she crossed him. So which one is it, big dog."

"I think that bitch had something to do with my brother getting killed."

"What!" Red said turning around. "That's the bitch. I will kill that bitch with my bare hands."

"Nah, nah. Calm down cousin. She will get hers in all due time."

"Damn girl. What's the matter with you. You back here shaking and crying and shit. Who is them guys." Alicia's coworker, Pam asked.

"My ex and some of his friends. It's nothing girl. I just got worked up but it's cool now."

"Are you sure."

"Yeah, I'm good now."

"C'mon Alicia. Let's get back to work."

Chapter 68

"So you really gonna do it huh." Tee asked Slump.

"Yeah man. I'm gonna marry her. I mean I know she is down for me and I know she loves me. But at the same time, I'm kinda scared cuz I never had these type of feelings for no woman but my momma."

"Well at least you know the love is real and that's all that matters. So other than that, what's new."

"Not shit. You know. Sucker ducking and dummy dogging. How about you?"

"Man just going through it with the bm. This crazy ass bitch acting brand new. Talking about Lil' Tee can't be around Jazz. But you know that's my Bonnie and Vicki is just jealous. Besides, she don't' be having shit to say when she be calling Jazz and asking her to borrow money and shit like Jazz ain't gonna tell me."

"Wait a minute. Your baby momma be calling your wifey, asking to borrow money. Man that's some Maury Povick shit." Slump said laughing.

"Tell me about it."

"You heard from Stone?"

"No, why?"

"Because I ain't heard from him in a couple of days."

"Shit he probably got some new pussy and laying up in it for a few days. I'm sure he alright. Who I'm worried about is Flip young ass. He been acting a little strange lately."

"What you mean?"

"I don't know. It's like he be in a whole nother' world sometimes. You know out of all those little niggas, he scares me."

"Why you say that?"

"Because he reminds me a lot of you, but worse."

"Well then, just be glad he's on our team." Slump's phone started to ring. He saw it was Lil' Lee.

"Hello?"

"What's up big bro! Momma K said you and Nicki getting married."

"Yeah, we thinking about it."

"Well congratulations."

"Good looking baby boy."

"The reason I called is because I got this move I wanna run past you."

"A move. What kinda move are you talking about?"

"You know exactly what I'm talking about. But I'm not going to talk about it on this phone. So where you at?"

"Me and Tee on our way to the spot."

"Why don't' you swing by Momma K's and pick me up."

"Alright. I'll be there in a minute."

"Who was that, Lil' Lee?" Tee asked.

"Yeah. He talking about he got a move lined up or something he wants to talk about."

"Oh yeah. I hope it's his weed connect."

"Well we about to find out."

They pulled up in front of Momma K's house about twenty minutes later.

"Shit. Why we're here. We might as well go in and say hi. You know how she get when she feels unloved."

"I already know."

"Boy you scared the shit outta me." Momma K said. She was on her way out the door when Slump and Tee was coming in.

"Where are you on your way to all dressed up." Slump asked hugging her.

Slumped

"None of your business boy. And Tee you better come give me some love while you're standing there acting all tough and shit."

"Nah, it ain't even like that." Tee said giving her a hug and kiss on her cheek. "You know I love you like my own mother."

"I ain't trying to run out on ya'll but I was headed out the door. And I know ya'll wasn't here to see me anyway so I'll talk to ya'll later."

"Wait a minute, Momma. Where are you going?"

"Boy why are you all up in mine."

"Because I need to know who I gotta kill if something happens to you." He said seriously.

"Boy you crazy. You know that. Don't you. But since you trying to be nosy. I'm going to pick up my future daughter in law and my grandbaby so we can go to lunch."

"Alright. Tell my ladies I love them."

"I will." Momma K said walking out the door.

"I thought I heard ya'll out here." Lil' Lee said coming down the hallway. "What's up bro!"

"So the only nigga you gon' speak to is your brother. Huh lil' nigga."

"Nah, Tee. You know you my dog. Even if you don't kill a cat. What's up. Ya'll ready to ride out."

"Why don't you tell us about this move first." Slump said.

"I can show you better than I can tell you. So like I said, ya'll ready to ride out."

"Let's go then."

Once they got into the Audi, Lee pulled the blunt from behind his ear and lit it.

"Ya'll know I been pushing this tree for a minute now. And I been lightweight getting my dough up."

"What that gotta do with anything."

"Damn. Calm down bro. I'm getting to it. Hit the weed. Like I was saying. I been doing my thang with these white boys but the whole time, it's been bigger than the weed. But now I'm in and they trust me. And they got a whole lot going on besides the weed thing."

"Oh yeah, like what?" Tee asked.

"They be moving that ice. And when I say moving. They got this house in the heights rocking nonstop. 24 hours a day. Every day. Nigga last week, I was with Eric."

"Who the fuck is Eric?"

"Oh, he the one that put me on with the tree. Anyhow, I'm with him and he said he needed me to ride with him right quick, so I did. You know where Parker Homes is right?"

"Back there off McArthur."

"Yeah. So we pull up to this house where all the Asians be on Kelly Court and this motherfucker was rocking. I mean it was motherfuckers going in and out that bitch spending money and once we went inside, these crackers had dope and money all over the place. It was like some movie shit. With all that cash, it had to be about a million up in that bitch."

"C'mon lil nigga. A million dollars. Just lying around. And he takes you up in there and let's you see it." Tee said.

"Hell yeah. I saw it. I told you, he trust me. But fuck it. Ya'll ain't gotta believe me. Just come and see for yourself." Slump got off the freeway at Marisville Blvd. and made a right onto McArthur.

"Keep going straight. And turn left at the second stop sign."

When they got to the stop sign, Tee said, "Damn, when they build a park right here?"

"I don't know. It's been a minute since I been back here."

"Pull up to the park bro. And let's get out." Slump pulled over, parked, and they got out the car.

"You got your heat." He asked Tee.

"What kind of question is that."

"Just asking. These Asians looking like we trespassing or something."

"Oh don't trip on them. They cool." They walked over by one of the bitches and sat down where they could see down the court to the house. It didn't take long before anyone with eyes could tell the house was a dopehouse.

"Damn! Look at all them motherfuckers." Slump said.

"I told you it's like some movie shit." They watched long enough to finish smoking the blunt. Then got in the car and left. Once back in the car, Lil' Lee asked. "So what's up. What you think?"

"So it was money all over the place." Tee asked.

"Man that shit was everywhere. And I mean everywhere."

"So what you think Slump."

"I think we can make it happen."

"But we don't' know how many people is up in there."

"It's only three of them. Eric, Brian, and Josh." Lil' Lee said.

"You sure?" Slump asked.

"Positive. They so comfortable with their shit, they wouldn't even see it coming."

"Ice? What's that. Meth?" Tee asked.

"Yeah. Everybody on that shit. It's the new crack. That shit's going for like 25 stacks a pound."

"This could be the one we been looking for Slump." Tee said.

"I was thinking the same thing. Now all we gotta do is find Stone."

Chapter 69

"So you sure you ready to do this?" Stone asked Flip.

"Man I was born ready for this shit." For the last few days, Stone and Flip been following Rick. Waiting for the right time to put him to sleep. And that time was now.

"Look. There he go. Do what you gotta do." Stone said to Flip.

Flip pulled on his hoodie and started walking toward Rick. Rick so caught up in the light skinned honey he'd been fucking with, didn't notice Flip until it was too late.

"What's up now you bitch ass nigga." Before Rick could reply, Flip shot him twice in the chest. The girl started to scream. "Shut up bitch." Shooting her once in the head. Then looking down at Rick, he said. "I'll see you when I get there." And unloaded the rest of his clip in his face.

He then turned and ran back to the base head rental. Stone was waiting for him. Once he got in the car, Stone sped away. There was no need to say anything. He just handed Flip a blunt and kept driving.

Chapter 70

"I don't know why we ain't been came here?" Money said to Red.

"I see why they call Cali the golden state. Shit, this is where it's at." They had been there now for a few weeks and it had been a non-stop freak fest. But now it was time to get down to business. Red still couldn't believe how small the world was. He would never have thought the niggas they were funking with three states away were the same niggas his family was going at it with and may even be responsible for the death of his little cousin.

"Yeah, I like it out here too. But I will like it even more once we kill them bitch ass niggas."

"So what's up. You ready to do this or what?"

"Yeah, I'm ready." They had been watching the spot where the five young niggas stayed.

"Tonight, it's only four of them up in there." Red said. "That little crazy one is gone somewhere with that fat nigga."

"So what are we gonna do, just air everything out then?"

"Yep!" Red said getting out of the car. He checked to make sure his desert eagle was locked and loaded.

"Just like old times." Money said doing the same thing. As they got to the house, the door opened and Ru and Spazz were coming out. They saw Red and Money.

"What's up blood? Ya'll lost or something."

"Nah, we ain't lost lil' nigga." And before the boys could say anything, they were pointing the gun at Ru.

"What the fuck." Ru said as Spazz saw the gun and tried to run back in the house. He took two steps before Money shot him twice in the back. One bullet tore through his heart. He was dead before hitting the ground.

Hearing the gunshots, Lil' Man and Junebug grabbed their pistols and went to see what was going on. When they made it to the front door, they saw Ru coming in with his hands up.

"What the fuck is going on Ru? Oh shit. What happened to Spazz?" Junebug asked.

"I happened to him?" Money said stepping into the house. Ru still in shock from seeing one of his closest friends gunned down in front of him, still hadn't spoken a word.

Junebug and Lil' Man pointed their guns at the men.

"If you don't want to end up like your boy did. Then I suggest you put your lil' pea shooters down...or use them." Red said. For the first time, Junebug wished Flip was around.

"What do ya'll want?" Junebug asked.

"First I want ya'll to put them guns down. Then we can talk." Red said.

"Fuck you!" Junebug said before opening fire and running to the back of the house. Lil Man froze. He dropped his gun and started crying.

"Please don't kill us man!"

"Stop begging." Money said, shooting Lil' Man between the eyes. "I always hated a crybaby."

"Hey lil' nigga. Where is the money and dope." Red asked Ru who never answered. He just stood there with his hands in the air.

"Look at him. That nigga don't' even see us right now." Red said looking at the blank look in Ru's face.

"He ain't go see much of nothing when he get to where he going." Red said before shooting Ru point blank in the face.

"We been up in here too long my nigga. I know somebody done called the cops by now. So if we are going to find the work, I suggest we hurry the fuck up."

Slumped

"Fuck that shit. Let's get the fuck outta here." Red said.

(End of part 2 of digital copy)

Chapter 71

"They are all dead." Junebug said into his phone. "They killed them. All my niggas is gone!"

"What? What the fuck is you talking about nigga. Who's dead. Who killed who?"

"I don't know. Two niggas came up in the spot and started shooting." Junebug said crying.

"How the fuck did you get away then?"

"I started shooting and ran out the back window."

"Alright man. Calm down. Tell me where you at?"

"I'm at Tonya's house around the corner. I can't believe they gone. My niggas is gone."

"Look Junebug. Crying ain't gonna bring them back and I need you to man up. I will be there in a minute. Me and Tee on our way."

"Man what's wrong?" Tee asked.

"Fuck! Man somebody done hit the spot."

"What! Who was that?"

"It was Junebug. He said two niggas ran in the spot and shot everybody. He ran out the back."

"Is he sure everybody is dead."

"From the way he crying and shit, they all dead. Man this is some fucked up shit."

"It's all part of the game. Kill or be killed."

"Yeah I know all that but still. Them niggas barely started to live life."

"Did Bug say he knew who it was."

Slumped

"I didn't ask him but he can tell us when we get there. He's at Tonya's house."

"Man this had to be some shit them lil' niggas got into and just ain't say shit to us about it."

"I don't know what he fuck the reason is behind our lil' niggas getting hit, but I do know, whoever it was that did it is going to pay." Slump stated.

Chapter 72

"Oh shit!" Flip said when they turned onto the block. "Look at them cops. They hitting the spot."

"Calm down lil' nigga. They ain't gon find nothing. It ain't no way they know where the safe is."

"Man, what the fuck is that?" Flip said looking at the gurney being pushed out of the house by one of the officers.

"That look like a body nigga."

"C'mon Stone."

"Nigga what is you doing. Is you crazy or something. Close the fucking door. We can't do nothing for them now. And if your ass run up there, all they gon' do is question how you know them. What the fuck is you gonna say. You live there and sold dope with them. You gotta start thinking Flip. So just sit back and chill." They drove past the house trying to get a better look at what was going on. But the cops were everywhere. But what Stone did see were the three bodies in the back of the coroner's van.

"We gotta get up outta here lil' nigga." He was hoping that Flip hadn't saw what he did. "When it rain, it pours."

"What's that shit supposed to mean?"

"Nothing. You wouldn't understand."

"I'm gonna call Slump and see if he knows what's going on." No sooner than he dialed the number and put the phone to his ear, he was ending the call. "Man, something ain't right. Before I could say anything, Slump told me to meet

them at Tonya's and hung up. I hope my bros are alright."
Stone didn't' want to tell him what he saw in the coroner's
van.

"Yeah. I hope so too. Where do Tonya stay?"

"You know Tonya. The white girl with all the ass around
the corner."

"Oh yeah." Since they were only around the corner, they
pulled up a few minutes before Tee and Slump, who had Lil'
Lee with them.

"What's going on?" Flip asked.

"We will talk about it in the house."

As soon as they walked in the door, Junebug walked in
the house. "They dead man. Spazz, Ru, and Lil' Man. They
gone."

"What!" Flip yelled.

"Some niggas came up in the spot and just started
shooting. I ain't never seen these two niggas before man.
Never. It's just me and you left, Flip. The bros are gone. I
tried man. I swear I did. But it was two of them but the tall
one had a gun in Ru's face telling us to drop our guns but he
was out of it man. Then the one with the iced out grill just
shot Lil' Man. I started shooting back, ran out the window
and came over here."

"So it was two of them." Slump asked.

"Yeah a tall nigga and a short one." Junebug answered. "I
swear I ain't never seen these two niggas before a day in my
life."

"Wait a minute. You said one had ice in his mouth." Tee
said.

"Yeah, it looked like his whole mouth was iced out. And
not no cheap shit. This nigga had rocks in his mouth."

"It can't be."

"It just could be. What you thinking?" Slump asked.

"The way he said a tall one and a short one with an iced
out grill only brings two niggas to my mind. But what are the

odds of it being them. Shit they are way in Texas. Something ain't right dog. I got a bad feeling about this."

"Wait! Wait! Look." Tonya said pointing and unmuting her television.

Breaking News: I'm on Eddison Ave in front of a house where a shooting just occurred. Three young men whose names were not yet released were shot to death in their home. Some guns and a small amount of cocaine and marijuana were found inside the home as well. The police say it seems to be a robbery gone bad. If you have seen anything, please call the Sacramento Sherriff's office.

"Man turn that shit off. What the fuck are we gonna do?" Flip said snatching the remote from Tanya and turning the television off.

"Who could it be Tee?"

"Now is not the place or time for that Flip. We are going to all talk later." Tee said.

"Later. Man fuck later. My bros are all dead and you talking about later."

"Who is it man?"

"Just tell me who did it. I will kill them niggas myself."

"I know you are tripping right now little nigga, but don't just start running your mouth."

"I said that this is not the time or place. So just calm down. Alright?"

"Yeah I hear you. But you going to tell me who they are and I'm going to do them just like I did that bitch ass nigga Rick." Flip said.

"See Flip that's the shit I be talking about. You just be talking, and never thinking about what you be saying."

"What's he talking about Stone?" Slump asked.

"Like Tee just said. Now ain't the time or place, but I suggest that we get some where we can talk asap."

Slumped

"Slump is Tony T back? Or is he on the road again?" Tee asked.

"It don't even matter. Come on. We are about to go out there. Stone y'all follow us." Slump said.

Thirty-five minutes later they pulled into Tony T's yard.

"Damn." Tony T said, as they all got out the cars.

"Who died?"

"Or what died?"

"Y'all niggas look like hell with death as the warden."

"Only if you knew Unc. Only if you knew." Slump said.

"Well since you three niggas and these two little half ass niggas done brought y'all problems out here, you must need to talk."

"Shit. Since that's the only time y'all act like you can come out here to visit an old dog."

"Naw it ain't like that Unc. It's just been a lot going on lately, and now shit just hit the fan." Stone said.

"Man what you mean shit just hit the fan?"

"All my bros are dead." Junebug said.

"Man shut that shit up nigga. Crying ain't gonna bring them back. And I don't know why we are here. We should be out there trying to find out who did this and burn they asses down."

"First of all Flip, don't get too cocky nigga. The same way your gun bust, you see they guns bust."

"The same way you downed that nigga, your niggas can be downed."

"The game is real little nigga and there is only one way out."

Before Flip could think of anything slick to say, Stone turned to Tee and Slump, and explained how he took Flip to get his first body. He told them how he thought Flip was just talking and didn't really think that he was ready for that part of the game. He told them how he hoped Flip backed out. But to his surprise, the little nigga didn't. Instead he got out of the car and did his thang with no second thoughts about killing

Rick. That made Stone proud because Flip showed him he was not just talk like 95% of the little niggas his age.

Slump, Tee, Stone, Flip, and Junebug talked that night until early the next morning. They grew closer that night than ever before. They also vowed that any and everything that had something to do with the deaths of Spazz, Ru, and Little Man would pay. It was no longer about getting money. It was about getting revenge now.

Chapter 73

Nine Days Later

"I still can't believe they're gone." Junebug said to Flip.

"I can't either bro. But look around at how much love they are getting sent off with."

"I didn't even know we knew this many people."

They were standing in front of the three black, eighteen carat gold trimmed coffins, looking down at their brothers.

"I know from where they are sitting at looking down at us, they see the love." Flip said.

They were at Sunset Lawns off of Drycreek Road in Del Paso Heights. From all the people and the looks of the funeral, you would have thought that the Pope or the President had died.

"Hey y'all. How you feeling?" Slump asked walking up behind them.

"I don't know what I feel. It's just that I still can't believe they are really gone." Junebug said.

"Yeah I know what you mean. But think of it like this. They are all in a better place. And one day hopefully no time soon, we will all be together one more time." Slump said.

"Did you see all them bitches that came up here to kiss Spazz one last time? I mean damn. Either big bro had a golden dick or a platinum tongue." Flip said, trying to make the best of the situation.

Slumped

"I think that little nigga had a platinum tongue." Tee said quietly.

"I still think that Stone should have come to see the little bros off." Flip said to Slump.

"In his own way, trust me he has. He just don't do funerals and he has his reasons."

By that time 18 of the baddest bitches walked up to them and said, "Y'all ready?"

"Yeah let's do it." Slump answered.

Six women to a coffin. They picked up the three young princes and carried them out to the waiting hursts.

"Man when I go that's exactly how I want to be carried to my grave. Those bitches are bad." Flip said.

"Yeah I'm sure Spazz is loving every minute of that shit." Junebug said.

"Shit. I'm loving it just walk by." Slump said elbowing Junebug lightly.

"Baby you alright?" Angel asked Stone.

"Yeah ma. I'm cool. Just thinking about my little niggas."

"Well if you want to talk, you know I'm here to listen."

"Yeah I know."

The last funeral Stone had went to was his mother's. He told himself he would never attend another one. Instead he would just remember them as they were.

Grabbing the bottle of Privilege off the table, he thought that whoever it was that hit them little niggas didn't know what they got themselves into.

Chapter 74

"**M**an we should ride up in there and shoot that motherfucker up. That would be some grimey ass shit." Red said.

"Well we've been called worst than that." Money said laughing.

"Come on Red. I ain't with that shit. Besides our problem ain't with nobody but them niggas. Not everybody else." Munch said seriously.

They had been parked by the Old Forty-Niner Drive In watching the funeral.

"Let's get up out of here before somebody notices us."

"I got a surprise for tonight."

"Oh yeah. What you got planned cousin?" Red asked.

"I rented out the Zoku lounge and we are going to have a party in honor of them three little niggas."

"Man is you crazy? What if they show up?" Red asked.

"That's the whole idea. But you don't have to come if you are scared."

The look on Red's face turned deadly.

"I'm not scared of shit except God and bad pussy."

"Good. I'm glad you ain't gone soft on me."

"Man I'm curious. Why should Red and I of all people be at this party? Once they see us all hell is going to break loose." Money said from the back seat.

"This ain't the country my man. The Zoku is in downtown Sacramento."

"So what the fuck does that mean?" Money asked.

"Police. And I know how them niggas think. So they won't try anything. I want you and Red there as my special guests." Munch said.

"I knew I liked you for a reason." Money said.

"Well I still don't see why we should let them know we will be there." Red said.

"I kind of like the element of surprise."

"Yeah but tell me you don't want to see the look on them suckas faces when they see the two of you. After the party we will just go get lost in the Bay." Munch said.

"Well fuck it then. Party at the Zoku's." Red said.

"Just one more thing. What makes you so sure they will show up?" Money added.

"Oh they will be there. That I'm positive about." Munch replied.

Munch had called Alicia earlier that day and told her he was having a party in honor of Rick, Ru, Spazz, and Little Man. He even paid the local radio stations to announce it. But he was sure that Alicia would call and tell Slump, that it was him who was throwing the party. So he knew without any doubts, at least Tee, Slump, and Stone would be there. The two little niggas might not be there, but they sure would be close by.

Chapter 75

"Oh yeah." Slump said into his phone.

"Yeah. Jaylon I don't think that y'all should go." Alicia said.

"And why not?"

"Because I think that he is up to something. I mean a couple of weeks ago him and two other niggas came to my job. He was talking all crazy and shit. He was telling me what he was going to do to y'all."

"And you decided to wait until now to tell me about this shit?"

"Well you ain't been around in so long."

"So since I don't come around, you can't call me and tell me a nigga is making threats on my life?"

"I mean it's not like I didn't already know."

"But still you should have let me know."

"Well I didn't think your wife would like me calling you." Alicia said with a lot of attitude.

"So that's what this is all about? I should have known."

"What? You should have known what nigga?"

"All you did was use me to get Munch."

"Just like you used me?" Slump said.

"Oh so it's like that now?"

"Hey look Alicia. I don't have any time for no bullshit. I mean you act like you are my bitch or something. All we ever did was fuck. Nothing more nothing less."

Slumped

"So that's how it is now? All I am and was just some pussy to you? Well fuck you then nigga." She said hanging up the phone.

Chapter 76

"What's going on?" Tee asked.

"Alicia said the nigga Munch is having some kind of going away party tongith at the Zoku lounge in honor of our little niggas."

"What! Who the fuck does this nigga think he is? He trying to tell us something."

"I don't know but I was thinking the same shit. I know one thing. That punk is real smart nigga. The police is all over downtown and the fucking county jail is right around the corner. But he knows we will come. In fact, I'm almost positive that's what he wants us to do."

"We going to Slump?" Flip asked.

"Man, you little niggas can't even get in."

"So what. We still going."

"Calm down lil' bro. Ain't shit gonna happen tonight."

"That's not the point Slump. That nigga trying to be funny by having that shit. It ain't got nothing to do with Rick's bitch ass. His funeral was three days ago."

"I'm gonna kill that nigga. His momma, his bitch, his kids, the dog and the cat if he got one…" Junebug said.

"Look ya'll, I know you're hurt right now. Shit I know ya'll mad as fuck too. So are we but we still gotta do it right. We got to plan and think. So ya'll ain't going." Tee said.

"So what the fuck we gonna do then?" Flip asked.

"Nothing. We are going to let this nigga think we are shook from our loss and knock down everything he touches.

Slumped

Every nigga he got hustling for him starting tonight. So when we are at the Zoku you two do what y'all do best. Matter of fact, hit that spot he had Rick set up in. That's one of his main trap houses."

"I don't know about sending them to do that Slump. I mean don't get me wrong ya'll. I know ya'll with the shit. I just don't' think ya'll ready for something like that yet." Tee said.

"Well then it's only one way to show you that we are." Flip said looking at Tee.

"Yeah but you are the only one talking."

"That's because there is nothing to talk about." Junebug said.

"Alright then, let's go see what's up with Stone." Twenty minutes later, they pulled up to Angel and Stone's duplex on Bomark Way in North Highlands. Stone was standing outside with his big brindle Bull massive Blockhead.

"Oh shit. Look at ya'll in suits looking like the men in black or something."

"You sure seem like you're in a good mood." Flip said taking the blunt out of Stone's hand.

"You know how it is, lil' nigga. You got to smile to keep from crying and today I feel like crying."

"Shit, we all do." Junebug added.

"I heard that. So what's up."

"You ain't gonna believe the shit this nigga Munch don' pulled." Slump said.

"I'm listening."

"This nigga is having a party at the Zoku tonight in honor of our little niggas."

"So what, we gonna shut that motherfucker down then, right."

"See that's what the fuck I'm talking about. Go set that bitch off. Let that nigga know we ain't playing."

"Man shut up lil' nigga and pass the weed." Tee said. But Flip wasn't done talking yet. "Man Stone. Can you believe

Slumped

Slump and Tee are talking about going to the Zoku and not doing shit."

"No, I don't believe no shit like that. So what's the plan because I know ya'll got to have one."

"Well shit. Not really. I say we go to the Zoku, peep out what's going on and let Flip and Junebug shoot out that spot Rick was pushing out of."

"I still don't know about that." Tee said.

"Why?" Stone asked.

"Because he don't think we can handle it." Junebug said.

"Well…"

"Well what, Stone?"

"You know what, lil nigga. Can you handle it? Are you ready to start putting your gun game down? I know Flip is. I saw that with my own eyes. But are you?"

"Hell yeah I'm ready nigga."

"Well then. Enough said. And I got the perfect attire for the night. C'mon. let's go inside so I can show you. Blockhead, get in the house." Stone said to the big dog.

"Hey ya'll. See what ya'll doing to me. Got me messing my makeup up." Angel said as they came in the house. Then she started crying.

"You still beautiful baby. Now stop crying and get what I had you pick up earlier for me." Stone said hugging and kissing her on her forehead.

"Okay baby." She said walking toward their bedroom. She came back a few minutes later with five coke white Coogi sweatshirts and handed one to each of them. On the front of them was an airbrushed mirror of Spazz, Ru, and Lil' Man with the words, 'Never to be forgotten' on the back of them. For a minute, nobody said nothing. They all just looked at the three faces on the hoodies. Each lost in their own thoughts.

"I had those made a couple days ago. Angel picked them up this morning. What do ya'll think?"

"Perfect!" Slump said.

Slumped

"Yeah, these are clean as fuck. So what time are we gonna be making our move." Junebug said.

"Oh yeah, I almost forgot. I heard on the radio today that they were having a party at the Zoku tonight in honor of the four young men who got killed last week. So I guess they were talking about Robbie (Spazz), Devin (Ru), and Paul (Lil' Man) and the other kid who got shot. Anyway they said the drinks are free from ten to eleven p.m."

"Well shit. I guess we know what time we're going then." Tee said.

"They also said they would have extra security and twice as many police just in case something happened. So if ya'l go, please be careful." Angel added.

"We will!" They all said together.

"Yeah baby. We're gonna be alright."

"Okay Mike. I know that look but it ain't none of my business so I won't say nothing, but ya'll better not let nothing happen to these two." She said pointing to Junebug and Flip.

"Stop worrying woman and get out of here so we can do us."

"Nah, don't trip. We'll meet up with you later. We about to go take these hot ass suits off."

"Alright then, in a minute."

Once they got back in Slump's Audi, he said, "We need to go by the spot and clean out the safe. We been putting it off long enough."

"Man I ain't trying to go in there." Junebug said.

"If you worried about the blood, I had the place cleaned already."

"It's not that. Ya'll wasn't there man. I watched my niggas get blown the fuck away in that bitch. I don't never wanna be up in that motherfucker again."

"All we doing is cleaning the safe out and ya'll getting the wagon outta there. How else ya'll gonna do ya'll thang?" Slump asked.

Slumped

"C'mon bro. Let's just get it over with." They drove to the old trap house, cleared out the safe, and Junebug and Flip got into the Cutlass wagon. They agreed to meet at Slump's house at 8:30. They boys drove back to Tonya's, where they'd been staying since the shooting. She'd been like a sister to them since they started running the streets. After dropping Tee off, Slump went home to spend time with Jada and Nicki. When he got home, Momma K and Shawanna were there.

"Now that's how you supposed to dress boy."

"How, like I'm going to a funeral."

"Don't get smart with me. You know what I mean. You look good."

"Yeah, well I don't feel good."

"Yeah, I'm sorry you had to go through that. Them boys were just babies too."

"Well that's life. We all gotta die. Look Momma K, I'm tired, hot, and I don't really feel like talking. I'm gonna take this suit off, wash my ass…"

"Boy you watch your mouth."

"My bad Momma K. I'm gonna wash my butt and lay down for a minute. Get my mind together." Slump went into the bedroom, closed the door, and started to take his clothes off when Nicki entered the room, followed by Jadda.

"Go give daddy some love Jadda."

"Hey sweet pea. How my baby girl doing."

"O Tay Daddy!" Jadda said. He bent down, picked his baby girl up, and kissed her.

"You know your daddy loves you right."

"Yep, him love me dis much." Jadda said spreading her arms out as wide as she could.

"I sure do."

"How much does daddy love me?" Nicki asked.

"I love you more than you will ever know lady. More than you will ever know."

"So how you feeling, Jaylon?"

Slumped

"I'm alright. It's just fucked up them lil' niggas is gone. You know what I mean."

"A little. So now what?"

"What do you mean?"

"C'mon Jaylon. I'm not stupid. I know how shit works in the streets. I'm from the hood too."

"You don't know shit about the streets Nicki. Nothing!"

"Yeah well I know enough. And I know I don't want to be burying you next."

"Well you don't even gotta worry about no shit like that."

"Why? You bulletproof or something?"

"Look, not right now. Alright. I just wanna lay back and chill for a while. Can I do that without you all over me about some bullshit."

"This ain't no bullshit. We are supposed to be getting married. Building a family. How we gonna do that if you end up shot like them boys or end up in jail because you doing something stupid."

"What do you want me to do?" He said loudly scaring Jadda, causing her to start crying.

"Look at you. It's like you've become a whole nother' person since your little friends got killed and it's scary. You are so unpredictable. I love you Jaylon. A lot. And whatever you are going through, whenever you want to talk about it, just know I will be here for you." She said kissing him and walking out the room.

Slump finished getting undressed and walked into the shower. *Scary and unpredictable. She had no idea.*

First someone shot Tee and now this. He knew shit was about to get real ugly and before it was over, a lot more bodies would fall.

Chapter 77

Slump, Tee, and Stone walked into the Zoku around 10:30 after a very thorough search by the security and the place was packed.

"Man look at all these thirsty ass niggas and bitches." Stone said.

"The longer the nigga keeps breathing the more I hate Munch's fat ass." Tee said. They were wearing their never forgotten hoodies and it seemed like everyone who walked past had something to say to them about how sorry they were for their losses. They made their way towards the bar.

"Keep your eyes open for that nigga." Slump said. The bar was packed tight since the drinks were free for another twenty minutes. They each ordered drinks and watched the crowd closely when a tall dark skinned nigga walked up to Tee.

"How you holding up nigga?"

"Do I know you?"

"Nah, my name is Snake. I knew your lil' bros." Something about this niggas was all wrong and it seemed like Tee knew him from somewhere. He had that gut feeling.

Snake stood there eyeing them for a minute. "Ya'll have a good time." He simply stated and walked off.

"Man who the fuck was that nigga and why was he standing here with that smirk on his face like he knew something we didn't."

Slumped

"I don't know Slump but I got a feeling I know that nigga from somewhere."

"I do too." Stone said.

"Man, where is this nigga? I'm not trying to be up in this bitch all night." Slump said but was interrupted by the DJ.

"How ya'll doing tonight?"

"Alright!" Everyone said holding up their glasses.

"That's what I'm talking about. Well tonight we are partying for the dead and in they're memory, the host of this party would like everyone with an empty cup to fill and drink to this song. After the song, he has a few words he wants to say." Just then, Lil' Wayne's "Man I miss my dogs" sent the club into an uproar.

Chapter 78

"You ready to do this?" Flip asked Junebug.

"I'm ready." He responded as they jumped out the wagon with their hoodies on and started walking down Renick. There were a group of hustler standing in front of the trap house not paying the boys any attention.

"Lil Man, Ru, and Spazz sends their love." Junebug stated as he and Spazz opened fire on the crowd. Then ran back to the wagon and drove off.

Chapter 79

"There that nigga go right there." Slump said watching Munch and two other niggas walk over to the DJ's booth. From where they were standing, they couldn't get a good look at Red and Money.

"I don't know what it is about them other two niggas but I swear I know them. I mean the way the move is so familiar. Man, wait a minute. It can't be." Tee said pushing through the crowd with Slump and Stone behind him. Before they knew what was going on, Tee threw his glass like it was a baseball and went crazy. It wasn't long before Slump and Stone recognized the men but by then, security had all three of them. They were fighting security like their lives depended on it. Red, Money, and Munch just looked at them smiling. The police entered the Zoku and calmed Tee down with a taser. When the whole thing was over, the three men found themselves in the county jail on attempting assault and resisting arrest. After being booked and waiting three and a half hours in the holding tank, Jazz bailed them out.

"I can't believe this shit. Out of all people, he had them two niggas in there with him." Tee shouted.

"Yeah well at least now we know they are here." Slump said. Stone just sat there lost in his thoughts trying to put the night together.

"Who are you talking about baby and why are you so mad. I ain't never seen you this mad." Jazz asked.

Slumped

"Yeah well you ain't never gonna believe who I saw tonight."

"Who?"

"Our old friends." She didn't catch it right away, then it hit her. She started shaking so bad that she had to pull over to let Tee drive.

"How could they be here? How did they know where we were?"

"It don't matter how or why. All that matters is they are here and have hooked up with Munch." Stone said finally breaking his silence.

"For some reason, I think they are the ones that hit the lil' bros. In fact, I'm sure it was them. Remember Junebug said one of the dudes had an iced out grill. I knew we should have killed them dudes when we had the chance." Slump stated.

"Yeah well we will this time. And that lil' fat nigga too." Tee responded.

"If this crazy ass nigga wouldn't have thrown the glass, we might have gotten closer to them."

"Yeah you think it was the glass." Tee said with a smile on his face. "I thought it was the yell."

"Yeah, I was gonna ask you about that. But I had to make sure you really did it first. I thought I imagined it." Slump stated.

"I know ya'll was crazy but I never knew I was." Jazz said trying to show the shock had worn off.

"Oh you didn't. Shit woman, why do you think I love you so much." Tee answered.

"Yeah well you know what they say. It takes one to know one." Slump said as everyone started laughing. Each with their own crazy thoughts.

Chapter 80

Junebug and Flip pulled up at Momma K's house as Lil' Lee got out the back seat.

"Do me a favor ya'll."

"What's up?" Junebug and Flip asked.

"Don't tell my brother I was with ya'll tonight when all that shit went down."

"Why? You did your thing." Flip said.

"Because I don't want him to know yet."

"Alright. We got you."

"I'll hit ya'll in the morning."

Driving off, Junebug stated. "Did you see that lil' nigga tonight. That dude is a straight up killa."

"Yeah, he's just like Slump. Just younger."

"And colder. Did you see how he pushed that bitch's shit back. I'm glad he's on the home team."

"I need some pussy." Flip said outta nowhere.

"Wow. Where the fuck did that come from?" Junebug said laughing.

"I don't know but for real. Let's go see if that freak over there in Cevey Circle is up."

"Who? The one we ran a train on with Spazz?"

"Yeah, her."

"Shit fuck it. I'm with it. And if she ain't up, she getting up. Light that blunt up nigga." Flip lit the blunt and turned up Tupac's "Hail Mary" as they sang to the lyrics. *I ain't no killa but don't push me, revenge is the sweetest joy next to getting pussy.*

Lee didn't see Momma K sitting in the kitchen in the dark but she saw him and the look on his face said everything she needed to know. She already knew her youngest was a hustler but she also knew that look too well. She'd seen it in Jaylon's face many of nights as she sat in the same spot and the look had nothing to do with money.

"Please Lord. I know my boys are not perfect but they are still my babies and I did all I could do to raise them right. Protect my babies Lord. Please protect my babies.

Chapter 81

S nake was on Elkorn and Watt Ave in North Highlands
coming from the liquor store. He was walking toward
his blue Chrysler 300 when a black Chevy van pulled
up next to him. Before he knew what was going on, two
masked men jumped out and grabbed him. They threw him in
the van and sped away. It happened so fast that anyone who
saw wouldn't be able to say more than a black van and two
men wearing ski masks grabbed him. The windows were too
dark to see the driver or if there were anyone else in the car.

Once they got Snake into the van, they handcuffed and
blindfolded him.

"Man what the fuck is going on? Do y'all know who the
fuck I am? Y'all done grabbed the wrong mutherfuc…"
Snake yelled. But no one answered. That was all that he got
out before Stone hit him in the head with the tire iron.

"Damn Stone! You done killed the nigga." Slump said
pulling off his mask.

"Nah he ain't dead. He just sleep, but when he wakes up
he's gonna wish that he was dead."

They finally got to the barn in the back of Tiny T's house,
where he was watching as they drugged Snake inside and
closed the door behind them. Snake was still unconscious and
tied to a wooden beam in the center of the barn.

"Wake that nigga up so we can get this over with." Tee
said.

"Not yet. What in the hell are y'all doing? Never mind answering that. I don't want to even know what y'all are doing, but who is that nigga?" Tiny T said coming into the barn closing the door behind him and pointing at Snake.

"We think that he had something to do with the deaths of our little partners." Slump answered.

"You talking about the three little niggas y'all had working for you?"

"Yeah."

"So why did y'all bring him here for? You should have just shot his ass and went on bout your business."

"We got a few questions to ask his ass first before we do that." Tee said.

"Mmm, looks like he is starting to wake up. Unc you might not want to be in here when we question him. Shit just might get crazy." Stone said to Tony T.

"Nigga, I was skinning niggas and feeding them to my hogs way before you ever thought about chewing bubble gum. Besides this shit gets my old dick hard. So y'all do whatever you got to do and just act like I'm not even here." Tony T said laughing.

"Wake yo bitch ass up nigga." Stone said kicking Snake in the stomach.

"See that's the problem with you young niggas today. You don't have any fucking imagination. Here Slump plug this up over there." Tony T said as he pulled a battery charger in front of Snake.

After Slump plugged the battery charger up Tee was told to get a bucket of water and two sponges. Then Tony T squeezed the sponges out, put one on each clamp of the charger, and quickly touched the skin of Snake's arm shocking him.

"What the fuck?" Snake screamed.

"Shut yo bitch ass up." Stone said as he snatched the blindfold off his face.

Slumped

Once he saw who it was, they couldn't get him to shut up talking.

"Please! I didn't want to do it. He made me do it man. Please! I'm sorry." Snake begged and pleaded.

"Who made you do what?" Slump asked.

"Munch did. He paid me fifteen thousand dollars. I swear man I never had any problems with y'all. It was just business. I swear man. He made me shoot him."

"Shoot who?" Stone asked.

"Him. He made me shoot you." Snake said looking at Tee.

"So you are the reason I got these scars? They had to cut me open to get the bullets out of me. Stone is there anything else you want to ask this nigga?" Tee said lifting up his shirt, showing a big scar running down the center of his rock hard stomach and abs.

"Yeah. Who are those two new niggas he is always with?"

Stone replied.

"One of them is his cousin. But then you already knew that. Because they said that you tried to have some bitches set them up in Texas or something. But one of them, Precious or Porshea was just a money hungry bitch that slipped up and said that y'all were trying to get them." Snake answered.

"I knew it. I knew that bitch couldn't be trusted. I'm glad that I blew that bitch's face off." Tee said.

"Oh shit. So y'all niggas did kill J-Wood and Tiny." Snake said.

"Too bad you won't live to tell it. Fucking coward. He would turn over on his momma to save himself. What did you expect with a name like Snake?"

Slump said pulling out one of the twins and shooting him right between the eyes.

"Well now. I haven't had that much fun in years. Now y'all clean this shit up." Tony T said and then he walked out of the barn.

Chapter 82

Since the party at the Zoku, Munch's pockets had been getting hit hard. Not only most of his trap houses had been robbed but his clothing store ran by his wife was robbed as well. He had been hit for close to half of a million in cash

And almost double that in product. With all of the murders that have been going on it made it hard on his workers. As if that wasn't bad enough. No one had heard from or seen Snake in almost a month.

"I can't believe this shit." Munch said.

"What's that cousin? Red said.

"These niggas just hit the gambling shack off of 47th. I wish somebody would hurry up and kill them niggas. I don't know how much more of this shit I'm going to be able to take."

"I don't know how we haven't ran into these niggas. It's not like Sacramento is all that big. It's like these niggas just vanished." Money said.

"Naw they are around here somewhere. We just ain't looking in the right places." Munch said.

"Shit cousin. We got everybody looking for these four niggas. And not one person has told us shit. But we found out where that nigga Tee's baby momma is."

"Oh yeah."

"Yeah but the niggas we got sitting on that bitch ain't seem him come through there. Not once."

"I say we snatch that bitch. You know how ol' boy gets about his women." Money said.

"Yeah. Fuck it. Make that happen. But the nigga I really want is Slump's punk ass." Munch stated.

"I want the fucking country boy. Ever since that night in Texas when he took my money and Jack's little club. I can't let that shit go. That nigga made me look like a bitch paying for everybody's drinks." Red said.

"Man, that little shit was nothing. Them niggas done got me for close to two million in money and product and you mad about a few thousand. And where he fuck is this nigga Snake ass at?" Munch retorted.

"I hate to say it but that nigga ain't never coming back. Shit, I doubt if he lived through the first night, let alone a month. But I know one thing, all this talking about what, when and why ain't getting us nowhere. We need to start answering. Start letting these niggas know it's real."

"And how do we do that when we don't know where to look." Munch asked.

"They got family and starting with Tee's bitch. They are just going to have to do until we catch with them." Money stated.

Chapter 83

"**M**an look at all this shit. I ain't never seen this much dope or money before in my life." Flip said.

"Get used to it lil' bro because some of it is yours. Shit, ya'll been putting in just as much work as we have so it's only right you and Junebug get an equal cut." Slump said.

"That's a whole lot of money." Junebug said.

"Yeah, well don't' get too excited yet. Ain't no way I'm gonna watch you lil' niggas fuck off $130,000 a piece. You got to put some away for a rainy day and better believe it's a storm coming. So I'm gonna have Jazz open ya'll up a bank account. Since neither of you are 18, it will just sit there and we'll have her feed the account slowly. So eight stacks each." Tee said.

"Man why can't we just get a safe and put our shit in it?" Flip asked.

"Because you ain't gonna do nothing but fuck it off lil' hard headed nigga."

"But if it's ours, we should be able to do whatever we want. Even if we choose to fuck it off."

"He got you on that, Tee. Besides, they know how to handle their shit." Slump stated.

"Yeah! Besides, we can't take it with us when we die. So we might as well have fun while we can." Junebug stated.

"Man why you have to go there?" Flip said.

"I'm just saying. Anything can happen."

"Yeah, well I ain't dying."

"And how you know that?"

"Because nigga, I refuse to."

"I heard that. And I like the way you think." Stone said. "Man, enough with this death shit. We been going hard for almost a month. Done hit damn near every spot that nigga got. It's time to enjoy some of this shit. What ya'll wanna do?" Slump asked.

"I know. Let's go to Disneyland." Flip said jokingly.

For a minute, nobody said anything. They just sat there looking at each other.

"You know what I think. We should, shit. I mean who has ever been there? And it would be good to have nothing to worry about but having a fun trip. Shit, the more I think about it, fuck it. Hell yeah. Let's do it. I can even take Lil' Tee."

"So that's the plan then. Disneyland it is." Slump said.

"Look at that lil' nigga. Nah, don't try to act tough now nigga. It's too late. Looking like a twelve year old in toy factory. Happy as a...Oh shit. I was just fucking with you. What you crying for?" Stone said noticing the tears running down Flip's face.

"It just hit me bro. I ain't never had no one to ever care about what happen to me."

"Well you got us now." Slump said putting him in a headlock.

"Now turn them tears off. It's good cuz you got a family that will ride or die with you." Tee said.

"I love ya'll and I don't care how soft I look or sound. Ya'll all I got."

"We love you too. Now we going to Disneyland." Everyone said as happy as ever.

It took a few days to plan the trip but in the end, everyone was going, including Momma K and the family. And just for the hell of it, they brought Tonya too.

Chapter 84

"**Y**ou got to be kidding me." Slump said looking at Flip in his Mickey Mouse hat.

"What nigga? You ain't feeling the ears."

"It ain't the ears bro. I just forgot how young you really was."

"Well my nigga. Don't even tell nobody you saw me looking like this."

"We ain't gonna have to tell nobody. All we got to do is show them. Smile." Tee said laughing.

"What!" But it was too late. Tee had already taken the picture.

"Yeah. This shit speaks a thousand words." Tee said looking at the digital camera.

"Whatever! I used to dream about this shit, so fuck you nigga. Acting like ya'll ain't having just as much fun as I am. I ain't never seen ya'll smile as much as I have on this trip. And look at him." Flip said smiling pointing to Stone.

"I know shit. He done stole my little man from me." Tee said.

"Man, ya'll gotta get on that thing." Stone said walking up to them. Him, Angel, and Lil' Tee just got off the Ferris Wheel.

"Dad! You can see the whole world from up there. It's hecka tight. And look at what Uncle Stone bought me." Lil' Tee said holding up the big Mickey Mouse ears.

Slumped

"Let me see them, son. How do I look?" He said taking the ears and putting them on.

"Like a black Mickey Mouse with an afro." Lil' Tee said, causing everyone laugh.

"Smile Tee! I got your ass, my nigga." Flip said taking a pic with Angel's camera.

"Daddy! Daddy!" Jadda said running up to Slump.

"How you doing baby girl." He said picking her up.

"Gwama and Mama took to me to see the snow lady and the little men."

"You mean Snow White and the Seven Dwarfs."

"Yeah....Them and me took pictures with them. Then we went on the big ol' swings."

"Look Jadda. There goes Goofy! You and Daddy should go take some pictures with him." Nicki said.

"Yeah c'mon, let's go. Please. Pretty please!"

"And here. You dad can even wear my hat." Flip said with a smirk on his face.

"Yeah daddy. Put on the Mickey hat."

"I'm gon' get yo' young ass for this." Slump said under his breath as he took the hat from him.

"I ain't tripping. It will be well worth it."

They went from one end of the big park to the other, sparing no expense. And for the next four days, no one thought of the problems they had to go home to. But unknown to them, shit back home got real.

Chapter 85

"**S**hut up bitch!" Munch said to Alicia.

"Why are you doing this to me? I never did nothing to you."

"Bitch you think I'm stupid. I know you told them niggas how to get at me. And I know you told them how to get my brother too. So stop acting like you don't' know what this is about."

"I swear, I don't know where you…"

"I told you shut the fuck up." He said punching her in the mouth. He tied her to a chair in her kitchen. "You thought them two niggas fucking you last time was bad. Well if you don't tell me what I wanna know, that ain't gonna be shit." Alicia looked at him with anger in her eyes. She had been too much to be scared but she needed a plan. If it was the last thing she did, she would get Munch…and Slump too for getting her into all this shit in the first place.

"C'mon. Please. You don't have to do this. You know I love you. Tell me what I gotta do to prove it and I will. I swear I will."

"Oh I have no doubts about that." She knew he planned to kill her but the only way to get out alive was to escape while he had her there because if he took her away from her apartment, no one would hear her scream. She had to think quick.

"Please daddy. Let me make it up to you."

Slumped

"And how the fuck you think you gonna do that, huh? Do you know much money they took from me? Do you bitch? Do you? You have no idea." In a rage, he punched her repeatedly. But not once, did she cry out. With blood running from her nose and mouth, and one eye almost swollen shut, she sat there and took the beating. She didn't want to give him the satisfaction of hearing her scream.

"So you think you're tough. Alright we'll see about that." He said walking off down the hall. A few minutes later, he returned with her curling iron. He plugged it in and sat it on the counter. He then grabbed a butcher knife from the holder next to the stove. He cut up both pant legs that were tied to each chair leg while she sat in her laced panties. Once she learned what he was about to do, she fought the tape that bound her and screamed to the top of her lungs.

"Help me. Somebody please help me." He hit her as hard as he could, knocking out her front teeth. She kept yelling until he taped her mouth closed. All she could do was fight with the taped chair and pray the neighbors downstairs would hear the banging and call the police. Tears and blood ran down her face.

"I don't know what you are crying for bitch. Love don't live here anymore." He said picking up the curlers and touching the lace of her panties, causing her to jump. "Now I'm gonna take this tape off your mouth. If you say anything other than the answers to my questions, I'm sticking this up your funky ass, bitch. What a waste. Do we understand each other." He said ripping her panties off and staring at her pussy. Alicia just stared. Grabbing the curlers, he placed it on her inner thigh causing her to scream, although it sounded more like a muffled moan. A blister two inches long immediately rose on her skin.

"I said do we understand each other. I take that as a yes." He said looking at the piss running out of her.

Chapter 86

"So this is what it takes to get you to love me?" Nicki asked laying next to Slump in their hotel room.

"What you talking about woman. I love you all the time."

"I'm talking about you. It seems like you're a different person right now. I mean you are such a sweet and loving man. The man I fell in love with and want to spend my life with. Is this man here with me right now?" Instead of ruining the moment with words, he leaned over and covered her mouth with his. The kiss was something out of a love story. One that lingered and lasted forever. He kissed her mouth, eyes, and nose as he slowly undressed her. Once their clothes were out the way, he kissed her body down to the silky light patch of hair between her legs. With his fingers, he parted her fat pussy lips, exposing her clit as he kissed it too causing her breath to catch.

"Make love to me baby."

"Shh…I will. But first…" without saying anything, he made love to her clit with his tongue. He started with slow light circles, then faster as he put two fingers inside her.

"I can't take it anymore. Please." But he kept going until a fierce orgasm rocked her. He kissed his way back to her mouth as her thick, sweet juices covered it. Tasting her sweetness on his lips, she grabbed his hard dick and guided him inside her. They made love well into the night before they feel asleep into each other's arms.

Chapter 87

S lump's phone about 3a.m that morning.
  "Hello?" He said sleepily.
  "Yes, this is Dr. Xzong at the UC Davis hospital.
I'm looking for a Jaylon Garrett."
  "This is him?" Slump said sitting upright.
  "I have an Alicia Smith in ICU and you are her only
emergency contact."
  "What's wrong? What's the matter with her?" By now
Nicki had awaken and asked Slump about the phone call. He
just held his hand up to her face.
  "Ms Smith has been through a severe emergency
operation. She was beaten into a coma and has been raped
and sodomized with something very hot. She has third degree
burns to her vagina and anus."
  "What! Do they know who did it?"
  "No sir. She was found in her apartment by police after
neighbors reported a lot of loud banging."
  "So nobody knows what happened?"
  Nicki was wide awake and watching his every reaction.
When he finally got off the phone, she asked. "So who is she,
Jaylon?"
  "Just a friend."
  "Just a friend my ass. You look like you wanna kill
somebody."
  "She's just a fucking friend. Alright."

"Nigga don't get mad at me cause somebody fucked up one of your little bitches."

"Look. It's not even like that. Me and Alicia go back a long ways and now she is laying in the…"

"Alicia! Ain't that the girl who was raped by her uncle. The guy you killed." He never told her about that.

"How do you know about that?"

"Since you are so closed mouth about everything. I asked Momma K why did you go to the CYA and she told me the story."

"Yeah well my momma need to keep her damn mouth shut sometimes."

"Where are you going?"

"Out. I need to think." He said throwing on his clothes.

"Out where? This is fucking Disneyland."

"I don't know. I just need some air. Go back to sleep. I'll be back in a little while."

"Jaylon, you need to get back in bed. There is nothing you can do for that girl."

"Go to sleep, Nicki." He said exiting the hotel door. As soon as he entered the hall, he called Tee.

"Nigga. Do you know what fucking time it is?"

"I do. But I really need to talk to you. Meet me in the lobby."

"Give me five minutes." Tee said hearing the edge in Slump's voice.

When he got down to the lobby, Slump was in a chair staring at a cup of coffee.

"What's up my nigga?"

"He got her dog."

"Who is he and what her are you talking about?"

"I'm talking about that bitch nigga Munch. He got Alicia."

"What are you saying? He killed her?"

"No, he put her in a coma and stuck something hot in her pussy."

Slumped

"Damn that's fucked up. Is she alright?"

"I don't know. All I know is that she's in a coma and even if she got out of it, she probably will never have kids."

"Well we leave the day after tomorrow, so until then focus on that soon to be wife and that cute little Goddaughter of mine, alright. You can't protect her forever my nigga. Besides, she knew what she was getting into and we paid her $50,000 for her part in all this." Slump said nothing. "You're about to get married. Sooner or later you will have to cut off all feelings you have or had for her, man."

"I know that Tee but I can't help but feel it's my fault."

"Well it's not. It's just the dirty part of the game we are playing."

"Yeah, I guess you are right. But on Momma, that nigga and the other two will pay with their lives when this is all over. That I promise."

Chapter 88

"**S**o when you gonna tell him?" Flip asked Lil' Lee. "I don't know blood but on momma, it's gonna have to be soon."

"I don't see what makes telling him so hard." Junebug said.

"It's not telling him that's hard. It's letting him down by choosing this lifestyle."

"I mean I know he ain't my brother but he treats me and Flip like we are. So I think you should just put it out there. After all, it ain't like he ain't gonna know something's going on. I wouldn't be surprised if he don't already know."

"Shit you be with us every fucking day" Flip added.

"I know huh. Fuck it. After we make this move, I will tell him." The three of them had been at Tonya's house for the last few days plotting to hit the white boys. First, Lil' Lee wanted to wait on his brother's crew but Flip talked him into letting the younger boys do it to show they were just as good as anyone else.

"So what's up ya'll. Ya'll ready to do this tonight?" Lee asked.

"Hell yeah." Flip stated.

"It's whatever with me." Junebug added.

"Alright then. This is how we are gonna do it. I've been fucking with these woods for a while now so they trust me.

And that's where they fucked up. I'm gonna call him and tell him I need some tree."

"Why don't we just go in there and rock they're shit back." Flip said.

"Because nigga. If we just go in there guns blazing, we might not make it out. So we gotta play it smart."

"Man, we've been over this shit a thousand times already. So why is it hard for you to understand?"

"Fuck you nigga. I understand. I'm just saying if we don't rock them now, we are just gonna have to do it later."

"I don't think it's gonna come to that with these fools. They ain't even built like that."

"Well I don't care nigga. All I'm saying is if I even think one of those crackers are on some funny shit, I'm gonna push his shit back. Period."

"As long as we stick to the plan, we ain't got to worry about none of that. So stick to the fucking plan." Lil' Lee said.

"Man, here we go with this shit. Everybody always telling me to be cool."

"Whatever man. Just call them motherfuckers and let's go get this money." Lil' Lee made the call. And just like he thought, Eric told him to meet at the spot. He told Eric he had two cousins with him from out of town.

"Let's go!" Lil' Lee said getting off the phone. He then went and got Tonya's car keys.

"Man, I gotta know. Is you fucking Tonya? Because every time me or Junebug ask to use her car, she's quick to tell us no."

"Did anybody ever tell you that you ask too many questions?"

"All the time. But are you? And if you are, just tell me. Is the pussy any good?"

"It's great my nigga."

"I knew it. I told you nigga. Now give me my money." Flip said to Junebug.

Slumped

"You two niggas is crazy. Flip, don't shoot nobody." Lil' Lee said as they checked their clips and went to the car. "I know. I know. Stick to the plan. I got you."

Chapter 89

Twenty minutes later, all hell broke loose and sticking to the plan was the last thing any of them were doing. Because when they pulled up to the house, Red was coming out the door.

"Oh shit! That's one of them niggas right there who killed the bros." Junebug said.

"What!" Flip said about to jump out of the car.

"Wait a minute." Lil' Lee said.

"Fuck that." Flip said jumping out the car and opening fire on Red, who ran back into the house. By then, Junebug and Lee were both out of the car and running up to the house. Lee kicked the door in and the first person he saw was Eric. Pointing his gun in Eric's face, he said, ""Where the fuck did that nigga go?"

"I don't know man. He came and bought a half pound of weed."

"I didn't ask all that. I said where the fuck did he go?"

"Out the back door bro. I swear. He ran out the back door."

"I think I hit that nigga. There is blood on the doorknob." Flip said.

"Man Lee. What's this all about. I thought we were cool."

"Shut the fuck up." Lee said hitting him across the head with the 45 caliber Beretta causing the skinny white girl who had been sitting on the couch to start screaming.

Slumped

"Shut up or die bitch." Flip said placing the barrel of his 40 glock on her forehead. She stopped screaming instantly.

"So much for the fucking plan! But since we ain't got too much time left before the cops get here. Hey white boy. You know what's up. So make it easy. Where is everything at?" Junebug said.

"Where is what at? I don't know what you're talking about. Lee man, what's he talking about." Eric asked.

"Make it easy E man. Just tell us where the money is so we can leave without hurting you."

"It's in the back room on the storage bin in the closet. Please don't hurt me. I won't say anything. I swear." The white girl said.

"Shut up you stupid cunt. These fucking niggers don't care about you." Eric yelled.

"Man shoot that fucking cracker." Flip said.

"Go get the money and whatever else is back there and let's get out of here." Lil' Lee said

Junebug and Flip ran to the back of the house and came back both carrying a 20 gallon plastic storage tub. "We got it. Let's go." They ran out the house but before they could make it to the car, Lee turned around and ran back toward the house.

"Fuck man. C'mon nigga." Flip and Junebug yelled.

"Start the car. I'm coming." He said back.

"What do you want, my fucking wallet too?" Eric said.

"Nope!" Lee said shooting him between the eyes. The girl started to scream, but no sooner than the scream left her mouth, a bullet went in and out the back of her head. Jumping back in the car with Junebug behind the wheel, they sped away.

"Fuck man. We are gonna be on the fucking morning news." Lee said.

"No we aren't. We had on gloves."

"But people saw our faces."

Slumped

"Who? All them fucking junkies. Man, we're good. Besides with all this money, we can buy our way outta jail." Flip said.

"I'm just mad I didn't get that nigga. We gotta tell Slump what happened." Junebug said.

"So who is going to call him."

"I'll call." Lil' Lee said.

"Yeah, but don't' tell him shit. Just tell him to meet us at Tonya's house right now." Lil' Lee made the call and by the time they were pulling in front of Tonya's house, Slump and Stone were getting out of Tee's truck.

"So what was so fucking important?" Slump asked looking at Lee.

"Yeah, what the fuck is in those tubs." Stone asked.

"Money! Now can we go to the fucking house?" Once they were home, they pushed everything off the coffee table, then emptied the bins onto it.

"Where the fuck did ya'll lil niggas get that? I know ya'll ain't robbed no bank or no shit like that." Tee said as Stone looked at Tee and smiled.

"Well you know I used to fuck with Flip and Junebug. I use to fuck with all of them so I've been in on what's been going on lately." Lil' Lee said.

"What you mean you been in on it?" Slump asked.

"C'mon on bro. you know what I mean."

"No I don't. So be a man and tell me." Slump said.

"I've been in on every lick as well as the other shit. I know this ain't the lifestyle you wanted me in, but I'm not in it. It's in me. Always has been. So now as a man, I'm telling you."

For a minute, Slump just looked at his brother.

"I told you that lil' nigga was just like you. Always has been. I don't know how you're the only one who couldn't see it." Tee said.

Slumped

"Where did the money come from?" Slump asked as he watched Tee stack bundles of fifties and hundreds on the table.

"Well remember the house we checked out?"

"The white boys. Yeah, I remember."

"Well tonight, we went and did that."

"Just the three of you?"

"Yeah nigga. Just the three of us? And we almost got one of them niggas that killed the homies." Flip said.

"What are you talking about?" Tee asked.

"Well when we were pulling up to the house, one of them niggas came out."

"He was by himself?"

"Yeah and I almost got him."

"How do you almost get a nigga?"

"When we pulled up, Junebug recognized him and I jumped out on that bitch ass nigga. I think I hit him too but he ran out the back door before we got in the house."

"And you niggas ain't told us shit. What if something would have happened to one of you. Or all of you. We wouldn't know shit." Slump stated.

"Yeah, well it didn't." Lil Lee said.

"Yeah, he just like you my nigga. Doing shit and not giving a fuck about how anybody feels." Tee said.

"So what happened to the white boys?" Slump asked Flip.

"Hell don't ask me. He shot em'." He answered pointing to Lee.

"Don't trip. Where they are, they can't speak."

"Yeah, that's your brother." Tee said laughing.

"Now that it's out the way, let's move on to something better. And this I know ya'll ain't ready for?" Flip said.

"What!"

"Guess."

"What nigga?" Stone asked.

"Guess who Tonya's fucking?"

"Man, c'mon Flip. You talk too much." Lil' Lee said.

Slumped

"Hell no! Lil' nigga, you don't know what to do with all that." Tee said.

"Whatever nigga. Fuck that. How much money do we have?"

"I ain't the smartest nigga in the world but by my count, $630,000." Flip said.

"I thought you said they had a million up in there?"

"Well shit. I was damn close."

Chapter 90

"That lil' nigga was trying to gun a nigga down." Red said to Money as Money did what he could to stop the bleeding in Red's shoulder. "I think it went in and out so you should be alright as long as it don't get infected."

"Man, you should have seen that little motherfucker. He was really trying to push my shit back. I didn't even notice them at first. By the time I did, it was almost too late. If them square white boys would have locked their door when I came out, I might not be here right now."

"Yeah, well you was slipping my nigga leaving your heat in the car."

"Ain't that the truth. I bet I don't do that shit no more. I don't' give a fuck if I'm just taking a shit, I bet it's in my hand while I wipe my ass."

"Well son." Money said smacking him on the shoulder.

"Oh fuck, nigga. Why you playing? What's so funny nigga?" He asked watching Money laugh.

"You my nigga. Almost got your ass blew off but you still got the weed."

"Hell yeah. I knew I was gonna have to burn something after all this shit."

"But seriously. We gotta keep our eyes open for them lil' niggas. They are really with the shit. It was probably the one that jumped out the window on us."

"Nah, it wasn't him. I know what he looks like. This lil' nigga can't be no older than fifteen or sixteen. A little bitchy motherfucker with braids."

"Well, we gon' give it a few days then go holler at the white boy and see if he can tell us anything about the lil' nigga."

"Man fuck this. I need a drink. C'mon let's go get a bottle or something."

"Nigga, you do realize it's after 3a.m., don't you? What you need to do is relax. Matter of fact..." Red said getting up.

"What?"

"I just remembered I still got that bottle of Skyy ol' girl left over here the other day."

"Is you crazy nigga or just stupid. The alcohol is going to thin out your blood and keep your dumb ass bleeding."

"But at least I'll be too drunk to feel the pain."

"Yeah, I thought so."

"Thought what nigga?"

"You ain't crazy. Just stupid."

"Fuck you, Money."

"Yeah yeah yeah. Just go get the bottle while I roll up some of this weed."

After coming back with the bottle and getting comfortable, Red asked, "What's up with cousin. You talked to him today?"

"Nope, I ain't seen him since yesterday. I still can't believe he did ol' girl like that."

"Man what you talking bout. We done bitches way worse than that. You only saying something because he burned up her pussy."

"Hell yeah nigga. That was a bad bitch."

"Well, I can tell you one thing." Red said laughing.

"What's that?"

"That bitch got that fire." They both laughed.

"I was wrong my nigga."

"About what?"

Slumped

"You, because you're ass is crazy and stupid."

"Yeah, well you ain't wrapped too tight your damn self."

Chapter 91

Alicia woke up a week after being admitted to the hospital. Her body was overwrought with pain. Her vision was blurry and her mouth was dry.

"Hey sleeping beauty." She heard someone say. Focusing on the person sitting in the chair next to her bed, she asked.

"What are you doing here?"

"I'm making sure my friend is alright."

"Oh, so now I'm your friend nigga?" She felt pain just breathing. "You are only here to find out what I told him before he did this to me. Well I ain't tell him shit so you ain't got nothing to worry about."

Before Slump could respond, a doctor walked into the room with two detectives. Seeing the cops, Slump stood and kissed Alicia on the forehead. "I'll be back."

When he walked out the room, it took everything in him not to look back. He could feel the detective's eyes burning holes into his back. The last thing he needed was to have them start questioning him about anything. The last thing he wanted was to go home but it was the best thing for him.

Headed to the car, he called his soon to be wife.

"Hello?"

"What's up beautiful."

"Nothing, just chasing your damn daughter around the house."

"Oh yeah. What's my mini me up to?"

"Shit, everything."

"Well, I'm about to be at the house in a minute. You feel like going out to get something to eat?"

"Jaylon, what's up babe?" why you sound like your best friend just died or something."

"Ain't nothing wrong with me and my best friend is on the phone."

"Boy you know you can't lie to save your life but if you don't want to talk, I ain't gonna push you."

"I love you too baby."

"Yeah whatever nigga. Love is an action word."

"What's that supposed to mean."

"Nothing. Just hurry up and get here. I'm about to put some clean clothes on Jadda and myself so by the time you get here, we should be ready."

"Alright. I'll see you in a few then. Love you."

"Action word." Nicki said before hanging up. An hour later, they were sitting at Applebees.

"Hi, my name is Pam and I'll be your server for the night. Here are your menus. Could I get you something to drink now or would you like to look over for a minute."

"Let me get a Strawberry Daiquiri for myself and an orange juice for the baby." Nicki said. And he will have a Long Island Iced Tea."

"Alright. Anything else?" Pam said looking at Slump.

"No that will be all. Thank you." Nicki said pulling her attention back.

"What's wrong with you?" Slump asked when the waitress walked away.

"Nigga don't act like you didn't notice that bitch was flirting with you."

"Nope, didn't notice." Slump smiled.

"Alright boy. Don't get Ms. Thang fucked up in here."

"Yeah daddy. Don't get Ms. Thang fucked up." Jadda said like she knew what she was talking about.

Slumped

"Girl, what I tell you about cursing." Nicki said trying not to laugh.

"I'm sorry mommy."

"She get it from you. Every third word out of your mouth is fuck, shit, or bitch." Slump said.

"Boy you got your nerve."

"Damn. Every time I see that, the world seems perfect."

"What...every time you see what?"

"That smile."

"What? Mine or hers. Whose?"

"Here you go sir." The waitress said with 'fuck me' in her eyes. She sat his drink down in front of him, then sat Nicki and Jadda's in the center of the table. "Just wave your hand when you're ready to order." She said looking at him before walking away.

"Ohhh...see that bitch is lucky my daughter is sitting right here or I would snatch all the weave out her head." Nicki said loudly drawing looks from the other customers.

"Calm down woman."

"Oh no. Fuck that. We need a new waitress. That bitch ain't gon' keep coming over here flirting with my nigga all up in my face like I'm not sitting here."

"Where you going?" Slump asked when she stood.

"To talk to a manager or somebody."

"Girl come here and quit tripping. I don't give a damn about that bitch."

"I'm gonna tell that hoe about herself next time." Nicki said reseating.

When the waitress came back to take their order, Slump put her in check. "Now check it out, ain't nothing wrong with a little harmless flirting every now and then. But that's my wife right there so could you do me a favor before you get yourself in trouble and just do your job."

Instead of answering him, the waitress simply stated. "Can I take your order?"

"Yeah, you can. Can I get the riblet platter with fries and a salad. And the kids chicken strip meal." Nicki said with attitude.

"And you?" She asked Slump.

"Yeah, let me get the T-Bone with shrimp, a basket of fries, and another long island."

"Okay, it will be a few minutes for the food but I'll be right back with your drink."

"Now all we gotta do is hope she don't spit in our shit." Slump said when she walked off."

The rest of the meal went well. they talked about their future and colored the kids mat with Jadda. They even laughed at how the waitress's once she was brushed off.

Chapter 92

Flip, Lee, and Junebug got $110,000 a piece from the lick and gave Slump, Tee, and Stone $100,000 each as well.

"Man look at all this shit. I got over $200,000 cash right here in front of me and I'm only sixteen. I can buy whatever the fuck I want. Do whatever the fuck I want. And can't nobody tell me shit."

"Man, I would give all this shit up to get my niggas back." Junebug said.

"Yeah, we all would." Stone added.

"But we can't so we are gonna ball for them. What's that old song by Master P. 'Stack your chips, get your paper, ball til' you fall, young niggas. Fuck them haters'. I know what I'm about to do." Flip said.

"What nigga. Go buy up every gun a nigga got to sell."

"Nope, I already did that. Look." He said showing them a big duffel bag he got from the back room. Inside was a new Mossberg 412 and a modified 50 round drum.

"Man. That damn gun is bigger than you, lil nigga. But I like the way you think. Stay ready, you never have to get ready." Stone said.

"I'm just making sure next time I see one of them bitch ass niggas, I got something that's gonna knock a body part off."

"Well that for damn sure will do the trick. I got one question." Tee asked.

"What?"

"Where the fuck is your little ass gonna carry that?"

"That's what I was getting to. Since we sold the wagon, we need to get us some new wheels because frankly, I'm tired of riding around in Tonya's little bucket. Besides, the only one she let drive it is Lee ass. So what's up big bro. Why don't you take me to the tow yard so I can flip me something."

"Nigga. You got all that damn money in front of you and you wanna go to the tow yard to get a car. You gotta really be crazy. If you don't get your young ass on Tonya's computer and see what they got on E-bay and flip your own shit the way you want it."

"Man, ya'll know Flip can't read." Junebug said trying to be funny.

"Fuck you. At least I ain't no bitch." Flip said a little too seriously.

"Damn nigga. I was just playing with your sensitive ass. Why you getting all serious on me and shit."

"Why you always cracking jokes on me. So what if I can't read."

"Hold on. Hold on. Wait a minute. You mean to tell me you really can't read, lil' nigga." Stone asked.

"No. I mean I can read a little but not that good."

"Yeah, well we're gonna have to do something about that."

"At least we all know he can count." Tee said trying to lighten up the mood.

"Shit a nigga gotta be able to know how to count them dollars."

"Come here my nigga. This shit is easy once we get to the site. All you gotta do is look for what you like, see how much it costs, then go get it." Lil Lee said sitting in front of

Tonya's computer. Junebug rolled up a couple blunts as they got their smoke on.

"That's it! That's the one I want." Flip said excitedly pointing at the screen after about thirty minutes. It was a baby blue 1968 Caprice Classic. A glass house. "The only thing is I don't like the color."

"Well shit, if you buy it, we can paint it any color you want." Tee said.

"How much do they want for it?" Stone asked.

"Fifteen thousand. That ain't shit."

"Well if that's what you want, let's call them and talk to whoever." Flip dialed the number and gave the phone to Stone. After a few minutes, Stone hung up.

"Dude said we can look at the car anytime."

"Oh yeah, where does he stay?" Tee asked.

"Up in Gault."

"Damn! But fuck it. We can slide that way now. We ain't doing nothing else.

"So what's up Flip, you ready now or what?"

"Hell yeah. Let me put all this away and it's good." He went into the backroom he shared with Junebug and put everything in the safe minus the fifteen thousand. Lil Lee and Junebug decided not to join on the ride.

"Man, I thought I was gonna have to pull that lil nigga off your ass." Lil Lee said.

"I know huh. He was really mad over that reading joke."

"Shit, if you would have been anybody else, that crazy lil' nigga would have probably tried to shoot your ass."

"Well, we would have two shot up mothefuckers in this bitch."

"Whatever nigga." Lee said laughing.

Chapter 93

I t had been three days since Slump left her bedside and now she wished he was there. So what he was getting married soon, she still loved him like no other.

"Hey what's up. You sleeping?" Slump walked in the room as if he could read her thoughts.

"No. And to be honest, I was just thinking about you."

"Oh yeah. I hope they were good thoughts." And she finally did what she wanted since she opened her eyes. She cried.

"Jaylon, do you know what he did to me?" She asked through her tears.

"I know what the doctor told me."

"He questioned me about you, Stone, and Tee. He asked where you lived and if you had any family and when I didn't answer him, he beat me up. He had me tied to a chair. When he realized I wouldn't answer him, he plugged in a curling iron and..he..he..he.."

"I know Alicia. I know what he did to you. I don't' know how I could ever make this up to you but somehow I will. I promise, somehow I will."

"He sat there and held her until she dozed off. When she fell asleep, he looked through her closet for her personal stuff. Not finding it, he looked in her nightstand next to the bed. He found her purse and took her phone out. Then he left.

Slumped

Once in the car, he turned on the phone and searched for the number he was seeking. He pushed the call button.

"Hello?" Someone said on the forth ring. He recognized Munch's voice instantly.

"You better spend all your time with your kids because when I see you, I'm gonna make you scream like your kids did." Then he hung up. It wasn't long before Munch called back but instead of answering it, he threw it out the window, breaking it. In a rage, Munch called Red.

"What's up fat boy?"

"Go get that bitch and that nigga's son."

"Whoa whoa whoa. Calm down. I can't understand you."

"Go get that bitch nigga Tee's baby momma and his son. I don't care how ya'll do it but tonight, I want that bitch at the trap house." Then hung up before Red could respond.

"It's show time, my nigga," Red said looking at Money.

"Oh word. He wants to grab the bitch."

"And the nigga's lil' one too. And he wants it done tonight."

"Well then, what the fuck are we still sitting here for. C'mon."

Chapter 94

"Oh shit. Check out the motherfucking wheels. This bitch is clean as fuck." Junebug said looking at the car Flip just bought.

"I know. That's why I bought it. So what's up. I know ya'll gon' come paint the town with ya' lil' nigga."

"Hell yeah!" Stone said.

"We with you lil' bro." Lee added.

"Not tonight. I gotta get back to the house. Since we got back from Disneyland, I done had Lil' Terry staying with me and shit. His punk ass momma got some sucker she been fucking with. She can blow up in her car for all I give a damn but he ain't about to be around some other nigga." Tee stated.

"Well alright. Good looking on taking me to cop this motherfucker."

"Don't trip my young nigga. Just know you owe me a ride. Now let's get up outta here cuz I know my son done drove Jazz half crazy but I'll holler at ya'll later."

"Alright. Holler at me." Stone said.

"You and your niggas don't kill nobody." Tee said laughing.

Chapter 95

"Yeah she up in there. It's her and some nigga. Well some white boy up in there." Scooter said getting in the back seat of a gray Camero.

"Good looking out nigga. Here. But remember."

"Yeah, I know. I ain't seen ya'll right." Scooter said taking the three hundred dollars from Red's hand.

"Yeah. Now get out of here. You ready my nigga."

"As I'll ever be. How about you. How's your should." Money said pulling on his ski mask.

"It's good. Besides, I don't plan on wrestling." They got out the car and walked quickly to the door. Vicki's apartment faced the street and it would be just their luck the police drove by.

"Remember no talking. I'm popping ol' boy. You grab the bitch and lil' dude and we up outta there." Money said screwing on his silencer.

As soon as Red kicked in the door, Money shot the white boy, blowing his head off.

"Scream bitch. I dare you." Red said carrying the big Smith and Wesson to Vicki's head. Money made his way through the small apartment not seeing the little boy.

"Where's the little boy?"

"He's with his father."

Slumped

"Come on. If you even look like you wanna scream. I'm gonna kill you." Red said pulling Vicki out the door. They made it to the car and drove away.

"Put your head between your legs and don't look up." Money yelled at Vicki as he and Red took of their ski mask and drove to the trap house. Once on the freeway, Red called Munch.

"It's done. We will be there in a minute." Then he hung up. Since Munch called him, all he could think about was what he said. Now he knew for sure they killed J-Wood.

"Don't worry lil' bro. I'm gonna get them all for you." He said aloud.

Chapter 96

"Now I'm about big block drop tops, white guts in them with much knock." Too short sang through the ten thousand dollar stereo system.

"Now all I gotta do is paint it and I'm gonna be the cleanest thing on four wheels."

"Maybe the second." Stone said.

"What you talking about. Who shit is cleaner."

"Mine."

"Your what nigga. You don't even got no car."

"I ain't got no car out here but back home, I'm sitting high lil' nigga. Better yet, look." Stone said pulling out his cell phone. Flip looked at the candy apple green 69 Caprice Classic on thirty inch rims.

"Man that looks just like my shit. Well now I can't paint my shit green. So I'll paint mine red. And what kind of rims is them. Some fucking 50s or something. That's cool. For right now, I'll take second best but when I get through with my shit you gon' have to step your game up."

"Yeah, we'll see. But it ain't no competition."

"Man, let's get a bottle and some more blunts then slide through the south and go fuck with these bitches that's been trying to get me there for the longest."

"I'm with the bottle and smoking but I ain't about to get caught up with some little girls."

"Man, I know you ain't trying to say I fuck with lil' girls." Lil' Lee said.

"Lil' nigga you ain't nothing but sixteen so yeah, that's what I'm saying."

"Shit, you must have forgot about Tonya then."

"Well, I guess you got a point. Fuck it. When you can't beat em, join em. But if we get over there and these bitches talking about playing dress up and having a tea party. We up outta there." He said laughing.

"Ha ha ha fat boy. You ain't funny." Lee said laughing.

Slumped

"Well, since you said please. Sergeant come here." Munch commanded the big dog who was foaming at the mouth.

"Shit bitch. you must got some good ass pussy. I've never seen him do that and he done got a lot of pussy. Shit I see you two looking and Money over there almost foaming at the mouth too."

"Shit my nigga. I guess I got a little dog in me too."

"So what's your name?"

"Vicky."

"Well Vicky. Do you have any idea why you are here."

"No!"

"Well, first because your baby daddy and his friends took my money. Then they killed my brother and took more of my money. Do you know where my money is?"

"No. I swear I don't."

"Well I think you might. But you wouldn't be lying to me, would you after how nice I'm being to you?"

"No, I swear, I don't know where your money is but if you let me just call him, I know he would give it back."

"You think he'd just give up a half million dollars for you. Shit, I think we all gonna have to try that pussy if it's good enough for a nigga to pay $500,000 for it. What do ya'll think." Munch asked Red and Money laughing.

"I think if she take them drawers off and them pussy lips ain't platinum then she is a dead bitch." Red said.

"Yeah. No more baby momma drama." Money added. Getting up for the first time since she'd been there, Munch walked to her with his phone and the dog close by.

"I guess we about to find out. Call him and tell him I want all my money back." She dialed the number and just as she pushed the call button, Munch snatched the phone. "I changed my mind. I think you need to see just what is at stake if I don't get my money." He then pulled out a chrome Colt 45 and pointed it to her face. "Stand up and take off your clothes."

Slumped

"I ain't never seen no shit like this before." Red said as it played out in front of his eyes as Munch sent the video to Tee.

Chapter 98

"Who is that babe?" Jazz asked when Tee picked up his phone.

"I don't know. It's a blocked number but it's a video message." When he played the message, the first thing he was a big ass dog eating some woman's pussy. "What the fuck."

He stared at his phone until Vicki's face came into view. He heard some niggas in the background talking about how the woman was about to come. Then it jumped to her being fucked by the dog.

"Ain't nobody safe." He heard as Red walked over and shot Vicki twice in the back of the head.

"You're next nigga." Munch said and he and Money showed off their guns. He had seen a lot in his life but the video was by far the sickest. Dropping his phone, he sat on the couch. Although he couldn't stand the bitch, she was still his son's mother. Jazz then picked up the phone and watched until she saw Vicki's face. She started crying thinking about what Porshea and her went through.

"I'm gonna kill them niggas." Tee said getting off the couch. "Jazz, when I leave don't open the door for nobody. I don't care if it's the fucking pope. You hear me."

"Yes!" She said knowing he was dead serious. When he came out the room, he handed her a baby glock 9mm.

Slumped

"If anybody comes in there that don't belong, you know what you gotta do." She nodded that she understood.

"Tee, come back to me, alright."

"I will baby. I will." He said walking out the door. Inside his truck, he really broke down. He didn't hate Vicki. Just over time, they grew apart. He started his truck and drove to no destination. He put in Lyfe Jennings CD and played the song "Cry." As Lyfe Jennings sung, cried is what he did. Once he got it out, he called Slump.

"What's up bro."

"I need you to meet me." Not caring that it was almost 3a.m.

"Where?"

"At my house. I should be back there in thirty or forty minutes."

"I'll be there." He said before hanging up. He could tell by the way Tee sounded, something was wrong.

"Where are you going?" Nicki asked as he put on his sweat pants, his black hoodie and grabbed his gun.

"I'm going to meet Tee. I'll be back." He said not waiting on a response.

"Be careful baby. You know we need you too."

"I need you more." Slump said coming back to the bed to kiss her. Walking past Jadda's room, he slipped in and kissed her.

As soon as he got to Tee's house, he could tell something was serious by looking at his face.

Tee handed him the phone and Slump watched the video.

"What the fuck is this shit. Some kind of sick joke."

"Just watch it."

Continuing to watch, he finally noticed it was Vicki in the video. By the time the message ended, he was sick to the stomach.

"It's time bro."

"Time for what?"

"Time to get up out of here."

Slumped

"Look man. I can't even begin to imagine what you feel right now. But I'm not running from nobody."

"I didn't say anything about running. But you have to think, if they found Vicki, how you know they ain't found Nicki or Momma K. Shit nigga. What about your little sister. What if they do something like that to one of them. All I'm saying my nigga is that we need to make sure our family is safe and as long as they are still in the hood, they aren't safe. What them niggas did to Vicki let us know they ain't got no limit to what they will do to get at us. I mean damn. We got all this money and we ain't did nothing with it. And believe me, Jay. Running is the last thing on my mind but I refuse to let them niggas take anything else from me."

It had been years since Tee had called him Jay. When he was younger, that's what he used to call him.

"I hear you Tee but we can't just up and move."

"Why can't we?"

"Because nigga. I mean how? It's not that easy."

"All we need nigga is money and we got plenty of that. So tell me why we can't just up and go."

"Does Stone know about that?" Slump said changing the subject.

"No. But like I said, we need to think about it."

"Think about what?"

"Getting out of here nigga."

"Look, I'm gonna see how Momma K feels, I mean she been living in that house before she had me and I don't think she's just gonna pack up and go."

"She would if she knew what was really going on."

"Man fuck all that. What are we gonna do about them niggas."

"Oh they as good as got but first I need to make sure…we need to make sure our family is safe."

"Are you alright bro?"

Slumped

"I'm good. But I'm serious about this and as soon as I find somewhere out, I'm gonna move mines up out of here and you need to do the same."

"I know I do bro and like I said, I'm gonna get at Momma K. But right now I want to know if you are cool."

"I'm good. All I can do now is wait for her body to pop up and bury her. I mean it's fucked up. I know she is gone but I can't call her moms and let her know. So all I can do is wait. But otherwise, I'm good."

"Alright. Well I'm bout to go home. But first thing tomorrow, I'm going to lay it all out there for Momma K."

On his way home, Slump thought about all Tee had been saying. And he knew Tee was right. It was time to get away from here because it was only a matter of time before death came knocking at his door. That morning the only thing on the television was the murder of David Young in Watercrest Apartments, and the missing woman who lived as well as managed the apartment complex Victoria Sweet. The news went on to say how a witness saw two masked men walking her to an unknown type of grey Sadan. When the news went off two police officers knocked on his front door. They questioned him about the last time that he had seen Vicky and his where abouts for last night. He explained to them that he hadn't seen Vicky since two days before they had left for Disneyland, and only talked to her twice since they had been back. They asked about his son and if he knew of any illegal activities that Vicky was in. He told them that since she had gotten a new live in boyfriend his son had been staying with him and his fiancée, and he didn't know of anything illegal that she was in to. They told him that if she contacts him at all to contact them. Once they had left, he leaned against the door, took a deep breath, and exhaled.

"You did good baby." Jazzmine said.

"I think they bought it."

"Shit. I sure hope that they did."

Slumped

Two days later, she was found naked in William Land Park, across the street from the Sacramento Zoo. Three days after she was found, he gave her a nice funeral, took her mother out to eat, and promised her she could see Little Tee whenever she wanted to.

Chapter 99

It had been almost two months since Vicky was killed, but today was the big day Slump, Nicky, and Momma K sat on Edgehill Drive in Eldorado Hills, looking at the big five bedroom, three and a half bathroom, two car garage house.

"So this is it, huh?" Momma K asked.

"Yeah. This is it. What do you think?" Slump replied.

"It sure is big, but I guess it will do."

"Ma, why do I get the feeling you like it more than you are letting on?"

"Shut up boy." It had taken him almost a month to explain everything to her about what was going on, but finally she agreed to make the move, but only if they stayed together at first. He was against living under the same roof as his mom with his wife, but that was the only way that she would leave her house. So this is where they ended up.

"Well let's go look inside." Nicky said. After they had walked through the house Momma K said, "I guess y'all will get the master bedroom." At first Slump thought that she was going to stat some shit until he noticed her smiling.

"Well baby, it looks like we got a lot of work to do turning this house into a home." She said to Nicky.

"Yeah we do. But I think that it will be fun. Besides he said that we could spend as much as we wanted." She whispered in Momma K's ear.

Slumped

"Man, what are y'all whispering about?" Slump asked.
"Your money." Nicky said laughing. And for the next few
weeks several delivery trucks came and went from the big
house.

Chapter 100

"**M**an bro you have no idea how much money my mom and Nicky have blown through buying shit for that damn house." Slump said.

"Shit, I think I do. Because Jazz ass done went crazy too with that shit." Tee said. Dealing with the same real estate agent, Tee and Jazzmine had ended up in Eldorado Hills at his four-bedroom house, which was ten minutes away from Slump's on St. Andrews Drive.

"But don't lie. How does it feel?" Tee said.

"I can't lie my nigga. I never felt this good in my life. I mean for the first time I don't have any worries. I mean, yeah them niggas will always be a problem until they are done in by us or someone else. But just being inside that house lets me know that it has not been all for nothing. And dealing with all those women in one place at one time is crazy." Slump said.

Tee started laughing and said, "Yeah, I feel sorry for you on that note."

"Man you have no idea. It's not really Mom or Nicky's. It's Shawanna and Jadda's. If it's not one, it's the other whining about something. I mean my daughter; she's still a baby, but my sister, man she acts like I'm her damn daddy or something."

"Shit you have been…"

Slumped

"I know, but she always asking for something, and her ass is almost 18. She better go get a job or something, shit."

"What's up with Stone?"

"I don't know but you know he always like fucking with the young niggas."

"I'm not talking about that. I mean why don't he get out of the way. He feels him and Angel are cool, I guess."

"So what's been up with you and Jazz? Shit, we're five minutes away and I barely see your ass."

"Oh, you know we good. She's been really playing mom to Lil' Tee."

"Well shit, now she is."

"I know. It's just that lately, she's been going somewhere and when I ask her where she been, she says shopping or something. But I ain't seen nothing new other than the shit for the house. And last night, I walked in the room with her and I know she was on the phone but she tried to act like she wasn't."

"Well shit. What you think is going on? She fucking with somebody?"

"That's the thing. I don't think so but with bitches you never know."

"Well, I don't know what to tell you bro, but you already know I got you. Look at these fools. What the fuck you niggas out here doing?" Slump asked getting out of Tee's truck.

"What it look like. We are having a block party. Today's my bunny's 23rd birthday so you know I gotta do it big for her." Lil' Lee said.

"Oh shit. Look who's here." Stone said coming out of Tonya's house."

"What's up my nigga? What you got in that cup?" Tee said.

"Nigga it's a party and you already know that Stone don't drink no water." Flip said giving Slump and Tee brotherly hugs.

Slumped

"Shut your young ass up lil' nigga." Stone said smiling, giving Tee his cup.

Looking around, Slump said, "Damn, everybody out here today."

"Wait til' you see what Lee bought Tonya." Flip stated.

"Oh what. You niggas couldn't come tell me that the bros were here? What's up with ya'll?" A drunken Junebug said coming out the house.

"Not shit." Tee said.

"Trying to feel like you." Slump added.

"Well then, shit. You better go in there and make you a cup."

"What all ya'll got up in there?" Tee asked.

"Shit, what don't we got." Lee answered.

"Well in that case, c'mon Slump. Let's go catch up." Tee said. While they were in the house pouring their drinks, a little girl about twelve ran into the house.

"Lee Lee, hurry it's here." She said excitedly.

"Don't let her come out here yet." Lee said to Flip and Stone before going to the door.

"Don't let me go where? Nigga I'm grown." Tonya said. But when she tried to walk out behind him, Stone and Flip blocked the door.

"Nah sis. You stuck for now." Stone said.

"Nigga if you and your protégé don't move, I'm gonna fuck both of you big headed niggas up."

"Yeah, but you still won't go out this door." Flip said.

"Here birthday girl. Hit this and shut up before we kick your ass for your birthday." Junebug said handing her a blunt.

"It looks like you might as well give it up lady. We got you five to one." Slump said.

"Ya'll don't scare me but I know when I'm beat. Right now, I'm beat." She said laughing and choking from the weed.

"Come here baby. But first, close your eyes." Lil Lee said when he came back in the house.

"Close my eyes for what?"

"Fuck it then. You just won't get your gift."

"Okay baby. You know I was just playing."

"Well close your eyes then."

"Alright. You better not let me walk into nothing or I'm gonna fuck all six of you niggas up." Lil' Lee led her out of the house while everyone followed.

"Alright. Open them." When she did, she saw the pearl white Lexus ES 350. Taped to the driver window was a big birthday card with the key inside.

"I love you!" She said kissing him.

"Ya'll need to go in the house or get a room." The little girl said.

"And you need to stay out of grown folks business." Flip said.

"Shut up. You ain't grown."

"Whatever lil' girl. Go play."

"Come here Meka." Lil' Lee said handing her twenty dollars before she walked off.

"Thank you." She said before running off to a group of girls her age.

Tonya couldn't wait to take her new car for a ride. "Come on Lee. Let's go somewhere."

"Ya'll have fun. I know I am." Lee said.

"I still don't know how he did that." Flip said watching them drive off.

"I don't either." Junebug added.

"Yeah, well he did it. And it was worth it." Slump said with pride in his voice.

Chapter 101

"Hello?" Jazzmine said into her phone.

"Can you talk?" the man on the other end asked.

"Yeah, I can talk. He ain't here right now."

"You know I miss you Jazzy."

"Don't call me that."

"I'm just saying. You know how many nights I've laid in the bed hoping you came back."

"Look Shawn. I thought you were going to help me but if not, then we have nothing to talk about."

Shawn had been Jazz's first love. He had been one of the biggest cocaine dealers in South Richmond, California. He still ran one of the biggest drug rings in Richmond. He'd just taken over the drug game when he met Jazz, who was seventeen at the time. Young and dumb. Back then, she was so in love with the attention of being a kingpin's chick and everything that went with being with a d-boy's brought. The money, clothes, and jewelry. But one night, her mother was kidnapped and held for ransom. Shawn had to pay to get her back. The money was paid but her mother was still murdered. After that, she told herself she would never been with another man in the game. Then she met Tee and everything changed.

"Yeah, I'm gonna help you. In fact, I got that info for you already."

"You do. But it's only been a week."

"Have you forgot who I was Jazzy?"

Slumped

"No I ain't forgot and could you please stop calling me that."

"Yeah I got you. But I'm not gonna give you this info over the phone. You are gonna have to come meet me."

"I don't know if I can do that?"

"Why, you don't trust me?"

"No it ain't that...I have to call you back." Jazz said hearing the garage door open before hanging up.

She made it downstairs just as Tee was staggering into the door.

"Ughh...look at you."

"I know." Tee said smiling drunkly. He grabbed her kissing her neck.

"Don't start anything that you ain't gone finish." She said huskily.

"Do I ever?" He shot back palming her ass and grinding into her so she could feel the erection in his jeans. He was hungry for her so without giving it any thought, he picked her up and put her on the kitchen counter. All she had on was a big T-shirt and boxers from lounging around the house. In one swift motion, Tee pulled out his dick and put it inside her, causing her to moan and bite down on his lip. Then thoughts of her hiding something from him made him get rough. Without giving her time, he plunged his eight and a half inches inside of her forcefully.

"Slow down baby. I ain't all the way wet and ready for that yet." But he didn't. The thoughts of her cheating mixed with the alcohol made him not care.

"Please. You're hurting me." Since being raped by Money and Red, for the first time, she felt violated. He'd always been gentle with her. Even when she wanted to get a little rough. He came inside of her with a violent growl before pulling out. Coming to reality, shame filled him as he looked at the tears that ran down her face. He put his dick back into his pants, walked out of the kitchen, and sat on the couch in the den.

Slumped

"What's wrong? What was that all about?" Jazz asked sitting next to him.

"Where have you been going?"

"What are you talking about?"

"When you leave here saying you went shopping, where have you been going, Jazz. You never come back with anything. I've been shopping with you and I know you can't go without buying anything. So where have you been going? Are you seeing someone else? Just be honest with me. Are you?"

"No I would never cheat on you Tee. Never."

"So what's been going on?" On those days, she'd been going to her mother's grave thinking about what she'd plan to do. She didn't' want to tell him about Shawn and what he doing for her.

"I've been going to the cemetery to my mother's grave."

"I never knew your mother was dead. What happened? How long has she been dead?"

"For six years now. She was murdered when I was 21."

"Oh baby, I'm sorry. I should have trusted you."

"Tee, I would never do anything to disrespect what we have. So please don't ever think I would."

"I'm sorry Jazz. I mean the alcohol and the thoughts of you…"

"Shhh. No worries baby. No worries." She said placing her fingers to his lips.

"What do I have to do to make up for what I just did?"

"Come upstairs and make me forget it ever happened." Standing up, he picked her up and carried her to their room where he made love to her repeatedly.

Chapter 102

"Shorty wanna ride wit me. Let your hair down. You said that you want a thugg. Don't be scared now." Young Buck could be heard singing in the background of Flip's painted sixty-eight Caprice Classic. He and Junebugg had been splurging all day. His car was full of bags everywhere from the banana republic to true religion.

"Nigga we got dumb ass gear, and nowhere to go." Junebugg said.

"Shit there is always somewhere to go when your money long and ya gas tank's full." Flip said.

"I know all of that, but that's not what I meant."

"Well stop talking in circles and say what the fuck you mean nigga. Now pass the damn weed while you over there babysitting the blunt and shit." He passed the blunt to Flip and said, "Nigga I'm talking about us. Right now, we are going back to Tanya's house. I mean damn we got money my nigga, more money than any two niggas our age and we still stay up in somebody else shit."

"So what are you saying bro? Do you think that we should get one of the bros to rent us an apartment?"

"Why not? Shit, we are doing grown men shit. So why not have our own? I mean don't get me wrong. I love Tanya like a sister, but she and Lee have been real serious and I know that they are tired of us all up in their space."

Slumped

"Man Lee ain't tripping like that. Shit, he's our bro."

"I know that he's not tripping on us. I'm just saying that I think that we should get our own spot."

"Well I'm with it. Fuck it. We could probably get Stone to do it for us too. Matter of fact, call him and see where he's at."

Junebugg called Stone, and he said that he was at home fucking with his dogs. So they drove to his house. When they got there, Stone was outside with his dog Blockhead.

"Man, I hate that damn dog." Junebugg said.

"Aww man, there's nothing wrong with Blockhead." Flip said getting out the car. Once he was out of the car and walking up to the yard, Blockhead ran up to him, almost knocking him down.

"What's up big boy?"

"What's up with y'all?" Stone asked.

"Not shit big bro. You know. Just doing us." Flip said.

"Shit. I see y'all have been buying up shit again." Stone said pointing at all the bags in the car.

"Yep. You know that we are some fly young niggas." Junebugg said.

"Hey. Look though bro. We are trying to get us a little apartment or something."Flip said.

"I was wondering when y'all was going to want your own spot."

"Yeah, this nigga thinks that Tanya and Lil' Lee are getting tired of always being around them."

"I didn't say that they were tired of us. I'm just saying. What if they want to just get naked and fuck all over the house?"

"They can't because we are in their shit. What if I want to bring a bitch to the spot and do something freaky? Shit, you feel me?"

"Yeah, I feel you. Every now and then a nigga do want to just let his nuts hang." Stone said.

Slumped

"That's what I've been trying to tell this fool. But you know that he doesn't listen, unless you, Tee, or Slump tell him something."

"Even then his little ass doesn't listen." Stone said.

"Man, How are y'all gonna talk about me like I'm not even here? Anyway, we need our own shit. So what's up? Are you gonna help us?" Junebugg asked.

"I don't see why I can't. Is there somewhere particular that y'all want to be?" Stone said.

"Not really." Junebugg said.

"Shit, if we are getting us a spot then I want it to be in Notomas. There are bitches out there. I think that I saw something like pay the first month's rent and the second month was free on the gate. Shit, what time is it? It's 2:45. Come on. Let's go in the house. I'll have Angel call and see what's up." Flip said.

"What's up y'all?" Angel said. Blockhead's tail knocked over the glass of Arbor Mist that she had been sipping on that Saturday on the coffee table. "Damn it Stone, put his ass outside."

"C'mon Blockhead. Momma doesn't want you in the house no more." Stone said.

"That damn dog doesn't do anything but eat and break shit every time that you let his big ass in here. Flip, could you hand me that rag by the kitchen sink?"

"Yeah I got you big sis." After Angel had wiped off the table and around herself, she asked for another glass.

"What y'all been doing today?"

"Nothing just out buying gear." Junebugg answered.

"Oh yeah, and y'all didn't bring me anything?"

"Yeah we did." Flip said.

"Oh yeah. What?"

"This." Flip said pulling a blunt from behind his ear.

"Boy. You are just like Stone's ass. Always got some weed ready to smoke."

"Weed! Who got some weed?" Stone said as he was coming back into the house.

"Your little protégé."

"Damn. Burn that shit little nigga." Stone said.

"You ain't said nothing but a word bro." Flip replied.

"Momma, do you think that you can you go online and see how much the rent is at the Point Natomas Apartments?" Stone said to Angel.

"For what?"

"For these two. They are trying to grow up."

"Yeah. I guess I could do that. But first, I need to get my mind right. I hope that this ain't no boo boo."

"Aww come on sis. You know that we don't smoke nothing but that fire." Flip said.

"We are going to see. Yeah. This is some good."

"What's up Junebugg? You trying to win your money back?" Stone said as he turned on the Xbox 360.

"I was just about to ask you if you felt like losing some." Junebugg replied.

"Well if I remember right. I'm up $700.00."

"Man you got lucky last time. I was high."

"Yeah, blame it on the weed lil' nigga." Stone said laughing.

"Baby, they got some pay the deposit and first month and the second month is free." Angel said looking up from the computer.

"How much is the rent?" Flip asked.

"$875 for a two bedroom. You want me to call them."

"Yeah and see how soon we can move in."

After talking to them, she announced, "They have a same day move in fee. If you pay it then you can get the keys today."

"Well?" Stone said pausing the game.

"Well what nigga. Me and Junebug can't just walk in there with some money and say here."

"No shit lil' nigga. I'm saying do ya'll wanna do it?"

Slumped

"Hell yeah!"

After it was all said and done, the boys gave Angel $1500 a piece to put it in her name.

"I don't want ya'll money but ya'll better not do no crazy shit. Especially yo' ass Flip."

"We ain't." Junebug said. She kept staring at Flip.

"Damn, why does everybody think I'm gonna do something crazy."

"Because you always do lil' nigga. And if you do, I ain't fucking with your ass no more."

"I got you big sis. I promise, I ain't gon' do no dumb shit." After Angel left to handle the business with the apartment, Stone took another $200 from Junebug. Then Stone and Junebug grabbed their things from Tonya's house.

"Man, I can't believe ya'll leaving me." Lil' Lee said.

"Nigga please. You know you and sis getting tired of us crowding ya'll space." Junebugg said.

"Yeah. Now ya'll can run around naked." Flip said smiling.

"Well shit. Don't think ya'll getting away from me that easily. You niggas been living here almost a year and ya'll better still come see me." Tonya said.

"You already know we gon' be over here. Don't nobody make tacos like you do. Plus, our bro here." Flip said.

"Yeah, well don't let that be the only reason, you little asshole." They boys then packed their clothes and guns. They packed Flip's car then met Angel for their key. Their apartment was downstairs in apartment 184.

"So now what?" Flip asked after bringing all their things inside.

"I know one thing. I ain't about to be in here without no TV and X-Box." Junebug said.

"Yeah on my momma I feel you on that shit. C'mon. Let's go to Fry's. I'm gonna get the biggest TV I can for my room. When they got there, they both bought 50-inch flat screens. Junebug got an X-Box 360 but Flip got a Playstation

3 and a home entertainment center complete with surround sound. They split the price for the 70-inch flat screen, the microwave and the computer.

"Let's hit up one of these furniture stores that's still open said." Junebug said after paying for their items and delivery fee for the next day. They then went to American Furniture where they tried to buy up so much the woman thought they were kidding including a 2 piece living room set, a 5 piece dining room and a six piece bedroom set for Flip.

"That's too much for me. I'm gonna keep it simple. Just a bed or something." Junebug said.

"Whatever, I'm going all out."

"I can tell." Headed to the register, they paid for their purchase.

"How will you be paying for this?" The clerk said.

"Um...ya'll take cash." Flip said pulling out a wad of money trying to be funny.

"You have to excuse my little brother. It's our first apartment and Mom and Dad are paying for everything."

"I wish my mother and father is half as nice as yours." The clerk stated. After confirming their delivery time, they left.

"Man you gotta stop doing that shit?"

"Doing what?"

"Pulling out money like that everywhere we go."

"I wish a nigga would try to jack me."

"It ain't got nothing to do with that. Nigga, you're 16 and I'm 17. How do we explain where we got this kind of dough from if the white folks put the real white folks in our business. Nigga, we spent almost $17,000 in the last 4 hours. All cash."

"I didn't think about it like that bro. My bad."

"It's good my nigga. Now what are we gonna do?"

"First I'm hungry as fuck so let's get something to eat. Then hit Walmart and get whatever else we need."

"Damn my nigga. You are a regular Martha Stewart."

Slumped

"Fuck you!" Junebug said laughing and lighting a blunt.

"Well shit, if we going to Walmart, we might as well go to In and Out Burger."

"Shit I'm with it. I could go for one of them classic double cheeseburgers."

"Shit me too." They boys spent the rest of their day buying any and everything they thought they needed for their apartment. The first night in their place they slept passed out on an air mattress. The next day, the others came to help them get everything together.

"Damn, I'm really proud of you two lil' niggas. Ya'll done really stepped it up." Tee said looking around at the now plush apartment.

"I know where I'm gonna be spending my time. Who picked out these couches. These motherfuckers are nice." Stone said.

"You wouldn't believe me if I told you." Junebug stated.

"Did you see that lil' nigga's bedroom set. That motherfucker makes me wanna get a new one." Slump said.

"Yeah, he really showed his ass coping that motherfucker." Stone said.

"Now all we need is some cable in this bitch and we're set." Flip said.

"Shit cable is the easy part. Ya'll done got the hard part out the way. Matter of fact, my homeboy Carl works for Comcast, let me see if he can come and get ya'll online." Tee said getting on the phone.

Chapter 103

"**D**amn girl. Look at you. You sure have grown up since I last saw you." Shawn said to Jazzmine. She agreed to meet him so he could tell her what he found out.

"That was six years ago, Shawn."

"I know and I've thought about you every day since Jazzy. My bad…Jazzmine."

"Look Shawn, I shouldn't even be here right now. So could you please stop trying to play catch up and tell me what you found out."

"Damn, I see one thing ain't changed."

"And what's that?"

"You still got that sexy ass Boss Bitch attitude. Well since you're here you might as well have a drink."

"No, I'm good. I gotta pick up my son when I leave here."

"Oh what you got a son now? What's his name?"

"Terry. He's named after his father. Look this was a bad idea." Jazz said standing up.

"No wait. Hold on Jazz. You can't be mad at a nigga for trying though. Can you? But I should have already known once you give yourself to a nigga, you are a loyal bitch. You've always been that way so I'm gonna stop wasting your time. The nigga Munch you were asking about. His name is

Slumped

Anthony Jordan. He is from the lower bottoms in West Oakland. He been getting money in Sacramento for a while now. Are you sure you don't want to tell me what this is about?"

"No it's my business. I can take care of it."

"Well here. That's all his info. I don't' know how up to date it is but it's the best I could do. I know his wife owns a little clothing store out there somewhere. The name of it is on the paper. The other two clowns I don't' know too much about. One of my people said Munch is related to one of them. They are from back east somewhere. D.C. I think. But as far as they go, I couldn't get too much information on them. But like I said, on that paper you got all you need to track Munch down." He said handing her a piece a paper.

"Thank you Shawn. It was nice seeing you." She said folding the paper and putting it her purse as she kissed him on the cheek.

"Anytime you need me Jazzmine. No matter what for. You know how to reach me."

"I know." Jazz said walking out the hotel room. Now she had a way to find Munch. Now all she had to do was come up with a plan to get them all at once. She wished her girl Porshea was still alive because she would know exactly what to do.

Chapter 104

Back at Flip and Junebug's apartment. Carl just finished hooking up the cable and internet.

"There you go Tee."

"Good looking my nigga. What I owe you?"

"Just a seventy five dollar service fee. If it was just the cable, I would tell you to pay the bill but since it's the internet too, I got to charge ya'll for that."

"It's good. Ya'll ain't gon' give him a tip for doing ya'll a favor." Tee said giving him a hundred dollar bill and looking and the boy.

"Yeah, good looking my dude." Flip said as they handed him a hundred a piece.

"If ya'll have any problems, just have Tee hit me and I'll come take care of it."

"For sure. And here...for when you get off work." Junebug said handing him about an eighth of purple.

"Oh for sure. You guys have a good day." Carl said giving him dap.

"Nigga, why you give him all the weed?" Flip said.

"Calm your ass down. That wasn't all the weed. We still got some left."

"Well, ain't nobody else in here hungry but me?" Tee asked.

Slumped

"Nigga your big muscle head. You stay hungry." Flip said.

"And your little skinny ass need to start eating more, shit. But I'm serious. What's up on a pizza or something? A nigga starving in here. Ya'll got everything in here but food. Fuck that, I'm ordering a pizza."

"Well shit, stop running your mouth and order some then. I knew my stomach wasn't the only one fighting my spine." Slump said laughing.

Forty minutes later, three extra large Pizza Hut pizzas were delivered and just as quick as the lids were open, they were gone. Out of nowhere, Flip started laughing.

"What's wrong with you?" Tee asked.

"You ain't noticed. Since these pizzas got here, ain't nobody said one word. All you hear is smacking."

"Yeah. And niggas was acting like they wasn't hungry."

Chapter 105

Alicia had been out of the hospital now for two days.

"So how you feeling?" Slump asked.

"I'm good, I guess. I mean I'm still alive right."

"I would have slid through to see you yesterday but I had something I needed to do."

"Jaylon, you ain't got to lie to me. Your wife probably didn't want to let you outside."

"Oh so you got jokes now, huh."

"No, I'm serious. She say jump and you say how high. And now you don' moved all the way to El Dorado Hills. Who idea was that?"

"Actually it was mine. You know a lot has been going on, and since that shit with Vicki, I just needed to make sure my family was safe."

"So what am I Jaylon, huh. I'm not family. I remember when we were young, you used to tell me you would never leave me or let me be hurt. Do you remember that?"

"Yeah I remember."

"So tell me, what happened? Why did you let him do me like he did."

"So now it's my fault. If I remember correctly, you got paid for the role you played."

"Yeah, well I didn't get paid enough to go through all this."

Slumped

"Ha! So that's what this is all about. Some fucking money. I never thought you were the type."

"What type nigga? What you trying to say?"

"I'm saying I never figured you to be a gold digger. I thought you were different." Slump said walking to the window.

"So you calling me a hoe now?"

"I didn't say that. You did."

"Fuck you nigga. You sure have changed since you started fucking with that bitch."

"Watch your mouth Alicia."

"Watch my mouth nigga. I've been raped and fucked with a hot curling iron all because of you and you have the nerve to tell me to watch my mouth. Fuck you and that bitch, nigga. Matter of fact, just leave. Go home to your wife and kid." Walking up to her, he tried to hug her but she pushed him away. "Don't touch me nigga. Don't ever touch me again."

More hurt than angry about what she was saying. "Do you want me to find you somewhere else to stay?"

"No nigga. I don't need you or your money. I can take care of myself. Just leave."

"C'mon Alicia."

"C'mon nothing nigga. Just get the fuck outta my house. Stay out of my life. I don't ever want to see you again."

"You don't mean that." He said hurt.

"The fuck if I don't. Now please, leave my house."

"If you need anything, just call me." He said walking to her door.

"Leave motherfucker." She said throwing a lamp at him as he walked out the door.

"Fine. If that's how you want it, it got it." He said slamming the door. One of her neighbors came outside to see what the noise was. They looked at Slump.

"What the fuck you looking at bitch." He said to the lady who quickly went back into her apartment and closed the door. By the time he made it to his car, he told himself he was done. Fuck Alicia.

Chapter 106

Shawanna got a job at Foot Locker in the Sunrise Mall. On her second day of work, two of the flyest niggas walked in the store. It was time for her to take her lunch break but she decided not to hoping one of the men would notice her. She would be eighteen in a week and now that Slump lived in Eldorado Hills, she didn't have to worry about him cramping her style.

That nigga sure makes it hard for a bitch to get hers, she thought. "Is there anything I can help you with?" She asked as she walked up to the men.

"I don't know. What I want they might not sell here." Money said looking her up and down and licking his lips.

"Well if it's not here, maybe I can still help you find it."

"And what makes you think you can do all that?"

"You would be surprised at all I know how to do."

"You got a phone shorty?"

"Yeah, I got one. Why?"

"Let me see it then." She handed him the blackberry as he locked his number into her contacts. "Don't lose it but don't forget to use it either."

"I won't." She said as her young pussy got wet thinking about fucking a baller. She knew they were ballers by the way they dressed, not to mention the diamonds in the mouth of the guy who gave up his number.

Slumped

"So Mr. Man. You know my name but I don't know yours."

"Who me? I'm Money. And that fly nigga over there. That's Red."

"Man, I don't even see the new Jays up in here. What's up with that?" Red said complaining for no reason.

"We sold out. But we got some coming in tonight or in the morning. I'll just put two pair to the side for ya'll. Just give me your sizes." She got their sizes and watched as they left the store. She couldn't wait to call her girl Misty and tell her about them.

"Man, that girl probably ain't even eighteen yet?" Red said leaving the store.

"So nigga. You act like you ain't never fucked no young bitch. You just mad I beat you to it."

"Nigga you got me fucked up. I hope she got a friend though."

"And even if she don't, you know how we get a bitch in the mood."

Once Shawanna got off, she decided she would go out on a limb and hook up with Money. She didn't care if he thought she was young or not. Her pussy hadn't stopped throbbing since he walked out the door.

"Damn girl. It took you long enough. I been out here waiting on your ass for the last twenty minutes." She said to Misty, who had been her friend since junior high.

"So what's up with these niggas you were talking about on the phone?"

"Girl, these niggas is fly as fuck and they got money. I'm trying to put this young snapper on that nigga and have him buying me all the flyest shit."

"See girl. That's your problem. You ain't nothing but a little gold digger. You don't think about nothing but some dick and some money."

"And you don't?" Shawanna said with attitude.

"I'm different bitch. I don't got no brother who can buy me anything I ask him for. Not to mention if he finds out you fucking with these niggas, he's gonna kill you and them."

"Bitch, I'm not even worried about Jaylon's ass and he ain't worried about me."

"Whatever bitch. I'm just saying be careful. That's all. Now you said the other one was just as fly as the nigga you was talking to because you know I don't do no ugly."

"Trust me. You will not be disappointed. Now let's get ready. I already talked to Money and he said him and Red, that's the one I'm hooking you up with, will be ready when we call.

Chapter 107

"**F**uck that bitch. I mean yeah it's fucked up that all that shit happened to her, but nigga remember all that you have done and been through behind her punk ass. And now she wanna act like it's your fault. That bitch knew what time it was. That's why we had to pay her." Tee said to Slump.

"I know but still, I can't help but feel like it's my fault."

"Well it's not nigga. So get over it and forget that bitch. I never liked her punk ass anyway. She was always too high maintenance for me. I told you in the long run she would be an issue but I told you so. Now we need to focus on finding these niggas and putting an end to this shit once and for all." He said passing the blunt.

"Bro, you know if it ain't one thing, it's another."

"What the fuck is that supposed to mean?"

"I'm just saying. Look at what all has happened over the last two and a half years. You done been hit. Our lil' niggas been killed, and now Vicki. I'm just saying even after we get them niggas, we still won't be even."

"It's not about getting even bro. it's never been but these niggas have to die."

"Oh trust and believe. They will all die. No question about that. But afterwards, what do we do. I mean we got money and just bought our first house. But we been so focused on killing these niggas that we forgot what we started to get money for in the first place."

"So what you trying to say. After we kill these niggas, you want out."

"Bro, I'm already too far in to ever get out. But I've been thinking and now that Lee is a part of this and I'm gonna be getting married soon, all this work I got tucked away, I'm gonna give it to him, Flip and Junebug and play the background for a little while. You know do the family thing and open up some type of small business."

"Yeah, it all sounds good but be honest, it won't be the same. The rush won't be there or the thrill of the game and sooner or later, you'll come back. It's who you are. It's who I am and like it or not, it's who we always will be."

"People change Tee."

"Yeah but niggas like us stay the same." Just then, Tee's phone rang.

"Hello?"

"What's up." Stone said on the other end.

"Not shit. Just out bending corners with Slump. Blowing on some of that good and talking about life."

"Well shit. Since ya'll already out, ya'll might as well come over. I got something I wanna run past ya'll real quick."

"Alright. We will be there in a few."

"In a minute then."

"Who was that?" Slump asked when he got off the phone.

"Your cousin. He said he needed to run something by us so we bout to go holler at him unless you got other plans."

"Nah, it's cool. I been needing to get at Angel about a wedding gift for Nicki anyway."

"I still can't believe you're going to get married next month."

"I can't either bro." They pulled up to Stone's about twenty five minutes later and as always, Stone was in the front yard with Black head.

Slumped

"Man what's up with that nigga and dogs?" Tee asked Slump.

"Shit, ever since he was young he liked dogs."

"Keep that big headed motherfucker over there." Tee said getting out the car.

"Man how many times I gotta tell you. He ain't gon' bother you if you don't bother him."

"I don't give a fuck about none of that shit. Just keep him away from me."

"Come here Blackhead." Stone called to the dog that had been watching them since they pulled up.

"What's up cousin?" Slump said.

"Not shit. You know just looking at it."

"I can dig it. So what's up?"

"Come on in the house and I will let you know."

"What's up Angel?" Slump said once the three men were inside.

"Hey Jaylon. What's up. Tee?"

"What's up Angel."

"So Jaylon, you ready to be a married man?"

"As ready as I'll ever be, but before I leave, I gotta holler at you about a wedding gift."

"Alright." She said before going back to whatever it was she was doing.

"Why don't ya'll come to the backroom."

"Put that damn dog outside before he breaks something." Angel said before they left the room. Stone put the dog in the backyard. "You ain't gonna put him in his pen?"

"Hell, he'll be alright for now.

Once in the backroom, he got down to business.

"So check it out. I've been thinking about going back to Texas and taking the lil' niggas with me."

"Oh yeah."

"Yeah, I mean shit. We got thirty kilos and we ain't been doing shit. Just sitting on work. I know you about to get married next month and now Tee got Lil' Terry full time and

I think it would be a good move to take them out there so we can push the work."

"I don't know. We got a lot going on.

"But at the same time we do need to get rid of it and it's been too hot out here to push the coke." Tee added.

"I planned on ya'll being here for my wedding."

"Man we wouldn't miss that for nothing in the world. But I be with these lil' niggas almost every day and I can see the hunger to do something in their eyes."

"Yeah, I guess you right. When did you plan on leaving?"

"I don't know. Probably next week. Angel said she wanted to come and Lee said he was bring Tonya if he goes."

"So you already ran past them?" Tee asked.

"Yeah, we been talking about it."

"Well shit. Ya'll do your thing then."

"And hopefully by the time ya'll get back and it's time for Slump's wedding, we will have our little problem taken care of." Tee added.

"So it's all good then."

"Yeah, I'm good with it." Tee said.

"I am too. Don't let nothing happen to my brother Mike."

"I'm not."

"And don't let your little protégé kill nobody." Tee added.

"So it's good then." Stone asked again with a smile on his face.

"Yep, it's good. Now I need to holler at Angel." He had her pick up something special for Nicki. "So what's up Angel, did you do that for me?" He asked walking in the living room.

"Yeah I did it. They said it would be ready for the wedding."

"I knew I could count on you."

"I don't see why you just don't let her go pick it out herself."

"Because I want to surprise her with it."

Slumped

"I guess." Nicki had been talking about wanting a new Escalade so he had Angel put a down payment on one and had it painted pink, which was Nicki's favorite color. But the interior was a one of a kind with Hello Kitty. That was an extra $11,000 but he didn't care. It would be well worth the smile when she saw it.

Chapter 108

"Ooh girl! You wasn't lying. These niggas are fine as fuck." Misty said. They had just got to Applebees on Truxel in Natomas.

"I told you bitch." when they got to the table, Money stood up and gave Shawanna a hug.

"What's up shorty."

"Nothing. This is my girl Misty. Misty this is Money. And that's his boy Red."

"So Misty, how old are you?" Red asked.

"I'm old enough to know better but still young enough to not care." She answered sexually.

"Is that right?"

"Yeah that's right."

"Oh I like you. You got attitude."

"I got something else too."

"And what's that?"

"I'm gonna keep it to myself because I don't know if you're good enough for it or not yet."

"Well hopefully I am."

"So shorty, you're gonna make sure me and my dude get them Jays right." Money asked.

"I am but do I get."

"I don't know. What do you want?"

Slumped

"I don't know but I could think of a few positions…I mean things."

"You couldn't take it if I gave it to you."

"Don't be surprised at what I can take."

"So ya'll want something to drink or are ya'll too young to be drinking?"

"Oh so you got jokes huh."

"Nah shorty. I ain't trying to be funny. I'm just saying, back where we come from if you got the money to pay for it, you are old enough to drink it."

"Oh yeah. And where are ya'll from?"

"From D.C. but for the past few years we'd been staying in Texas."

"And what brought ya'll out here?" Misty asked.

"Business. And we decided to stay since we liked what we saw."

"Shit what we still seeing." Money added.

"Well, we got no IDs so we can't order no drinks in here. But that don't mean we can't drink afterwards unless ya'll had other plans."

"Alright. That sounds good to me." Money said.

"Shit, me too." Red added.

After they ate their food, they went back to Misty's apartment since she only stayed up the street in Gateway Oaks in the New Natomas. They stopped at the liquor store and got a fifth of Hennessey and Hypnotiq.

"Bitch if you give this nigga some pussy, you better make him use a rubber." Misty told Shawanna when they arrived at her apartment.

"I will."

"You will what?" Money asked coming through the door."

"Nothing!" She said smiling seductively at him.

"So who stay here with ya'll?" Red asked looking around the spacious apartment.

"Nobody but us. Why?" Misty answered.

"Cause I don't wanna have to hurt nobody's boyfriend or brother."

"Well you ain't gotta worry about none of that. So you can relax and get comfortable." Shawanna played "My Chick Bad" by Ludacris and Nicki Minaj. Misty got some glasses so Red could mix the drinks.

"So do you think I'm good enough yet?" Red asked handing Misty her drink.

"I don't know. The night is still young." Around 11:30, her phone started to ring. She saw it was Slump and pushed the ignore button.

"Who was that, your lil' boyfriend?" Money asked.

"No. Just my bigheaded ass brother. He always be trying to act like he my daddy or something. Shit, I'm grown." She answered as the phone rang again. This time she just turned it off.

"Oh shorty. He just looking out for you. There's a lot of bad men out in the world." Money said with a smile on his face.

"Are you one of them?"

"Who me? Do I look like a bad person? I mean come on. Look at this smile."

"Nah, you don't look like a bad guy."

"Good, I'm glad you feel that way but I got a question."

"And what's that?"

"Why you so far away?"

"You the one acting like you scared to touch me or something."

"Shorty I told you that you couldn't take it if I gave it to you."

"Yeah you talk a good one but that's about it."

"Let's go in the room and see who is all talk." Money whispered in her ear.

"Misty, I'm bout to go in the room." She said getting up.

"Have fun then." Misty said giving her a look.

Slumped

"Come lay down with me for a little while." She said grabbing Money's hand.

Shawanna went into the spare bedroom as Misty went into hers ten minutes later as they tried to hook the two men.

Chapter 109

"**I**'m gonna fuck her ass up." Slump said to Nicki.

"For what? The girl damn near grown. Shit let her live a little."

"Yeah well the key words are damn near grown. Her ass ain't eighteen yet and as long as she living here, she better let me or Momma K know where she is if she ain't gonna be coming home."

"Your acting like you're her father instead of her brother."

"See that's what the problem is. Living in a house full of women."

"What?"

"Ya'll all stick together."

"Boy shut up and go to sleep. I don't know what's the matter with you but you been in a funky mood all day."

"I know what I'm bout to do."

"Where are you going?"

"She could only be at one place. Misty's."

"Jaylon, get back in the bed and leave that girl alone."

"Alright. But tomorrow when she brings her little hot ass home. I'm gonna tell her about herself." He said laying back down.

"Why don't you tell me about this?" Nicki said straddling him.

Chapter 110

At 3am, Money rolled over opening his eyes. Shawanna laid naked next to him. When he got out the bed, she woke up.

"So that's how you gon' do me. Hit and it and sneak off while I'm sleep?"

"Nah it ain't even like that shorty. But I got a lot going on. Time is money. You feel me."

"It's three o'clock. Just keep it real. I'm grown."

"It ain't like that shorty. Me and you gonna be spending a lot of time together."

"You promise." She said sitting up, letting the blanket and sheet fall around her waist with her perky little B-cups fully exposed.

"Yeah I promise." He said taking one of her nipples and putting them in his mouth.

Money and Red left that morning telling the girls they would see them real soon. After they were gone, Shawanna turned her phone back on and had nine missed calls. All from Slump. She knew he would talk shit but thought the night had been well worth you. She laid back down and was soon back to sleep, dreaming of what her and Money had done to each other.

Chapter 111

Jazz walked into Top Notch, the clothing store that
Munch's wife ran. There were two women working. One
too young to be married so that left the older woman,
who was about forty and could use a major makeover, not to
mention some weight loss.

"Can I help you ma'am?"

"No, I'm just looking right now."

"Alright but if I can help you, just let me know. Okay."

"Okay." There was someone coming in the store. She saw
it was no one other than Lil Lee and Tonya.

"What's up big sis."

"Nothing. Just out and about. What about you?"

"Aww shit. You know. Just trying to stay fly. Oh shit.
Jazz, this is my lady Tonya. Tonya, this is my bro's girl,
Jazzmine." The two women spoke and shook hands.

"Well I don't see anything up in here I want. So I'm bout
to go. But it was good seeing you Lee and nice to meet you
Tonya."

"Likewise."

"Tell Tee I said what's up." Lil' Lee said.

"I will but you will probably see him before I do." When
she was inside of her Lexus coupe, she thought it would be
easy to get Munch's wife. Slowly, a plan was forming in
Jazz's mind. She'd already driven by the house where Munch

lived and saw him both times she went by. Of course she could just tell Tee and let him, Slump and Stone deal with it. But she wanted Red and Money for what they did to her and Porshea. So once she got them, she would tell Tee where they could find Munch, but not before.

Chapter 112

"**N**igga I'm telling you that young bitch got the best head I ever had in my life. And her pussy. Nigga I'm telling you it's off the hook."

"Oh shit. Don't let me find out Mr. Dirty Dick himself got sprung on some young pussy."

"Call it what you want my nigga. I'm sprung. So what's up with you and ol' girl?" Money said reciting the line from T-Pain.

Slumped

"She's alright I guess."

"Alright! Shit. She was thick as fuck."

"I know. She likes it in the ass too."

"Well maybe we need to set up shop at their spot. Since we've been here, all we've been doing is spending money and not making any."

"Yeah, I've been thinking about that too. And the only thing on my cousin's mind is getting them niggas. He doesn't even give a fuck if he goes broke in the process of doing it either."

Yeah, I've noticed."

"So how do you want to go about doing this?"

"Shit. The easy way. How do you think? I mean the only thing bitches their age want is a nigga with a little bit of doe and treat them to the glamorous life. So I say we spend a little to get a lot."

"I'm with it."

"So when do we start?"

"Shit. Now nigga."

"I called shorty this morning. She said that she was on her way to work."

"Oh yeah? And what about her girl?"

"She works at the Toys R Us around the corner from the mall."

"So I say that we slide through. Maybe take em' lunch or something, and while we are at it. We can cop them new Jordan's too."

"Fuck it lets do it." Red said as he began to break down a Swisher Sweet. So he could roll up a blunt while Money drove.

Chapter 113

"So we are really going to Texas?" Flip asked Stone. "Hell yeah little bro. And we are going to get this money too."

"That's what I'm talking about." Junebugg said.

"So when are we leaving?" Flip asked.

"Day after tomorrow." Stone replied.

"Are we driving?" Junebugg asked.

"How else are we going to get the work out there?"

"I was just asking."

"Shit well stop asking dumb ass questions nigga. And pass the damn weed." Stone said smiling at him.

"How long does it take to drive out there? I'm taking my car too." Flip said.

"I't takes about three days. And nah you not driving out there lil nigga."

"Well then where am I going to put my car? Because I sure ain't about to leave my shit parked out there while we are gone."

"You can park it in the garage at Angel's house. Since we are going to be taking her car."

"Alright. That's what up." Flip said. Just then, the front door opened and Little Lee walked in.

"What's up with my niggas?" Little Lee said.

"Not shit. Just chilling." They all said as they were talking about the trip.

"Yeah about that. I talked to Tanya and she said that she wouldn't mind driving."

"So then it's good." Stone said.

"Yeah. It's good, but don't nobody mention the work. Because I didn't tell her that there will be fifteen kilos in the trunk. So we need to watch what we say."

"You hear that Flip?" Stone said.

"Yeah. I heard that. And why do ya'll always have to single me out when it comes to shit like this? Don't shoot nobody Flip. Watch what you say Flip."

"Because nigga. You always are doing something." Stone said.

"Whatever. Ya'll just be doing that shit because I'm the youngest."

"Age ain't got shit to do with it. So what we all need to bring with us?" Junebugg asked.

"Some clothes and enough doe to get you by until we start getting money." Stone answered.

"What about our heat?" Flip asked.

"To be honest. You don't need to worry about that. Because I got a dumb ass plug on burners out there."

"That's what's up."

"So we leave the day after tomorrow. Unless something comes up. And we will fly back out here for Slump and Nicky's big day. Now Junebugg, are you ready to lose some of your money in Madden?"

"I'm always ready to beat yo' ass." Said Junebugg.

"Yeah. Well money talks little nigga.

Chapter 114

When Money and Red got to Shawanna's job, she was with a customer. But when she saw them, she smiled and waved to them. A few minutes later, when she was done with the customer. She walked over to them.

"What's up shorty?" Money said giving her a hug.

"Nothing. What ya'll doing?"

"We were just in the area and thought that we would come say hello."

"Aww. How sweet. Oh yeah. Hold on. Here are them shoes that ya'll want." She said as she went in the back of the store to get two boxes.

"That's what's up." Money said.

"Yeah. Good looking out." Red added.

"Well don't thank me until ya'll pay for them."

"How much are they?" Red asked.

"Two hundred dollars. But I'm gonna let ya'll use my family discount. So they will be thirty percent off."

"Aww shit. Look at my shorty hooking a nigga up." Money said.

"Yeah baby. I'll take care of you." She responded.

"Well since we are here. What time is your lunch break?"

"Actually it's in about ten minutes. But I can take it early. Why?"

Slumped

"Because I'm going to take my woman to lunch."

"Oh so I'm your woman now?" She got her purse and they picked Misty up. Then they all went to McDonald's for lunch.

"Can I help you sir?"

"Yeah, I need to speak with Shawanna." Slump said to the woman that works with her.

"Oh shit. You just missed her. She left like ten minutes ago with her boyfriend and his boy. I think that they were taking her to lunch."

"Oh! It's that right? Her boyfriend huh."

"Yeah. Or I mean I think that he was. But I could be wrong." She said. Hoping that she hadn't said the wrong thing.

"Well when she gets back. Could you tell her to call her brother? Please."

"Yeah. I'll do that." She said relieved that he was her brother and not somebody that she was fucking with.

"So what do ya'll have planned for tonight? Misty asked Red.

"Shit. Nothing I don't think. Why?"

"Because me and my girl planned on cooking for ya'll tonight."

"Oh yeah? Ya'll was going to make us dinner? That's what's up. I don't remember the last time that a woman cooked for me."

"Then you ain't been fucking with the right kind of woman."

"I guess not." Shawanna got up to go use the bathroom. But before she did, she told Money in his ear to come with her. He didn't have a problem with that. When they came back to the table, their food was there.

"Ya'll are some freaks." Misty said with a smile.

"Ain't nothing wrong with keeping your man pleased is there?" Shawanna asked Money.

Slumped

"Hell no!" Money said smiling. They ate their food then Money and Red dropped them both back off at work, twelling them that they would see them later. When Shawanna got back to work Linda her coworker said, "I didn't know that you had a brother?"

"Yeah. I got two. Why you say that?"

"Because one of them came by here like ten minutes after you left. And girl he was fine as hell. Why don't you hook a bitch up?"

"What did he say?" Shawanna asked her. Ignoring her last comment.

"He told me to tell you to call him when you got back from lunch." It had to be Slump. Because Lee young ass wasn't worried about anything other than Tanya's ass Shawanna thought.

"So what's up? Can a bitch get hooked up or what?" Linda asked.

"Girl, that's my older brother Jaylon. And he is getting married next month. If my sister-in-law found out about that nigga cheating, she would kill him and your ass too."

"Can't blame a bitch for trying though. Can you?" She said walking off to go help a customer.

Shit. Let me go and call this nigga. So he can quit worring me. Shawanna thought.

"So you don't know how to answer your phone now? Huh?" Slump asked.

"Damn nigga. You can't say hi first?" Shawanna replied.

"Hi. Now who the fuck you got taking you out to lunch and shit?"

"None of your business nigga. You ain't my daddy nigga. You are my brother. So stop trying to run my life."

"Oh, so now that you got a job. You are all grown now. Huh? And you don't need me anymore?"

"All I'm saying Jaylon is that I'm grown now. I ain't no little girl. And you need to stop treating me like one."

Slumped

"Yeah. Well as long as you are staying up in my shit. You are going to respect my rules."

"Well maybe I won't be staying in your house anymore."

"Oh so what you are going to do move in with some nigga you just met? And don't know shit about."

"And if I did it's my business. Look Jaylon. I have to get back to work and I might not be coming there tonight. In fact, I know I won't be. I will be staying at Misty's. So tell Momma K not to worry. I'm alright." She said hanging up the phone. She planned to take Misty up on her offer to be her roommate. Misty had been asking her for a while now. She always turned her down. But now she thought that it was time to get away from her crazy ass brother. She felt like a little kid waiting on recess. She watched the clock. As 4:30 p.m. came she was running out the store to go meet Misty. Who for once didn't take forever to pick her up.

"Hey girl." She said to Misty.

"What's up shorty?"

"So what are we gonna do first?"

"First we are going to the grocery store to buy dinner."

"But I don't know what we should cook."

"Steak bitch."

"How do you know they are going to want steak?"

"Girl all niggas like a big thick steak."

"I hope that you are right. Because if they don't. I'm blaming you."

"Bitch please. Anyhow I need to talk to you about something serious."

"Talk then bitch."

"Well you know how you been asking me to be your roommate and go half on the rent with you?"

"Well is it still good if I do that?"

"Hell yeah! It's cool. You know that you are my girl."

"Good. Because, I can't take my brother's shit anymore. That nigga done worked my last nerve."

"Just because you move in with me, doesn't mean that he is going to stop trying to play yo' daddy."

"I know. But at least now I can tell his ass to mind his own business."

"I heard that shit. But don't have his crazy ass popping up on no bullshit."

"He ain't. But enough about that nigga. Let's talk about you and Red."

"Oh girl, that nigga put it down last night."

"Uhh, I thought that the plan was to get them sprung? Not get sprung."

"Who said that I was sprung? I'm just saying that he had some good dick. And if his pockets are as deep as he was in my ass last night. Then there's not going to be any problems. And what about you?"

"Bitch I had that nigga calling my name, his momma name, and anything else that he could think of to call." They got to BelAir and got what they were going to cook for dinner. Then they went home to cook, get ready, and wait for Red and Money to get there. After they cooked and both took showers, Misty said, " Shawanna I know that you ain't trying to hear my bitching. And after this I don't have anything else to say. But I know that you didn't let that nigga go raw up in yo' shit."

"Bitch I ain't trying to have any kids."

"Bitch I ain't talking about you getting pregnant. That shit we can deal with or fix. I'm talking about Aids."

"Girl this nigga doesn't have Aids or nothing. Bitch are you crazy?"

"No hoe. I'm not crazy. I'm just being real."

"Well yes Ms. Thang. We used a condom. Shit girl, we used two or three of them bitches."

"Bitch you ain't the only one." Red and Money were knocking at the door about fifteen minutes later.

"That's them." Shawanna said excitedly.

"Damn bitch. Calm down. You act like you ain't just pull the nigga dick out your ass. And where ever else you let him put it at."

"Shit. He can put it whereever he want to, but in my ass. That's you with all that in the booty shit."

"Don't knock it until you try it." Misty opened the door for Red and Money.

"What's up ya'll?" Misty said.

"Shit. Hungry as a mother fucker." Red said with a smile on his face.

"Hell yeah. We are hungry. So I hope that ya'll ain't on no eating light shit. Because you know real niggas eat steaks and shit." Money added.

"See bitch. I told you." Shawanna said.

"What did you tell her Shorty?" Money asked.

"Shit. Why don't ya'll sit down at the table and find out?" Misty said.

"Yeah baby. Sit down and let me treat you like a king is supposed to be treated." Shawanna said.

"Oh shit. Did you hear that shit Red? A king nigga." Money said.

"More like the dark prince." Red said.

"Don't hate me nigga. Shit if I'm the king then you know that you are a king too nigga." Misty and Shawanna brought the food from the kitchen and sat it down on the table.

"That's what the fuck I'm talking about. Treat ya nigga like he mean something. What are those? T-bones, baked potatoes and salad? Shit, you feed a nigga like this every night. You don't have to worry about him leaving." Red said.

"Shit. All this shit will turn a cheater faithful." Money said.

"So that means that you are all mine then? Right?" Shawanna said.

"Yeah Shorty. You got me now. What are ya'll going to do? Make us look at the food or feed us?" Money said.

Chapter 115

"Calm down boy. Momma K told Slump. "How are you going to tell me to calm down ma? When you know just like I know that bitch Misty..."

"Watch your damn mouth boy when you are talking to me."

"My bad ma. But we both know that Misty isn't going to do anything. But have her ass all up in hella nigga faces and doing whatever."

"She is grown Jaylon."

"She is only eighteen."

"That's the point boy. She is eighteen. After all, What are you going to do? Go over there and fight the boy that she is up in there with? If that's what she is doing."

"Hell yeah. Beat his ass and then hers too. And if Misty have something to say. I'll whoop her ass too."

"Jaylon listen to yourself. Will you? Both of you are grown now. You are about to be married. Hell you got a child of your own to be worried bout. You can't keep saving your sister's ass. Shit. If you always there to catch her when she falls. How in the hell is she going to ever learn how to pick herself up? If she wants to run behind Misty and give her goodies to whomever. Whenever she feels like it. Then her staying here and you always on her back, ain't going to stop her from doing just that."

"Momma K is right Jylon. I know that's your sister. And since forever, you've been her older brother. As well as something like her father. But if she doesn't want to be here, then you making her is only going to push her farther away." Nicky said.

"So what I'm not supposed to do? Nothing then. Just say fuck it?"

"No I'm not saying that. All I'm saying is just stand back and respect what she decides to do. And if she needs you. Just be there for her."

"See I knew I liked you for a reason." Momma K said.

"So what both of ya'll are saying is just because her ass is eighteen or will be eighteen. I should let her throw her life away and end up pregnant by some nigga who is not going to be there."

"Well if that happens. You are not gonna have to worry about kicking her butt. Because if she haves a baby before she gets married. I'm going to kill her ass."

"Alright. We will do it your way for now. But if I run into her and this mystery nigga somewhere, I can't make any promises." Slump replied laughing.

Chapter 116

Friday June 13, 2012

"**M**an. What the fuck is taking you two niggas so long?" Stone asked Flip and Junebugg. "Nothing nigga. Damn. Shit its four o'clock in the fucking morning. Shit let a nigga wake up before you start bitching and shit. Fuck." Flip said."

"Don't make me fuck you up Flip. I told you niggas last night I was going to be here at four. And I told you to be ready. When I got here, you two little niggas are still fucking sleep." Stone said."

"Our bad big bro. Right after you and Lee left last night, some work popped up. And we got lost in the moment." Junebugg said.

"Shit. I don't know about no moment! I was lost in some pussy." Flip shouted.

"Now ya'll are running around trying to pack up some shit." Stone said as he rushed them.

"Man fuck it. I'll just buy what I need when I get there." Flip said dropping his bag.

"Yeah. Fuck it." Junebugg repeated.

"Well then. Ya'll come on. Shit." Flip and Junebugg both grabbed an extra three thousand dollars from the safe that they had hidden. And Slump told them that would be the reason why they wouldn't get their security deposit back.

"Fuck it. They can keep it." Flip said boasting as usual.

"Man. Just come on. Those two little niggas are riding with you." When they got to the parking lot, Lee rolled down the passenger window.

"Shit Flip. What have you done now?

"Man it's too early for that shit. That shit would not have happen if bro had listened to me last night when I packed the load in his garage. " Flip said.

"Nigga please. As much noise yo ass be making. Nobody would have gone to sleep. Now just shut yo ass up and get in so we can go. And I don't even want to hear anymore of your smart remarks." Stone sternly replied. Stone reminded Lee to tell Tanya to drive right. Because they were not trying to get pulled over. So then, Angel pulled off on to their trip. And sure enough, Tanya was cruising right behind her.

Chapter 117

Later that same day around 1:30 p.m. or 1:40 p.m., Tee sat in the passenger seat of Slump's car. They were in downtown Roseville.

"So what do you think?" Tee asked pointing off.

"About what my nigga? I still don't know what the fuck it is that I should be looking at." Slump replied.

"The building."

"Okay. So it is a big ass empty building. Nigga it is hella empty buildings out here. Why did you bring me out here to look at some fucking empty ass building?"

"Because nigga. That building is ours. I went through Vicky's friend to get it for me."

"For what?"

"For us nigga. Why are you looking at me like I'm crazy?"

"Nah. I already know your big muscle headed ass is crazy. This is my stupid look of you face."

"Alright. Look. Check this out. What's the one thing that Sacramento has a lot of?"

"Cops."

Slumped

"Ha. Ha. Ha. Nigga. Now let me finish. What's the one thing when you were younger that you couldn't wait until you was 21 years old to do? Well maybe not you. But normal little niggas."

"Oh. So I'm not normal?"

"Nigga if you are normal, then Popeye is allergic to spinach."

"Just get to the point Tee."

"The club nigga. All these young niggas and hot ass girls can't wait until they are old enough to go clubbing."

"So you are about to turn this building into a club?"

"Nope. We are about to turn this building into a club. But not just any club. The first 18 And Under Club."

"And some little nigga like Flip is going to come shoot the motherfucker up, on some dumb ass shit."

"Damn bro. Why you being so fucking negative? You always got to piss on a nigga's dreams."

"I ain't pissing on your dreams Tee. I'm just being real. Shit. You know how these little niggas get when they're on pills and drank."

"That's why there is not going to be any dranking and shit."

"Man how do you expect to stop that shit?"

"I don't expect to stop it. But they asses won't be coming in here high or drunk. Period. And they better be on their fly guy shit."

"Well it sounds like you got it all figured out. And you already know where I stand from the womb to the tomb. Whichever way the bullets fly. I got you."

"See that's what I was waiting to hear. Now let's get out of here before somebody sicks Johnny Law on our black asses."

Chapter 118

Across town, Jazz followed Munch to Carmichael and was parked on Little Oak Lane down from Sienna Vista apartments. She pretty much had his daily route down. She knew every Monday and Wednesday, he took his son to his karate class in Antolope on Watt Avenue. She knew every Friday, him and his wife took the money they made at Top Notch to the bank. And every spare minute he had, he spent it here at the big booty white girl's house. But not once had she seen him with Red or Money. It was starting to frustrate her because she didn't like hiding things from Tee and he was getting more and more suspicious of her daily store runs that took sometimes more than an hour. She was tired of lying to Tee.

"Fuck it. I'm gonna tell him everything tonight."

Chapter 119

They made it to Texas two and a half days later, pulling into Stone's driveway. It had been a little more than a year since Stone had been home and looking around, he wondered why he waited so long to come back.

"Damn baby. You own all this." Angel asked.

"Yeah. My grandpa left it to me."

Looking at the cars under the car cover, Flip asked. "Now which one is it?"

"The one under the gray cover."

"I think I been sitting on my ass too long because I can't feel it." Tonya said getting out of the Lexus.

Walking around the car to her, Lee slapped her on her ass.

"It's all still there."

"Boy you crazy."

"C'mon Lee. Let's unload this shit and I'll show you which room you and Tonya got."

"For sure, cousin. Man wake your sleepy ass up, Junebug." Lee said opening the back passenger door.

"Man I'm not sleep nigga. I was just resting my eyes."

"Well unrest them motherfuckers and help me with these bags.

"Where the fuck is Flip?"

"He's out back trying to see what a real glass house should look like. C'mon so you can see how a boss rides in the dirty." Stone said.

Slumped

"We want to see." Angel said.

"Shit speak for yourself. I need to wash my ass. A bitch feel like she been rolling around in the sand or something."

"The bathroom is the third door on the left."

"I'll find it." Everyone followed Stone out back where his cars were parked. Flip already pulled the car cover off the Chevy and was wiping the dust off it with an old rag.

"I know you gonna let me push this motherfucker around." Flip said.

"Maybe. But first, keep it real with me."

"About what?"

"So you wanna act dumb now huh lil' nigga."

"As of right now you got me. Your shit is clean as fuck."

"Come on. Follow me to the gas station." Stone said throwing Flip the keys.

"I'm riding with you Flip." Junebug said.

"And you ain't even seen my other toy." Stone said pulling the cover off his 1960 Super Sport Chevelle.

"I'll give you whatever you want for this motherfucker right here. Now this is a car. What is it, a 60? And I bet it got the big block 454 in it too." Junebug stated.

"What you know about cars?"

"I don't know shit about cars but I do know about this car. This is my dream car."

"If you're serious, I'll dump it to you." Stone said surprising everyone.

"Shit. Hell yeah I'm serious."

"Well ya'll gon' to the gas station. I'm gonna wait here." Lil Lee said.

"Nigga, you ain't slick. You trying to jump in that shower with Tonya's ass."

"Shit. I'm gonna jump into more than that."

"Oh boy, you so nasty." Angel said laughing.

"Well we'll be back in a minute."

"Shit cousin, take a few minutes." Lee said walking back toward the house as they left for the gas station.

Slumped

"Hey Mike. I ain't seen you in a while. Where you been hiding?" Old man Guss said coming out of the station's garage. He'd own it since Stone could remember.

"C'mon Guss. You know I don't run or hide from nobody. I've been in California with my future." Stone said pulling Angel close to him. "And that's my two brothers. My cousin and his girl are back at the house."

"So how ya'll like old Texas?"

"Don't know yet. Ya'll got anything cold in there to drink?"

"You got some money boy?"

"More than you know old man." Flip said pulling a wad of hundreds from his pocket.

"You know what Mike. There was a time when you were no bigger than that. And I'll be damned if that little sucker don't remind me of you. Come on son. I got a cold pop inside. They filled up both cars and headed back to the house just as Lee and Tonya finished a quickie.

"Anybody call Slump and tell him we are here."

"Shit. I knew I needed to do something." Stone said pulling out his phone.

Chapter 120

"So what is it we're doing Money?" Shawanna asked out of nowhere lying naked next to him in bed. "I don't know what you call it. But I call it having sex."

"No crazy man. I mean us. Me and you. What are we doing? Is it just good sex or something more?"

"I don't know. Is it?" Money asked.

"See that's what I'm talking about?"

"What?"

"Why is it every time I ask you something, you come back with a question?"

"Hey shorty. Why don't you just come on and say whatever it is you're trying to say. I'll just tell you if I can do it and we can go from there."

"Well, I'll be eighteen tomorrow and what I really want from you more than anything is for you to be my man. Not just some nigga who pops up to get some pussy or his dick sucked but the man in my life. I want to be your woman. Not your bitch or your shorty. I want to be a priority. Not just something to do."

"Damn, how long it take you to come up with that?"

"See. You never take what I say seriously. It's always a game with you."

Slumped

"Well check me out shorty. I done been from here to the fucking moon and everything started off cool, but in the end, it's only about what you can get. But motherfuckers never want to give..."

"So you think that I'm only after your money?"

"Well then, if that's how you feel."

"See you later. Bye. Fake niggas do fake shit. And sweetheart, money can't buy a real bitch." For a while, those fourteen words played repeatedly inside Money's head, before he got up from the bed and went to the bathroom. Shawanna was in the shower and had the whole bathroom steamed up. Money stood there for a minute admiring her beauty through the doors. "Can you hear me?"

"Perfectly."

"Could you be loyal to me and nothing else?"

"Nigga, I've already walked away from my family to be with you. My momma tripping. My fucking brother tripping. So to answer your question. Yeah nigga, I could and I have." She said opening the shower door.

"Shorty, you be loyal to me and I'll die being loyal to you." Money said stepping in the shower.

"No matter what?"

"No matter what."

Chapter 121

Over the next few days, life couldn't have been better. Tee and Slump worked around the clock hiring contractors, designers, paying electricians, and plumbers. The others were still in Texas doing the damn thing and the money was already starting to pile up. Money had taken Shawanna to Jamaica for her eighteenth birthday and treated her to whatever her heart desired. Meanwhile, Momma K and Nicki made all the last minute plans for their wedding, which was only a week away.

Chapter 122

"**M**an, I ain't never going back to Sac. The money is better out here. The pussy is better. Shit nigga, even the food is better. And I ain't even had to push nobody's shit back yet." Flip said.

"Bro, you know you got real life issues, right?" Junebug said.

"And you don't?"

"Yeah, you do got a good point. But we still need one thing."

"And what's that?"

"Weed nigga. Because this tree bark these niggas be smoking ain't the business."

"Yeah, you ain't never lied."

"What ya'll in here talking about?" Lee asked walking into the only room no one slept in. They called it the vault because it was the room with the money.

"Shit, nothing but the tree bark these country niggas have the nerve to call weed."

"I know. That's why I'm gonna try to get a few pounds and bring it back."

"And who you gon' get it from?"

"That white boy."

"I wish. That cracker had fire."

"Anyway so what's up. Ya'll ready?"

Slumped

"Ain't nothing else going on." The three of them planned to go to the mall in Lufkin, Texas to buy a wedding gift.

"So who driving? Because I know I'm not."

"I'll drive." Junebugg said. He gave Stone ten stacks for the Chevelle and still owed seven more.

"Well shit. Let's go." Lee stated.

Chapter 123

On the day of the wedding, everyone was there but Shawanna. She had called from Cancun to give her congratulations and to tell her the surprise gift should arrive any minute. She explained how her flight was delayed and how she was sorry she couldn't make it and how she hoped her and Jaylon loved the gift.

"I can't believe that girl."

"It's alright Momma K."

"No it's not. That little cow knows that she was supposed to be here. Jaylon is never gonna forgive her for this. How could she be so selfish as to miss ya'll wedding?"

"It's not her fault Momma K. Her flight was delayed."

"Chile couldn't lie to save her life. Ain't no flight late. She just running behind that boy, whoever he is, and she ain't worried about nobody but herself. But you know what?"

"What?"

"She doesn't even matter. This ya'll day and ain't nothing gonna mess it up. Look at you. My son sure did win when he met you."

"I won too."

The boys made it back from Texas and they all clowned around with Slump.

"I can't believe this nigga up in here in a tuxedo and shit." Tee said.

"I know. I thought just him getting married was unbelievable, but a tux. I done seen it all now." Stone said smiling.

"But fuck what ya'll talking about. I look good. You niggas is just hating."

"Nah, we ain't hating. It's on you if you wanna look like a fly ass Poindexter." Lee and Junebugg started laughing.

"Go ahead. Laugh and make jokes. But don't forget, one day, ya'll gonna be the ones in the tux and payback is a bitch."

"I ain't never getting married." Flip said seriously.

"Lil nigga. You barely started fucking."

"Shit, I been fucking since I started walking. And I'm gonna keep on fucking. But now you stuck with the same coochie for the rest of your life." Just then, Momma K came in the room. Everyone got quiet.

"Oh, look at my baby. You look so good. It seems like only yesterday that I had to pick out your school clothes and make sure your socks matched." She said with tears running down her face.

"Aw, come on momma. Why you gotta go there?"

"I'm just saying boy. Standing here looking at you all grown up and about to be married makes me feel like an old woman. Anyway, I was just coming to see if you were ready to get this on the road."

"Yeah, I'm ready. Is my sister here yet?"

"No, but she called and apologized, she…"

"But, it don't matter. You're here and all my brothers are here." On the inside, he was really hurt that she wasn't there.

"C'mon big bro. Don't let her mess your day up. Forget about her. You know how stupid she is."

"Well. I'm gonna go tell the pastor we are ready to start." Momma K said. Twenty minutes later, the couple was standing at the altar saying their 'I Do's'. The wedding was a hit. They danced, toast, and opened the gifts people bought for them. When they left the church, a pink Escalade was parked at the curb. He kissed her and told her the gift was from him. A kind of thank you for showing him what love was.

Slump and Nicky spent the next ten days honeymooning in Las Vegas; making love, gambling, and making more love, thinking about nothing other than each other. Towards the end of their honeymoon, Slump had a strange feeling that everything had been going too well. Not knowing at the same time he was feeling that, Jazz was telling Tee her real objective.

Chapter 124

"So you have known for almost a month now where he laid his head every night and instead of telling me, you kept it to yourself hoping he led you to the other two niggas?"

"You make it seem like…"

"No I don't make it seem like shit, Jazz. What if he did lead you to them, huh? What then? What would you have done or tried to do, huh? Tell me that? Or better yet, tell what you would have done if he found out you were following him and set you up, huh? What then? You saw what he did to Vicki. What do you think he would have done to you? Not to mention the other two. We both know what happened last time."

"I'm sorry Tee. But no one knows what it's like, how it felt to go through that, how it feels every time the person you loves touches you. I just wanted to put it all behind me. I don't wanna be scared that one day they will pop up again." After hearing her say that, all his anger left. All he wanted to do was protect her. He wanted her to know she didn't have to be scared anymore. He would never let anything or anyone hurt her again. Jazz didn't know it, but he always blamed himself for what happened to her. And he still had a secret of his own. One he prayed she would never find out.

Slumped

"Jazz, please don't go looking for them anymore. Let me take care of it. I don't know how I would go on living if something happened to you. Let me handle it baby, please." He said with tears running down his face holding her hand. "I promise. I won't go off on my own anymore. But you got to promise me for Porshea. That when you do get them that I get to watch."

"I promise Jazz and I promise that I will lay their bodies at your feet. Now tell me everything that you know about Munch." For the next hour, Jazzmine had told Tee everything that Shawn had told her. And all she found out on her own. Sparing no details.

Chapter 125

It had been two days since Jazzmine told Tee about Munch. And he couldn't think about nothing else. It seemed like it took forever for today to get here. But it was finally here. He had called Slump and told him he would meet him and Nicky at the airport. Because he needed to talk to him. Now he sat parked in front of Sac Internationals American Airlines waiting on them.

"What's up my nigga? What's up sis?" He said giving them a hug.

"Tired and ready to go home and relax." Nicky said.

"I know that's right. So how did you like Sin City?"

"I had a good time."

"Shit you better have. As much money as you lost." Slump said.

"Shut up boy because you told me I had no limit. Don't start crying now."

"You should have seen her eyes Tee. Taking hits at Black Jack with twenty showing."

"Aw, come on sis. I know you ain't done no shit like that?"

"Just once."

"So what's been up Tee?" Slump asked once they were on the highway. He could feel there was something on Tee's mind.

"You know. Same shit. Different flies."

"Have you talked to Stone and them?"

"Matter of fact, I talked to Junebugg last night. He said everything was good but other than that, you know, just taking care of business as usual." From Tee's look and tone, he could tell something was wrong. He had to hurry and get away from Nicky to find out what was going on.

Once they made it to the house, Tee spoke to Momma K and little Jadda. He then motioned for Slump to follow him outside.

"What's up nigga? Why you acting so funny?"

"Bro, I don't even know how to put it in words, so I'm just gonna show you." They got in Tee's truck as he explained the best he could.

"Man, I thought you had something bad to tell me. This is great. Now we can finally get this shit over with." Slump said laughing.

"I don't think it's that easy. Jazz said she didn't see them one time when following Munch. We still don't know where them other two niggas are hiding." They just made it to the street Munch lived on.

"So that's the house right there, huh."

"Yeah, that's it. And I'm sure because I watched him pull in last night."

"I'm surprised you didn't get out and gun his ass down right there."

"You don't know how bad I wanted to."

"I think I do and to be honest, if it were me, I would have."

"Where would the fun in that be? I'm gonna make him beg me to kill him when I get him and now that I know where he lives, I'm gonna make him sweat a little."

"What you got in mind?"

"Well we know he got something going with the white girl."

"What white girl."

Slumped

"Oh I forgot to tell you that part?"

"Nah, I think you left that out on purpose." Slump said with a smirk.

"Well, he fucked over two women that we loved or had love for us and I think we should pay him back."

"I understand how you feel but I ain't into all that weird ass shit."

"I'm not saying we do the same thing. I'm just saying, you kill my dog, I kill your cat." Tee said, explaining what it meant on the ride home.

Chapter 126

"I didn't think that shit would move so quickly." Stone said as they all sat in the vault counting money.

"I wish it did last a little longer because I ain't ready to go back yet. I'm having too much fun out here." Flip said.

"I feel you." Junebugg said.

"I'm having a good time too. But ain't no place like Saktown." Lee said.

"Are you serious? We would have never seen this kind of money this quick unless we took it. Most likely, we would have had to kill somebody for it. Shit since we been out here, we ain't killed nobody."

"Oh yeah, what about that stunt you pulled the other day at that fucking club or did you forget?" Lee asked.

"We didn't kill anybody. I didn't say we didn't' fuck nobody up."

"We?" Junebugg asked.

"Shit. We saved that hoe ass nigga. He should be thanking us. That nigga had it coming. Getting at me like I'm some bitch ass nigga or something."

"Lil' nigga. All he did was ask you a question?" Stone said.

"I know."

"Since we talking about it, what the fuck did he ask you?"

Slumped

"That nigga asked if I was old enough to hang with the big boys and how my mommy would feel about it. So I showed him I was old enough and didn't care what my momma thought."

"So you pistol whipped him like that in front of all of Texas. Yeah my nigga, you crazy." Lee said.

"The nigga shouldn't have questioned my gangster. But really made me mad was that bitch ass nigga bleeding all over my fucking gun. That shit is brand new."

"So what do ya'll want to do that now that the work is gone?" Stone asked.

"Man shit. It really doesn't matter to me." Junebugg said. They all looked at Lee, who was the only one who hadn't answered.

"Well if we are going to re-up, we gotta go back to Cali anyway. So I'll tell ya'll what I'll do then."

"Nigga you going to do whatever Tonya want you to do." Flip said then sang lines from T-Pain's *Sprung.*

Throwing a bundle of fifties at him. "Shut that shit up. Don't hate on me because you too crazy to get a good bitch."

"Nah, I just ain't found one crazy enough I like. But I still gets mine nigga." They finished counting the money and talking shit to each other about any and everything.

Chapter 127

"All we have been doing since we came out here is spending and not making nothing back. And now that we are fucking with these broads, we are spending more cash." Red said.

"So what are you saying? You ain't feeling ol' girl?"

"Not half as much as you digging your Shorty. To be honest, I'm getting tired of her and your ass ain't making it no easier, always buying Shorty something."

"Well shit my nigga, what I do, and what you do with your chick is your business."

"I'm just saying. We need to figure something out because this shit is getting old and my cousin is on some other shit. Half the time, I don't know what he got on his mind."

"Yeah after that shit with the dog, I don't know about him. He is acting like he doesn't even care about them niggas no more."

"I know and he keeps his head so far up that white girl's ass."

"Shit, she sure got enough of it."

"She do, don't she?"

"I'm just saying, I'm ready to get up out of here and go back east somewhere where we can get our cash like we know how. I mean we don't got nothing tying us to this motherfucker anyway. Well, at least I don't."

"So what you saying is you are ready to go home now."

"I mean we have been gone from D.C. for too long. I think it's time we showed our faces and took back what is ours."

"That's the last place I'm going back to. I don't care how much time passed. We can go anywhere but there."

"Yeah well we need to figure something out. And we need to do it fast."

"What's the rush? It's not like we will be broke anytime soon."

"I don't know. I just got this feeling, that's all. And something just don't feel right." They'd been parked by the river.

"Nigga fire up one of those blunts so I can get a feeling too." Money said starting the car.

"Say what you want to my nigga. But I'm telling you something just ain't right."

Back at the apartment, the girls were talking.

"Girl you got lucky with Money."

"Why you say that?"

"Because bitch, he spoils your ass with everything. Red on the other hand, be acting like a bitch. He be asking for too much if 'she' say 'she' hungry. Lately I don't even like being around his ass."

"I've noticed. You sure have been doing a lot of overtime."

"Well shit. Ain't no telling when these niggas decides to leave."

"Shit, Money ain't never gon' leave me."

"Yeah, that's what his mouth says."

"No bitch. That's what I know."

"And how do you know that, huh? Ya'll only been fucking for a few months."

Slumped

"I just know. Alright. Don't ask me how or why. I just do, okay."

"Yeah whatever bitch. Just don't come crying to me cuz all I'm gonna do is tell you I told you so."

"Oh I ain't worried about that. I know my baby love me."

"Shit bitch. He loves the pussy. And I ain't mad at you. Do your thing girl. I'm just saying be careful. I don't want to see your ass get hurt. I'm gonna be the one up in here drying your tears."

"Awwww, you would dry my tears?"

"Yeah, laugh now. Cry later bitch." Then they heard the front door open. Shawanna jumped up to go to her man before Misty could say anything else.

Chapter 128

"**S**o you ain't heard from Shawanna?" Slump asked Momma K.

"No and I done called the girl and left her messages and everything. She don't never call me back. She just sends a text message, talking about sorry she missed my call. She has just been busy working and stuff. But not to be worried. She is okay and she loves everybody."

"Yeah well she is grown now. So she ain't my problem."

"Boy cut that out. You know you worried about her just as much as I am."

"No I'm serious momma. I'm done worrying about her ass." Just as soon as those words left his mouth, he knew he didn't mean them.

"Ya'll was always fighting and getting on each other's nerves when ya'll was young and ya'll always will. Now hush boy and leave me alone. You making me miss my stories."

"I don't know why you and Nicky even waste your time on that bullshit."

"Hush Jaylon so I can watch my bullshit in peace and quiet."

"If Nicky asked tell her I went to meet Tee and will be home later." He said grabbing his car keys. Not that she would even notice until them damn soaps were off anyway.

Slumped

"That girl ain't worried about you boy. Now would you leave or just leave me the hell alone."

"Momma!" He said walking out the door.

"What?"

"Nothing!" He said laughing and closed the door, still hearing her talk shit. He went to meet Tee at their club, which they named, Young Bucks, since it was for the younger crowd. By the time he made it, Tee just finished talking to the interior decorator.

"So what it's looking like?" Slump said as Tee met him.

"Shit this time next month, we will be in the club business." Over the last month and a half, they spent over a half million dollars for the club's grand opening. But truth be told, working on the club was the only thing that kept their minds off Munch.

"So have you talked to them?" Tee asked.

"Yeah, they called earlier this morning when they got back. I told them we would slide through later. I still can't believe they ran through thirty kilos in less than a month."

"Shit, let's Stone tell it. The work been gone. Those little niggas just didn't want to come back yet."

"Texas, eat the chicken, drink water, and get some pussy. You ain't never gonna wanna leave. They said they had a surprise for us too."

"Oh yeah. I can't wait to see what it is." Tee got into the Audi with Slump.

"I need to make a quick stop first."

"Do you bro. I'm just riding." About twenty minutes or so, they pulled into the parking lot of Sunrise Mall.

"So you still ain't heard from her yet?"

"Huh? No and earlier Momma K said she hasn't either. So I just wanna run up in here and see what her problem is."

"Shit me and Lil' Tee both needs some new shoes anyway. So you just saved me a trip." With her back to them, Shawanna didn't see them.

"Oh girl, that fine ass brother of yours and some big buff nigga just walked in."

"What! Oh shit. Here we go. What's up ya'll." She said walking to them. Slump looked at her as if she hadn't said anything.

"Shit, just need to get me and my lil' man some shoes. I think I see some I like over there." Tee said walking away from them staring at each other.

"So what's up? You don't know how to call nobody or something?"

"I've been busy."

"Yeah I bet."

"Jaylon, don't start no shit. Please."

"Nah, you ain't gotta worry about that. It's your life and you're grown now, right?"

"Look, my bad for missing your big day but I did send ya'll a gift."

"Nah, don't even trip. It's cool. I ain't here to start no shit. I'm just here to tell you to call Momma K because she is worried about you."

"I'll call tonight when I get off."

"Yeah alright. Whatever." Slump said walking towards Tee. "I'm gonna be waiting in the car, my nigga."

"Alright. I'm bout' to pay for these and I'll be right out there." Slump walked out, not looking back.

"I don't know what your problem is and I don't even wanna hear it but that nigga that just left, he will be there for you when your so-called boyfriend ain't." Tee paid for his shoes and left the store.

"She's gonna have to learn the hard way, my nigga. And you're just gonna have to let her." Tee said outside the car as Slump smoked a blunt. Slump nodded his head as they got in the car. While they were getting inside, Money was headed in the mall to take Shawanna to lunch. They never saw him and he never saw them but they were almost close enough to touch.

Chapter 116

"**D**amn. It smells like weed and feet up in here." Tee said as they walked into Flip's apartment.

"See I keep telling you that your fucking feet stink nigga." Junebugg stated.

"So what. Deal with it."

"No wonder you ain't got a fucking girlfriend." Slump said.

"I bet with the money we got now, a bitch will suck my dirty toes."

Lee came out the bathroom, gave his brother, and Tee a hug.

"Damn Flip, put your fucking shoes back on."

"You know what. Fuck all you motherfuckers. This is my shit, and if I wanna sit around here with funky feet then that's what I'm gonna do. If you don't like it, then the same door you niggas walked in, you can walk out."

"Damn Flip!" Stone said walking in the door. Everybody started laughing, including Flip. "Did ya'll show them already?"

"Hell no! We ain't had a chance to. The only thing these niggas worried about is my damn feet."

"Well you need to do something about that lil' bro because seriously, them motherfuckers on hit."

"Alright. Alright." Flip said putting on his shoes.

"That's crazy. You ain't even gonna take a shower with your lil' grimey ass, is you?" Slump said.

"It sure is nice to be back home where everybody loves me so much. Now I wanna see what ya'll say when I show you what we brought back with us." Flip stated. Flip went the safe and came back with two duffel bags. He handed one to Slump and Tee.

"Surprise. You smell me now."

"How much?" They asked looking in the bag.

"$855,000. Now I'm bout' to go wash my papered up grimey ass."

"Shit, throw those shoes and socks away." Lee said.

"Ha ha ha, nigga."

"Ya'll did this in thirty days?" Slump asked Stone.

"Less and I didn't do shit. Those three did."

"So what's up with this club or whatever it is Stone been telling us about. And when does it open?" Lee asked.

"Yeah, you know we gotta be the flyest young niggas up in that junt." Junebugg added. They smoked a few blunts and exchanged stories about the club and the trip.

"Well now that we got all the fun shit out the way. We got something serious we need to get at ya'll about. It will affect every one of us if it doesn't go right."

"Ahh, so fresh and so clean. What I miss?" Flip said coming out the shower.

"Nothing. You're just in time."

"Just tell me where that nigga stay and I'll push that nigga shit back. On me." Flip said angry after the situation was explained.

"All you gotta do is tell us what you want done and it's done bro." Lil' Lee said.

"What about them other two niggas. That's who I want." Junebugg asked.

"That's the thing. We don't know. That's the only reason Munch is still alive." Tee stated.

Slumped

"Didn't ya'll say something about a white bitch?" Stone stated.

"Yeah and I was just about to get to that. I don't know how any of ya'll feel when it comes to a bitch so I'll understand if you feel some kind of way."

"Hold up. Hold up. Are you asking if we scared to push her shit back too? If you are, then nobody needs to answer because this nigga right here will take God to war if he crossed anyone in this room and I put my life on that shit righ there." For a minute, no one said anything but they all felt like Flip.

"Why don't we get to the point and stop all this beating around the bush shit." Lee said looking at the men in the room.

"Yeah do we get the bitch or what?"

"I think we're gonna have to, even if it's only to send a message." Tee said.

"But if ya'll know where he lays his head, why not just get him and skip the bitch." Stone asked.

"Yeah. He might not even care about the white girl anyway." Junebugg said.

"The white girl is only bait. She is just the cheese on the rattrap. But his wife, she will be the reason he gives up the other two niggas." Tee stated.

"At least that is what we're hoping. One way or another, this nigga dies. He has done too much already and for some reason I think that when they hear about him, those other two niggas will do what they do best and run." Stone added.

"Well this is one time that I hope that you are wrong." Junebugg said looking at Tee. That night after Tee and Slump left. Stone and the rest of the crew stayed and made plans of their own.

"I don't know about ya'll, but to me Tee and Slump's heart just don't seem to be in it like they use to." Stone said.

"What are you talking about?" Lee asked.

"I'm saying that Slump is married now and Tee has his son to take care of. I know that both of them are cold-hearted killers. But they got too much to lose now. Personally, I think we owe them. No, let me change that. I think I owe them my life and then some. For all they have done for me. Because before I hooked up with them I was just a broke country boy, barely getting by."

"Shit. Before I met those niggas. I didn't have shit. No place to sleep. Shit I was eating out of the trashcans. Now look at me. It's all because of them. Never again do I have to worry about anything. Since as far back as I can remember for the first time I feel like I have a family. If anyone of ya'll bring this shit up I'm going to kill you." Flip said crying.

"Yeah right nigga. We love your funky feet ass too." Junebugg said.

"My whole life I've looked up to my brother. Wanting to be just like him. To walk and talk just like him. I've always wanted him to look at me as an equal and not just as a little brother. He has always been my protector and now I've have the chance to protect him. Shit. I will kill Munch, his wife, his bitch, and his kids. Because I know without a doubt at all, he wouldn't think twice about doing it for me." Lee stated.

"Well looks like we all feel the same way about what needs to be done. The only thing left to do now is, get it done, and enjoy spending some of this money." Stone said.

"I still can't believe that shit earlier though." Lil' Lee said trying to lighten the mood.

"What shit?" Flip asked.

"The way that your damn feet smelled." Lil' Lee shot back at him.

"Yeah lil' bro. The first thing that you need to do when this shit is all over is to burn those motherfuckers." Stone said.

"I knew wasn't gonna last long. It always has to be me. Why does it always have to be me? I know. I know because it's always me doing something." Flip stated as he started to pull his shoes off.

"Don't do it Flip. Stop. What are you doing Flip?" They asked.

"Fuck ya'll niggas." Flip replied as he looked at everyone with smirks on their faces.

Chapter 117

A	t home after a long week of running from one place
	to another, getting all the last minute papers filed and
	signed by all the right officials for Club Young
Bucks' grand opening in two weeks. Not to mention all the
different vendors who would supply all the food and drinks
for the big night. Tee had vendors coming from Coca-Cola
and Snapple. Momma K and a few of the women that she
played Bingo with, had said instead of having food vendors
that they would do all of the cooking on the spot as it was
being ordered.

"Now you know ain't no cooking like momma's
cooking!" Momma K said smiling thinking of how she had
conned him into it. He had all of the hottest local rappers
coming as well as a rap off contest. The winner would be
receiving a thousand dollars. He had a drop it like its hot
contest as well. It is scheduled for all of the young ladies who
wanted to show off their ass on the dance floor. Now finally
after all that running around, he was laid out on the couch
falling asleep. There was a breaking news alert on the
television. At first, he didn't think anything of it. But when he
saw Alicia's picture flash on the screen his phone began to
ring. When he answered it, Slump was telling him to turn on
his TV.

"I'm already watching it."

Oh my God! That's the clothing store that his wife works
in." Jazzmine said.

Slumped

Whose wife?" Tee asked. Then the newscaster answered all of their questions. Saying:

This is Channel 3 live outside of Topnotch Clothing Store. Where witnesses say that this woman, now identified as twenty-four year old Alicia Smith. She came in demanding that the store's owner call her husband and tell him to come to the store. When the owner refused, Smith pulled out an automatic handgun, out of a duffel bag that she was carrying. She then shot the owner at point blank range. Killing her instantly. Witnesses say that Smith then turned the gun on herself. The officers say that is in critical condition, and that they do not have any more information at this time.

"Man I know what you are thinking. But it's not your fault. She did what she felt that she had to. It's not your problem anymore." Tee said.

"Yeah. I know. But still I can't help but feel like I had played a part in it." Slump said.

"Yeah. Well don't. It's all part of the game. And now you don't owe her anything. And if you did then ya'll are even now."

"Yeah. I guess that you are right."

"Well don't guess nigga. Know. And know that you did all you could. She pushed you away. So it's all on her now."

"So what's up with the grand opening?" Slump asked changing the subject.

"Shit. We are all ready to go."

"That's what I'm talking about. We are businessmen now my nigga. Shit, we are bout to be the number one hot spot. My nigga ain't no looking back from here."

"From the bottom to the top my nigga. Hey Slump?"

"What's up Tee?"

"Forget about her. Worry about your family. Now that is all that matters."

"I'm good my nigga."

"Alright then. I'll hit you up later."

Slumped

"Aight then. Later."

Chapter 118

"I know that I should have killed that fucking bitch. I fucking knew it. I should have stuck my gun up that punk ass bitch's pussy. Instead of that damn curling iron, and blew the top of her fucking head off. Snake ass bitch. I hope that bitch is still alive so I can kill her myself." Munch said to Red and Money. Pacing back and forth in the living room of the white girl's apartment. Munch was looking for something to take his frustration out on. But then he turned to Red and Money and said, "Where the fuck have ya'll been?"

"Look cousin. We are family and all, but I'm not one of your little workers." Red said as he stood up.

"C'mon Red. Let's get up out of here before somebody says or does something that they will regret later." Money said without hesitating.

"Hey my dude. For what it is worth. I'm sorry for your lost." Red said before walking out of the house with Money after staring at Munch for a few seconds.

"I'm done. I'm out of here. Fuck this shit." Red said once they got into the car.

"Yeah. I feel you. I think that you are doing the right thing by leaving. Family doesn't kill family."

"That nigga ain't family anymore. And the next time that I see him. If I ever do again. My aunt's son or not. One of us is going to die." Red said with a look that Money knew that he was dead serious. Flip and Lee were parked in the back of the apartments. And they never saw Red and Money leave. But as soon as Munch came out an hour later, they saw him.

Chapter 119

They had been parked in Tanya's Lexus. And the dark tint on the windows would never have let Munch see inside the car. Even if he tried to look.

"Look at him. Like he don't have a care in the world. I should do him right now." Flip said.

"No. We are going to follow him and see where he goes. We need to find them other two niggas." Lee said. Pulling out behind Munch, but staying at least a car behind him. It didn't take long before he pulled into the Target on Madison Avenue. He got over in the passenger seat and a white girl got into the driver seat of the Benz. Then they drove off. Once they got onto the freeway, Flip called Stone. He wished that he had never made the call. Stone had told him not to follow him because it was too hot.

"He wants us to come to his house. He said don't follow that fat ass nigga. Because he said that it was too hot where he was going. He said that he would explain it when we get there." Flip said. Lee got off the freeway, turned around, and went to meet Stone.

"This shit had better be good. We had that bitch ass nigga." Flip said.

"And we will have him again. But where he was going, is going to be crawling with cops." Stone replied.

"What are you talking about?" Lee asked.

Slumped

"Alicia's ass has flipped out, went to where his wife's store, and blew that bitch head off in front of everybody inside the store. Then she shot herself."

"Damn it. That's good news. Lucky I didn't do it. What?" Flip said as Stone and Lee just looked at his crazy ass.

"You're crazy Flip. Did you know that?" Lee asked.

"Yeah I know. Now tell me something that I don't know."

"Well did you know that you were stupid as a motherfucker too?" Stone as he laughed.

"You are damn right. I know. STUPID MOTHERFUCKING CRAZY. But I can count, add, and subtract. And I know now, that's one less bullet that I got to waste proving my point.

"And what point is that?" Lee asked him.

"That I will kill any and everything that a nigga loves most. That's if he ever crosses me or my niggas." Flip replied as he stopped smiling. Both Stone and Lee knew without a doubt what he said was true. Because they felt the same fucking way that he did.

Chapter 120

"Stupid, fat motherfucker." Red said.

"Man are you still letting that shit fuck with your mentally?" Money asked taking a bite of his Big Mac. They were at the MacDonald's on Northgate Blvd.

"I ain't letting it fuck with me."

"Then what's it doing to you? Because from over here it sure looks like you got something on your brain."

"I just can't believe the way that nigga got at me like he just Don Juan or somebody."

"I know that's your family and all, but…"

"You are my family. That nigga is lucky that he is still alive." Red said interrupting him.

"Yeah. Well you what them old niggas be saying. *Friends will get you killed.*"

"And your family will make you want to kill them." Red said finishing Money's remark. They ate the rest of their food and left. They stopped by the liquor store, grabbed a box of Phillies, and a fifth of XO before heading to the apartment they stayed in with Misty and Shawanna.

Chapter 121

"So Mr. Jordan. You and Ms. Smith had a past affair. In which you had broke off to reconcile with your wife." The black detective asked Munch.

"Yeah. Something like that."

"So about how long ago was the break up?"

"A little over a year ago."

"Well are you aware of Ms. Smith being raped and sodomized a few months back?"

"Yeah. I went and saw her in the hospital a couple of times. Just as a friend. You know. I just can't believe that she would do something like this to me." Munch answered playing the innocent role.

"Well love sometimes makes us all a little crazy at times."

"Well if that is all officer. I have to get home to my son so I can explain to him why his mother won't be coming home tonight or any other night for that matter."

"Well Mr. Jordan if there is anything else I know how to contact you. And again I'm sorry for your loss."

"Yeah me too." Munch said walking off. He thought to himself that he was going to end up killing that bitch eventually anyway.

"Well I guess now you might as well go to my house. Since now we know that the wife is not going to be coming home no time soon." Munch told Amber the white girl, as he got back into the car laughing.

"Alright baby." She said as she thought, if his money wasn't so long, that she would get as far away from that nut as possible.

Chapter 122

"Come on Melvin. Stop acting like that." Shawanna said calling Money by his government name.
"Stop acting like what?"
"Like you are acting." Every since Money and Red came through the door. They had been smoking weed and drinking. Money had been following Misty's ass with his eyes every time that she moved or got up to do anything.

"Aww. Come on Shorty. There's nothing wrong with looking." Money said.

"Yeah. You know that it ain't no fun if the homies can't have none." Red said laughing.

"And what the fuck is that suppose to mean? Shawanna asked.

"I think that ya'll done had enough of this." Misty said picking up the bottle of XO.

"Bitch you are cute and all, but don't get fucked up touching shit that don't belong to you." Money said as he snatched the bottle out of her hand.

"Nigga you are up in my shit. So let's get that shit straight right now. Misty runs this shit not Red or Money."

"Aww girl he just playing." Shawanna said as she was trying to keep things from blowing up.

"Mind your business Shorty. Bitch I don't know who you thought I was. But I am not him. And as far as running something. You need to run your ass up in your room before I run this Jordan up your ass." Money said.

Slumped

"Nigga you ain't gonna do…." Misty said as for she couldn't finish her statement Because of the bottle broke across her head.

"Nigga are you crazy or something? I think that you killed her." Shawanna said pushing Money back and bending down towards Misty, and trying to stop the blood from gushing out of her forehead.

"That bitch ain't dead. And how the fuck are you going to stop the blood with your fucking hands. Go get a towel or something. With your stupid ass." Money said.

"Who the fuck is you calling stupid nigga? You crazy motherfucker." Shawanna said.

"Watch your mouth Shorty before I have to put my hands on you."

"Fuck you nigga. You don't scare me. My brother will break yo ass off in if you ev…."

"If I what? Huh. If I what bitch?" Money said chocking her. He had pinned her up against the wall. She was grabbing at his hands trying to loosen his grip enough to get some air.

"Oh what, your ass can't breathe? My bad." Money said letting her go as she fell to the floor.

"Get out! Get the fuck out nigga." Shawanna said. Before Money could do anything else Red grabbed his arm saying, "Fuck these hoes family. Let's get up out of here." At first Money just looked down at Red's hand on his arm.

"Clean this shit up. I will be back." Money said to Shawanna as if nothing happened.

"No you won't. Don't you ever come back nigga." Now Misty regained consciousness and was moaning in pain. Trying to sit up. Shawanna rushed back to her girl's side crying.

"You are going to be alright girl. And Money you are going to wish that you never touched me or my girl." Shawanna said.

"Yeah. Whatever. Like I was saying. Clean this shit up. I'll be back and I don't give a fuck what ya'll tell the cops.

But my nigga's name or mine better not come up." Money said.

"Fuck the police. I'm going to have you killed. Bitch ass nigga. You and your fucking flunky pulling you out the door." Misty said fully aware of what happened. By now, the neighbors in the apartment next door came out to be nosey. They looked at both Red and Money.

"Come on Money. Let's be up outta here before those people get here." Red said. Misty now had a towel to her head that was already covered with her blood. She was standing in the door screaming at Money and Red's backs.

"You are dead nigga. You hear me. Your ass is dead. Bitch I'm the one that's bleeding. Why is your ass crying?" Misty said.

"I'm pregnant." Shawanna said.

"What?"

"You heard me. I'm pregnant. Now what am I going to do?" Two and a half hours and nine stitches later, Misty and Shawanna sat in a hotel room that they had decided to check into. They were not going back to the apartment because they were afraid that the fellas would come back and get in. Because they had keys to the apartment. So until they changed the locks, they were going to stay in the rented room. It was either that or go to her brother's house. And they damn sure weren't ready to deal with all of the extra shit right now.

"So how long have you been knowing?" Misty asked Shawanna.

"Been knowing what?" She replied.

"Bitch don't play dumb. How long has your ass been knowing that you were pregnant by that fucking psycho?"

"For about three weeks now. What am I going to do Misty? What am I going to do?"

"I can't believe your ass. I told and kept telling your ass to use a fucking condom."

"I know. I should have listened."

Slumped

"Well you didn't. So now what are you going to do?"

"I can't kill my baby Misty. I've been thinking about it since I first found out. But I can't kill my baby. I just can't."

Well I know that you ain't about to keep fucking with that crazy ass nigga."

"Hell no. And I'm going to have my brother fuck his ass up too."

"Girl if you tell Jaylon about what happened today, you know that he is going to kill that nigga. Right?"

"That's why I'm not going to tell him. I'm going to tell Lee."

"And you think that he is not going to tell Jaylon?"

"Not if I ask him not to. He won't."

"if you say so." Misty said hoping that Shawanna was wrong and Lee did tell Jaylon. Because Shawanna's baby daddy or not deserves not to live.

"I still can't believe that your ass went and got pregnant by the American psycho. You know that I got your back even though you didn't have mine." Misty said smiling.

"Bitch you sound crazy. While you were laid over there bleeding he was chocking the shit out of me. I pissed on myself too. I still got on the pissy thong to prove it." Shawanna stated. After that, they started laughing.

"Ouch! He lucky that he caught me slipping, or I would have cut his ass up." Misty said.

"Don't trip. He is going to get his. I'm going to make sure that Lil'Lee and some of his little homeboys fuck him up. Matter of a fact, I'm bout to call him right now." Shawanna said as she pulled her phone out of her purse.

Chapter 123

"Oh yeah. Hit that pussy." Tanya said while Lee was fucking her doggy style on the couch.

"You like that shit?" Lee asked her as he deep stroked her hard and fast.

"I love this shit." Tanya screamed. His phone began to ring.

"Fuck!" He said.

"Yeah. That's what you better keep on doing."

"I got to get that. It might be my brother."

"I don't care if it's the fucking Pope. You better not stop."

"Oh, that's all that you are worried about. I got you. I ain't trying to come out of this pussy anyway." He said still getting his stroke on. But when he heard his sister on the phone crying, he pulled out of Tanya. She started to go bad on him until she saw the look on his face.

"Calm the fuck down sis. I can't understand you while you are crying and shit. What's going on?" He told Shawanna. While she told Lee what had happened. All he did was listened. After she finished, he asked her, "Where is that nigga at?" Lee asked her.

"I don't know. But they still have keys to the apartment."

"They?"

"Yeah. Him and his homeboy that Misty use to talk to."

In the background, lee heard Misty saying that he can get too!

"Where are ya'll at right now?"

Slumped

"The Motel 6 on Watt Avenue. Room 662."

"I'm on my way. I'll talk to you when I get there." When he hung up the phone, he started putting on his clothes.

"Are you alright?" Tanya asked.

"I'm good baby. I'm just bout to go check this clown for putting his hands on my sister."

"I know that is your sister and everything, but don't go and do anything stupid."

"I'm not. I'm going to go pick up Flip and Junebugg. And then we are going to go and stomp a hole in that nigga's ass for chocking my sister." After he put his clothes on and tucked his 40 cal in his waistline, he kissed Tanya and said, "We will pick back up where we left off when I get back."

"Just be safe Lee. And come back to me." Tanya said. He just kissed her and walked out the door. Lee had learned that a long time ago that the game was too unpredictable. And anything could happen, but he also knew that only death would keep him from getting back in that pussy. The thought of how good Tanya's pussy rushed him to get back quick. He called Flip and Junebugg and told them that he was on his way. It took him about ten minutes to get to them. When he got there, they were outside smoking a blunt.

"So what's up?" Flip asked as they got in the car.

"Shawanna's so called boyfriend done broke a bottle over Misty's head and chocked Shawanna out." Lee answered.

"Oh shit. Why didn't you say something? I would have brought my heat with me." Junebugg said.

"You are not going to need it."

"Why?"

"Because I got mine." Flip said pulling out the big Desert Eagle 50 cal smiling.

"So did you call Slump?" Flip asked Lee.

"No. And ya'll better not either." Lee replied.

"Damn. My bad. I was just asking." Flip said.

"Why? You don't think that we can handle these niggas or something. I mean if you are scared, I can take you back home."

"Oh so you got jokes now? Huh?" Flip asked.

"Who said that I was joking?"

"You must be. Because the only thing that I'm scared of is God and bad pussy. And don't forget that. Man why do ya'll gotta play? I'm the hardest all the fucking time."

"Let's just go stomp these niggas out right quick so I can get back to what I was doing." Junebugg said from the backseat.

"Here hit the weed. Calm down."Lee said.

"Wait a minute. Are you talking about Misty that works at Toys R' Us?" Junebugg replied.

"Yeah. Why?"

"Nigga I been trying to fuck with her for the longest. She always on something. Talking about she is too old for me. She ain't nothing but one year older than me."

"Uh oh." Flip said.

"What?"

"I think that I just saw your cape."

"Fuck you Flip."

"What are we doing here? I thought that Misty stayed by us." Flip asked.

"She does. But they are here because those niggas got keys to her spot. And they don't want to be there when the mad strangler show back up." Lee responded.

"That's a good one." Flip said.

"And no jokes either when we get up in here Flip." Lee said.

"And where is the fun in that at?" Flip replied. When they got to room 662 and knocked on the door, Shawanna looked out and saw who it was. Then she opened the door and asked Lee, "Why did you bring his crazy little ass with you?"

"Love you too. Here I am here to help you and that's how you treat me." Flip said walking past her and into the room.

Slumped

"Aww. I think that you done hurt the baby's feelings." Misty said.

"And you told me not to crack any jokes. And you got her looking like she fresh out of a Freddie movie, cracking all the jokes." Flip stated.

"Fuck you Flip." Misty said.

"I know that you want to, but I don't like old women."

"And why are you so quiet Junebugg?" Shawanna asked.

"Because he's in love with Misty." Flip added.

"Something like that." Junebugg said as he started singing Messy Marv's. "She keeps calling me a baby."

"Man we didn't come here to play fucking love connection. Where are the damn keys at?" Lee asked.

"Here you go." Shawanna said giving him the keys.

"Don't tear my house up." Misty said.

"Don't trip. We can pay for anything that we break." Junebugg said.

"I ain't paying for shit." Flip said.

"Man will ya'll stop running your fucking mouths and come on." Lee said roughly.

"We won't fuck it up too bad." Junebugg said as he walked out the door and closed it. After she locked the door Shawanna said, "I think that I called the wrong brother. Did you see how he was looking?"

"Yeah. For a minute I had to remember that it was Lee and not Jaylon." Misty said.

"I know huh."

Chapter 124

Creeping up to the door and seeing that there were no lights on in the apartment Lee said, "I don't think that nobody is here. Just in case that there was he pulled out his 40 cal and cocked it. He put the key in the lock and opened the door. He walked in and turned the lights on.

"Flip check that room while I check this one. Junebugg watch the door." Lee said.

"I got it." Junebugg said. Flip went to check the room while Lee checked the other one. Lee didn't see anyone. But as soon as Flip turned on the light in Shawanna's room, he said, "Motherfucker." Because on the dresser stood a picture of Shawanna hugged up with none other than Money.

"What?" Lee asked running into the room with Flip.

"This. Now do you think that it is time to call the bros?" Flip said handing him the picture.

"What the fuck is going on? What ya'll done found? Is that who I think it is?" Junebugg asked as he looked at the picture in his hand.

"Yeah it's him. And the whole time we have been riding around looking for these niggas. They have been right in our fucking faces." Lee stated. Bending down and picking the picture up, Junebugg said, "Let's get out of here before they come back. We got them now. No need for them to know. They're not getting away this time." They turned off all the lights and left the apartment. No words were spoken. Nothing needed to be said. They all knew what had to be done and couldn't wait to start doing it. Once he pulled into their apartment, Lee said to Flip and Junebugg. "I'm going to go to the house, grab some shit right quick, and then have Tanya drop me off over here.

"Nah. Fuck that. You wait right here. We will be right back." Junebugg said. Lee got back out the car.

"Go ahead. We will meet you at your house. We are going to be right behind you." Flip said. Once Flip got to the spot, he went to his room and grabbed the duffel bag he had the AA12 in. Looking down at the gun, he said, "It's time." He loaded the fifty round drum he had bought with all slugs, grabbed his hoodie with *Never To Be Forgotten* on it under Spazz, Ru, and Little Man's faces on it, and went to meet Junebugg in the living room.

"Are you ready?" Flip asked Junebugg. Junebugg smiled, ran in his room, grabbed his hoodie, and said, "I am now."

Chapter 125

2:30 A.M.

Red and Money stumbled inside of the apartment. They had been at Showgirls, a local strip club. They had been getting drunk and paying white girls for lap dances. Now all they wanted to do was go to sleep.

"I can't believe that these bitches are still not here yet." Money said.

"Nigga you broke a bottle over her fucking head. You better hope that bitch didn't bleed to death." Red said drunkenly.

"Nah. She is all right. It was just a little cut. At least they didn't call no fucking cops. " Money said laughing.

"I told you that my Shorty wasn't going to do no shit like that." Money had pulled out his phone and left what had to be his tenth message. Telling Shawanna that he was sorry and begging her to come home. So he could make it up to her. Hanging up his phone he said, "Fuck it. Another quailu and she'll love me in the morning."

"As much as you drank tonight, you ain't going to love yourself in the morning." Red said.

"Hey Red. Red you know that you are my nigga right?" Money said just before he passed out sitting up on the couch. Red was laughing and shaking his head on his way into the room saying, "Yeah. You are my nigga."

Chapter 126

"I can't believe this shit. The whole time that nigga been fucking my sister." The six men where sitting in Slump's living room trying to derive a plan instead of just running in there with their guns drawn.

"Why don't we just grab them niggas up and make them tell us everything?" Junebugg asked.

"I ain't got no questions I want to ask neither of them bitch ass niggas so just say kill them and get it over with. We already know where Munch is so why are we sitting here talking about nothing." Flip said furious.

"Gateway Oaks. Ain't that by the river?" Stone asked.

"Yep. Why?" Tee said.

"Well they say the best way to die is to drown or be burnt alive."

"See that's what I'm talking about. Let's go do something. Fuck this sitting around talking shit." Flip said.

"I got it. We grab them two niggas coming up out of them, that way, Misty and Shawanna don't know we had anything to do with them being missing." Tee suggested.

"I got a better idea. Why don't ya'll ride this one and let us four handle it. You just got married and Tee got his lil' dude and this club about to open. Now I know you want to do these two niggas bad, if not worse than we do. I'm just saying what does it matter who do it as long as they die."

For a while, no one spoke. They just sat around staring at each other.

Slumped

"How do you feel about it?" Slump asked Tee.

"I don't know Slump. I feel like I need to do it. I got nothing but love and respect for you lil' gangstas, but I made a promise to Jazz that she could and would watch them niggas die, and after everything they did to her, I think she wants to put a bullet in them niggas herself.

Slump walked to the wall safe hidden with a big picture of Jadda, he then pulled out twin Rugger P890s. "Well, we all do it together and this is how we're gonna do it. Me, Tee, and Stone will get Money and Red. Ya'll grab Munch and we'll meet at Tony T's. I think he's on the road right now anyway."

"Hell even if he ain't. He ain't gonna be tripping.. Unc is an old school killa. He likes that shit. Well now that that shit is settled, who wants to lose some money to Madden?"

Chapter 127

"**D**amn. My motherfucking head hurts and how the fuck I get out here on this couch? Money said the next morning.

"Nigga that's where your ass passed out at."

"And what type of bro is you to let me stay here?"

"What did you want me to do? Carry you to the bed, undress you, and tuck you in?"

"I would have did it for you."

"Shut your ass up nigga. I told you to slow down with all that drinking shit last night. So it's your damn fault. Now go clean your ass up and let's hit Denny's or something. I'm hungry as fuck."

"And you loud as fuck too." Money said walking to the room he shared with Shawanna. "I'll be out in about ten minutes."

"Yeah. What the fuck ever. Just hurry your ass up." Once in the bathroom, Money called Shawanna who still wasn't answering him.

"Come on shorty. Answer your phone. I said I was sorry. Damn." He then got into the shower. Twenty minutes later, he came out dressed and feeling better.

"I thought you said ten minutes nigga."

"Shut up nigga. Let's go." As they got into the car and Red started it, the driver's window exploded causing glass to cut into his face.

Slumped

"What the fuck?" He said as they tried to reach for their guns but were too slow as the masked man pointed two guns in their faces.

"Do it nigga. Act like you're gonna reach for something so I can push your face in that bitches lap." Tee said snatching open the door, pulling him out the car, and putting a big Smith and Wesson in his face.

"You miss me?" Tee asked. Stone pulled up into a blue cargo van. When Red saw Stone's face, his knees buckled.

"Nah playboy. Ain't gonna be none of that." Once they into the van, they drove off.

"So you want to touch my little sister?" Slump asked Money as he pulled of his ski mask.

"If I would have known she was your sister, I would have murdered that bitch..." Suddenly everything went black from being hit in the head with Slump's gun.

"What about you? On second thought, I don't even want to hear it." He said before punching Red in the jaw. Red's eyes glazed immediately. "That nigga had a glass jaw the whole time. Oh yeah, this shit is going to be fun."

"Why I gotta be the one who stays in the car and ya'll get to have all the fun." Flip asked across town.

"Fun? All we doing is grabbing this nigga and getting the fuck outta here." As the boys got out the car, Flip's phone rang.

"Change of plans. Put the whole house to sleep." Stone said.

"What you mean the whole house?" Flip tried to ask but Stone hung up. "Well, looks like I get to come in after all."

"What did they say?" Lee asked not liking the look in Flip's face.

"Maybe I should go in by myself. They said put the whole house to sleep."

"Well fuck it. I'm not Italian." Lee said.

Slumped

"Damn, the little nigga too." Junebugg said finally catching on.

"Sins of the father. Let's get this shit over with." Lee stated.

Chapter 128

When they got to Tony T's, they hung the men from the ceiling of the barn by hooks.

"So now what?" Stone asked.

"We wait until we know they killed Munch. Then piece by piece I'm gonna take this nigga apart.

"Did ya'll call Jazz yet?" He asked Tee.

"No. And I might have to break my promise. She still don't know and I don't think I want her to."

"Man, all this over some bitches? And I thought you niggas were gangstas." Red asked.

"Who these lover boys? Why don't you just shoot me and get it over with or did you just bring me here to hang out."

"At least you got more heart than Mr. Glass Joe over here? But don't trip. After I introduce you to my big headed friend, let's see how tough you are."

"I should have known you niggas was up to no good as soon as I saw that big ass van parked out back. And whose big ass dog is that tied up in the back of my damn house." Tony T asked coming into the side door.

"Man if I didn't know any better Unc, I would think you liked this type of shit." Stone said.

"Yeah, I thought it was your damn dog. It kinda looks like you."

"Yeah, and he eat like me too."

"Now that I gotta see. So what you two done did to be hung by my skinny racks?"

Slumped

"Man you gotta help us. They're gonna kill us." Red said.

"After all this time, you turned out to be a pussy." Money said laughing.

"Man fuck you. I told you to leave them damn bitches alone to begin with."

"Wait a minute. So you the two boys that did that coward ass shit to them girls." Tony T said having a revelation.

"Yeah, that's them Unc." Stone said.

"I was hoping I was around when they caught up to ya'll. I got something special I like to do to men who beat and rape women. I just ain't had the chance to try it yet. I seen in that movie *Casino Royale*."

"The James Bond movie?" Slump asked.

"Yeah. That's the one. And ever since I saw that shit, I wanted to try it. Hell I even made the chair and everything. Well something like the chair but it should work." He walked to the corner of the barn and grabbed a chair….well more like a toilet seat with four legs.

"So which one of these two boys got the biggest balls?"

"Why you gonna give me one last blow job old man?" Money asked.

"If that's what you wanna call it. Pull that one down for me, strip his ass naked, and tie him to the chair." Once they had Money tied down, Tony T took a thick rope from the wall with an 8-ounce deep fishing sinker attached.

"Oh shit. You niggas don't remember that part when he took James Bond and hit him in the balls with that rope?"

"Yeah I seen it but I never thought about doing it."

"Anything ya'll wanna ask before I give him a blow job?" Tony T asked then winked at Money.

"Nah. Do your thang Unc!" Slump said.

Chapter 129

Munch and his family sat on the couch while the boys sat in front of them with their guns drawn. "So who the fuck is you lil' niggas supposed to be. Kris Kross or something?"

"I'll see you in my sleep lil' nigga." Flip said putting the 50 caliber to Lil' Munch's head and spraying blood and brain matter all over Munch and his beloved white girl.

As the white girl screamed, the barrel of the gun was aimed at Munch's head, mixing his blood in with his son's. Then Junebugg shot the white girl before throwing up everywhere.

"Can you get DNA from throw up?" Flip asked.

"I think so. Now what. We can't go in there and clean that shit up. We gotta get out of here." Lee said.

"Hold on." Flip said jumping out and running back in the house. A minute later, he ran back out the door with flames behind him as he closed the door.

"Go nigga go before that bitch blow up." Flip said diving in the car. As Lee sped away, the whole house exploded.

"Now that's how you do shit." Flip said.

"What the fuck my nigga? You had some damn dynamite in your pocket?" Lee asked.

"Nah, I turned on the stove and there was some gas. And you know the rest. BOOM!" Nobody said anything about Junebugg throwing up. They all focused on Munch's son. He was nothing more than his father's son. But in the game, it

Slumped

was better to leave nothing behind than to have to look over your shoulder.

Chapter 130

"**M**an look at that nigga's nuts. They are the size of fucking watermelons. Not to mention, he done shit and pissed blood all over the place." Stone said.

"Say son. Wake up boy." Tony T said slapping Money.

"You…can't….break me…old man."

"I like this boy right here. He got some big ol' balls. You can learn a lot from your friend here. Well now I done had all the fun I think I can handle. So now I'm gonna let ya'll get back to what ya'll had planned. Burn that with everything else when ya'll finish." Tony T said dropping the rope on the ground.

"Now that nigga right there. That nigga is the motherfucking truth." Stone said.

"That nigga is scary."

"Man after he hit that nigga the first time, I damn near shitted on myself. So bro, how's hit hanging." Tee said walking in front of Red.

"C'mon. Please man. I can make ya'll all rich. Just let me go."

"Bitch ass nigga. Just like your cousin." Money wheezed.

"Man fuck you. It's all your fault. Everything from D.C. to Texas to this. So fuck you."

"So what are you saying? He made you do it?"

"Yeah he made me. I didn't want to. I'm telling you that sick motherfucker made me do it. And you said something about making us rich." Slump asked.

"Yeah. We got about two million dollars in the locker at the downtown Greyhound. I can take you to get the money and ya'll can just let me go."

"And you would just get on a bus and never look back?" Slump asked.

"I swear. You would never see me again."

"Well first, how do I know your word is any good?"

"Send someone to the locker and have them bring it back."

"I don't know."

"C'mon now. Please. Check it out. It's locker 11. The combination is 09-04-08."

"You get that Tee."

"Yeah." He said repeating the numbers.

"Where ya'll at?" Tee asked calling Lee.

"On our way to meet ya'll."

"So then it's all done."

"Yeah. It's good on our end."

"I never doubted you lil' niggas. But check this out. We got a bonus and ya'll need to get it and bring it here."

"Alright bet. Just say where." Tee gave Lee the information and hung up.

"Now back to you. If everything is what you say it is, then you will get a chance to run."

"You know they still gonna kill you right. And I just hope I'm still breathing long enough to hear you scream."

Chapter 131

Flip came out of the Greyhound carrying a green army duffel bag.

"I almost feel a little better now. But I was looking forward to using my new toy." Flip said.

"What's in the bag?" Lee asked.

"My second favorite thing in the world next to guns."

"Well it can't be no pussy so it gotta be cash." Junebugg said.

"And a whole lot of it too."

"Well he said it was a bonus. Now let's go out to Tony T's before we miss the real party.

Chapter 131

"Alright. We'll see you in a few. The money was right where he said it would be."

"I told you. Now ya'll can let me go right?"

"Don't trip. I told you that you would get a chance to run. I'm gonna keep my word. You'll get a chance.

"Damn!" Tee said looking down at his phone.

"What?"

"Jazz is calling."

"Well answer it nigga. Don't just look at the fucking phone."

"Hello?"

"What's going on Terry? I was just watching the news and they talked about how Munch's wife got killed at her store a few days ago and this morning, his house blew up. They said his son was in the house with him."

"I don't know what you want me to say. It's not like you didn't know how this shit was gonna end."

"But he was a child."

"Yeah but he was his father's son."

"Where are you?"

"Why?"

"Because I'm asking…you got them, don't you." She asked after a few minutes.

"I don't know what you're talking about."

"So now we are lying to each other Tee."

Slumped

"I'm just saying. All you need to know is it's taken care of and you don't have to worry about it anymore. It's over. We won."

"But you promised me."

"And I also promised that I would protect you. That's what I'm doing. If you love me, you would let me handle my business so I can spend the rest of my life keeping you and my son happy."

"Make them pay for what they did to me and Porshea."

"They will. They are. I promise." He said before hanging up then turned towards Money. "You like dogs?"

"Fuck you. Kill me and get it over with because nothing you do to me will ever change what I did to her and you know what, that bitch loved every minute of it..." Suddenly there was a gunshot as half of Money's head blew off.

"What the fuck?" Tee asked looking at Stone and Slump. They were all shocked of the gunshot. Looking around, they saw Junebugg's gun still smoking. He couldn't even be upset. He knew Junebugg still felt bad for running that day.

"Aw man. I missed it. I know what happened to the nigga's head but what happened to his balls. Better yet, who's gonna show me how ya'll did it."

"Yeah I know I'm crazy right. But then we already knew that. But what about ya'll."

"How's it hanging killa? Remember me? I almost got your ass coming out the weed house that night. No hard feelings. It's personal. Don't got nothing to do with business. You killed my brothers so it's only right that I tried to kill you." Flip said to Red.

"Leave him alone. I see you getting that look in your eyes." Slump said.

"What the fuck you talking bout' leave him alone. I know ya'll ain't gonna let this nigga go. Oh shit, ya'll are, ain't you. That's what the money was for, huh?"

"So you ain't as dumb as you look." Stone said.

Slumped

"Man fuck that. Ya'll can't let him go. What about Ru, Spazz, and Lil' Man? What about Jazz?"

"Look lil' bro. He didn't have nothing to do with it. It was all Money's doing. Why don't you go get Block head and brig him here real quick while we cut this nigga down." Kicking a headless Money's head.

"Whatever."

"So ya'll really gonna let me go?" Red asked once his feet were on the ground.

"Something like that." Stone said.

"But he said I would get a running chance." He said pointing at Slump, who stood there smiling.

"I still don't see why he gets to go free."

"He paid for a running chance and that's what he will get. Stone, untie his hands." Slump stated. Once untied, Tee pushed the barn doors open.

"Run nigga." Red took off like a track star racing for the gold.

"This shit is crazy. Ya'll really gonna let that bitch ass nigga run away?"

"Shut up lil' nigga and let the damn dog go." Stone told Flip.

"Get em' boy." Flip said taking Blockhead's leash off. The dog caught Red in seconds. By the time they caught up with Blockhead, he had Red's left leg bent at an awkward angle and screaming.

"Get the dog, please. Get the dog."

"How you let this big slow ass dog catch you?" Flip asked smiling.

"Release." Stone commanded whose head was covered in Red's blood. Slump gave a Rugger to Tee who shot Red in the head. Then Slump got it back and shot him in the chest. Each man got his turn at Red before handing the gun back to Slump.

"I'm out. It's over for me. I'm married with a beautiful baby girl. I got my reason now." Slump stated.

Slumped

"A reason for what big bro?"

"A reason to live baby boy. A reason to live."

"I feel you." Tee said nodding. He too had found his reason.

"Well, looks like it's on us now. But don't trip. I think we got it. What do ya'll say? Stone asked the boys.

"Yeah, we got it." They burned Money and Red's body like the garbage they were and cleaned up the barn. They gave Tony T a hundred thousand from the duffel bag and left.

Epilogue

"**M**an I never thought we would get here." Tee said to Slump looking around the club that was packed.

"Yeah my nigga. I thought we would be in too deep to walk away myself. But that's the game, you know."

"Nah, it ain't the game. It's just that the good die young and the bad live forever."

"I got no problem with that. I got no problem with it."

Now Available:
Paperback & E-Book

Slumped

On Our Bookshelf

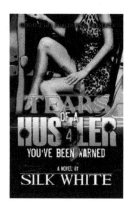

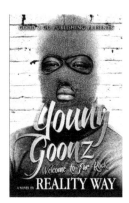

Slumped

  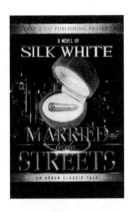

Good2Go Films Presents

Slumped

To order films please go to www.good2gofilms.com
To order books, please fill out the order form below:

Name:
_____

Address:
_____

–
_____

–

City: _____ State: _____ Zip Code:
_____

Phone:
_____

Email:
_____

Method Payment:
Check ☐   VISA ☐   MASTERCARD ☐

Credit Card#:
_____

Name as it appears on card:
_____

Signature:
_____

Item Name	Price	Qty	Amount
He Loves Me, He Loves You Not - Mychea	$13.95		
He Loves Me, He Loves You Not 2 - Mychea	$13.95		
Married To Da Streets – Silk White	$13.95		
Never Be The Same – Silk White	$13.95		
Tears of a Hustler - Silk White	$13.95		
Tears of a Hustler 2 - Silk White	$13.95		
Tears of a Hustler 3 - Silk White	$13.95		
Tears of a Hustler 4- Silk White	$13.95		
The Teflon Queen – Silk White	$13.95		
The Teflon Queen 2 – Silk White	$13.95		
Young Goonz – Reality Way	$13.95		
Tears of a Hustler 5 – Silk White	$13.95		
Subtotal:			

Slumped

Tax:			
Shipping (Free) U.S. Media Mail:			
Total:			

Make Checks Payable To:
Good2Go Publishing
7311 W Glass Lane
Laveen, AZ 85339

CPSIA information can be obtained
at www.ICGtesting.com
Printed in the USA
LVHW05s1139120518
576979LV00026B/554/P

9 780989 185967